This Animal Family

This Animal Family

MZ Pevsner

© MZ Pevsner 2021

To Peter and Alice

Guthrie 1

The day Oswald Guthrie's life imploded began like they all did at the time. It was mid-September, exactly two years since his retirement. He woke before Delia, slipped on his dressing gown, made two cups of tea, and left hers on her bedside table.

He was heading for the spare bedroom, the one he used as his office, when he remembered what day it was, and so he went back downstairs. A moment of calculation. This week was blue for recycling. He wheeled the bin out onto the pavement, paused to gaze up at the clear sky, then sniffed the air. Yes, it was still there, the foul reek from next door.

Ever since that family moved in, the drains had been on the blink. Foreigners, apparently. A dark-skinned man and a plump wife and half a dozen kids. There was a baby involved, so it was probably wet wipes, or grease from their pungent cooking poured down the kitchen sink. Guthrie threw their house a dirty look and tutted as he headed back inside.

They'd bought the house in 1981, him and Delia. After his apprenticeship, Guthrie had worked for Dawson & Griggs, a painting and decorating firm in Headington. He'd met Delia at a pub in Kidlington one Saturday in the summer of 1976. He was playing Aunt Sally for his local pub team, and Delia was there with her best friend. It was her smile that did for him, kind but with a hint of mischief. He surprised himself by striking up a conversation, he'd never been so forward in his life. By autumn they were engaged.

After the wedding, they rented a tiny bungalow in Barton. They lived frugally, saved every penny. He set up business on his own in 1979, and by the time Delia announced that she was pregnant one damp evening in the November of 1980, business was steady enough to think about a mortgage.

The new place was a three-bed terraced house on the Rose Hill estate, built in the late fifties to house the Morris Motors factory workers at Cowley. He supposed that some might call it an ugly house, like all the others on the street. Low ceilings and small bedrooms and too much pebbledash, though the oblongs of grass out back were decent in size. But if it was unsightly, he was blind to its flaws. All he'd seen all those years ago was a sanctuary, a place for the two of them and the nestling to come. He'd loved it then, and he loved it now.

After ten years, they'd extended the kitchen at the back, and later they squeezed a ground floor toilet beneath the stairs. He papered and painted the place to Delia's tastes, and was content to let her arrange the furnishings as she liked, right down to the framed Constable reproductions on the walls and the collection of china Beatrix Potter knickknacks on the mantelpiece. She was the boss when it came to domestic matters, not because she was hard-nosed, but because he loved her, and so shared in her pleasure at the choices she made.

If the interior was her domain, she gave him full rein in the garden. Along with the research into his family history, this was his chief passion, both before and after his retirement. He waged war on the moss in his pocket-sized lawn, nurtured the flower beds on either side of the grass, and grew leeks and onions and runner beans in the raised beds he built from railway sleepers at the back of the garden between the compost bins and the shed.

Thoughts of bins brought Guthrie back to the present. The wheelie bin was out so he could relax and get on with his day. Now where did he leave his cup of tea? He had a hunch he'd abandoned it in the bedroom. On the way up the stairs, he heard the toilet flush.

Up until this day in September, his post-retirement routine had followed a predictable pattern. His gardening and ancestry aside, he helped Delia with the weekly shop at the Sainsburys on the ring road, and joined her once a fortnight for a Whatsapp chat with their son, Eric, who'd emigrated to New Zealand with his wife, Lizzie, and their two young sons. He forced himself to take an hour's exercise a day, either a walk to Rivermead, the little urban nature reserve on the edge of Rose Hill, or a bike ride up the towpath. Once or twice a month he cycled over to the Kassam stadium to watch United.

The football matches were a habit he'd formed when his son was a child, and that he'd never quite shaken, though in the early days, before the new stadium was built in Greater Leys, he'd stood on the Osler Road terraces at the old ground in Headington. After his son grew up, lost interest and then moved away, Guthrie had taken to going to the matches with Barry, a neighbour from over the road. But a few years ago, Barry and his wife had moved up to Yorkshire to be closer to their grandchildren, so now if Guthrie went, he did so alone.

Up until February, there'd also been a regular Friday night in the pub after he'd had his tea, a chance to catch up with Dougie, his oldest friend, over a pint or three, and a game of dominoes. But Dougie had got sick and died, the journey just three short months from first GP visit with the stubborn cough, to his last night in the hospice.

Nowadays Guthrie stayed in on Friday nights and watched television with Delia. He didn't talk about how much he missed his old friend, but those Friday evenings at home were the only times he ever felt he'd rather be somewhere else than with her.

Later, after what happened to Delia in September, whenever Friday came around, he'd remember how powerfully he missed the evenings in the pub with his old mate, how mightily he'd wished he was not stuck at home with his wife, and he felt a cruel stab of guilt. He'd think, Well, you got what you wanted, you're free to spend every Friday in the pub now. You should have savoured those times with the wife. Now they're gone, and it serves you right.

On this September morning, he heard the flushing toilet and thought, Ah she's awake. Just then he remembered where he'd left his cup of tea, on the kitchen counter beside the fridge, and so returned downstairs. He had his morning all worked out. He'd grab the tea, then head back to the study to switch on his computer. He'd pop his head in the bedroom door to say hello to Delia, then crack on with his latest research. He'd discovered a relative on his mother's side who'd joined the army sometime in the 1860s and fought in India. He loved uncovering family links to the old days of British glory. He liked to imagine tales of derring-do in the colonies.

In sharp contrast to the blur that followed, he remembered the next hour or so with vivid clarity. He found Delia dressing in the bedroom, caught sight of the back of her naked thighs, pocked and puckered as she bent to slip on her panties, and offered a wolf-whistle. She pursed her lips in mock disapproval, but he knew she liked it when he reminded her that he still thought of her in that way.

"Can a man not compliment his wife on her figure?" he asked.

"Ah, stop your nonsense, man," she said. She never dealt well with admiring comments.

"It's not nonsense," he answered, and he meant it.

The sight of her dressing so carefully reminded him that today was not to be so run-of-the-mill. She was leaving on a trip, and he'd need to make sure she got off alright. Oh well, there was no rush, he'd have to leave his on-line research until later.

He watched her select and discard a handful of outfits before she settled on the floral blouse, the navy cardigan and matching slacks that made up her ensemble for the day. She had a small open suitcase on the bed, and she packed a few folded items. She didn't need much, she'd only be gone two nights.

"You sure you don't mind me not coming?" he asked, for the fifth time since she'd heard the news of her aunt's illness and announced that she wanted to see her before it was too late.

"It might be the last chance to see Agnes. She's ninety-one and fading fast," she'd told Guthrie after she'd come off the phone to the manager of the care home two days before. "She's got no one but me. I can stay with Trisha, I've already spoken to her."

Guthrie had been torn from the start. Sheffield was a long drive away, so he oughtn't to let Delia go off on her own. But she had her heart set on seeing her aunt, and though he hadn't met the daughter-in-law, he felt sure Delia would be well looked after. Besides, he was keen to deal with his latest ancestral findings. He used the osteoarthritis in his knee as an excuse, as he'd done so on several past occasions. When Delia first raised the visit, he made sure to limp a little more than was necessary.

"The arthritis giving you gyp, love?" she'd asked. "You don't need to come."

"It's alright," he said. "I don't mind."

"No, love. You rest up. I'll be fine."

"You sure?"

He could tell she was a little disappointed, but she was too kind-hearted to make a fuss. Later, he'd think, I allowed myself to be talked into letting her go alone. She gave me the pass. I didn't have to take it, but I did.

It was a decision he'd regret for the rest of his life.

They ate breakfast together. They had Radio 2 on in the background, as usual. *Penny Lane* came on, and Delia was still humming it as she went upstairs to clean her teeth.

He watched her leave the kitchen. She still kept herself in trim, he supposed. When they'd first met, she'd reminded him of Barbara Windsor, not just the curves, but the bubbles too. What a smile! Had she changed much over the years? If you hadn't seen her for decades, he supposed she'd show all the normal signs of age. But he was hardly ever apart from her. Well, not for long enough to register a change. No, she might be a little thicker, perhaps. And there were the wrinkles, on her hands and face and belly, not to mention her breasts. Well, what do you expect of a woman in her sixties? But he didn't think about that too much. In his heart, she was still his Barbara Windsor.

He carried the little suitcase downstairs and put it in the back of the hatchback. She wrote down Trisha's address on an old Sainsburys receipt. Afterwards, he kept that scrap in his wallet. Of all her things, he couldn't bear to throw it away, though he wasn't sure why.

Their last exchange, nothing meaningful.

"You sure you don't mind?"

"Of course not."

"Is the tank full?"

"I'll fill up on the ring road."

"Well, give my love to Agnes."

"I will."

"And drive carefully."

"I'll call when I get there."

And then she was off. He'd watched the car until it disappeared around the corner at the end of the street. Then he'd gone back inside and put the kettle on for another cup of tea. He was pleased to have got out of the trip, and was looking forward to some solid hours on the internet discovering what he could about a soldier's life in nineteenth-century India.

Less than an hour after she left, he got the call. She was still on the M40, she hadn't even got as far as Banbury. The voice identified itself as WPC Vicky Jarvis. There'd been a traffic accident. Delia was injured. Before he could form the question, the voice said,

"She's alive, but it's serious. She's in an ambulance, on her way to the John Radcliffe Hospital."

He thanked her and hung up. Later he'd learn about the line of traffic she'd joined, the roadworks up ahead, the lorry driver falling asleep, his lorry ploughing into the back of her.

For a moment Guthrie stood frozen, just a brief instant between processing the news, and the more sinister thoughts that followed: apprehension, fear, panic. Then the paralysis ended and the battle commenced, a fight to curb the raw waves of dread coming at him from all sides, an effort to steady his nerves enough to consider what he needed to do.

He thought, Car keys, but then remembered that she had the vehicle. He searched frantically for his mobile phone, then googled a local taxi firm with trembling fingers. He had to repeat himself twice as his mouth was so dry. He took his jacket, pocketed the phone, and stood in the lounge, peering out of the window until the cab arrived.

The clarity that had marked the start of Guthrie's day now shifted to a ghastly haze, not for minutes or hours, but long bleak days. The taxi arrived, and the driver was in a mood to talk, a monologue about Oxfordshire County Council and its latest traffic calming scheme. When they halted outside the Emergency entrance, Guthrie thrust the banknote into the driver's hands and fled without waiting for the change.

Inside the building, The A&E receptionist told him to take a seat. The waiting room was a quarter full. A teenage girl on Guthrie's left sat with her feet curled beneath her, headphones on, as she worked her way through a packet of cheesy quavers and a bottle of something orange. Opposite, a shaven-headed man in a tracksuit sat grey-faced and grim as a woman beside him pushed a buggy to and fro and made shushing noises to the infant within. The man leaned forward and began to rock back and forth in pain or boredom, it was hard to tell which. Guthrie stared at his shiny pate.

At last a female nurse approached and asked Guthrie to follow her. As soon as he got to his feet, his impatience disappeared and he was overcome by a wave of dread. He thought, Oh God, let her be alright.

She was lying on a bed, hidden from prying eyes by curtained screens. Nurses were still working on her, one checking the cannula in her arm that connected to an IV drip, the other monitoring the machine that stood to the left of the bed and made irregular, discouraging sounds.

A male doctor stood over Delia's still body. A blanket covered her from the neck down. Something like a gag or muzzle lay over her mouth, strapped around her head, and a tube led from it to a small self-inflating bag. A third nurse was squeezing the bag. Guthrie had seen something like this on television. There was a word for the procedure, the insertion of the tube down the patient's throat, the pumping of the bag to aid breathing, but he couldn't recall it now. When the doctor saw Guthrie hovering at the end of the bed, he waved him away.

"Not yet," he said. "You shouldn't be here. Please go back. I'll come and find you."

Guthrie stood the wrong side of the curtains and watched the frantic comings around him. It was his first ever visit to a resuscitation unit, and it stirred in him equal feelings of inadequacy and fear. As he walked back to the waiting room, he tried to make sense of what he'd seen of Delia, to gauge from it what he should prepare himself for.

When the doctor next appeared, he beckoned for Guthrie to follow him. He pulled aside the curtain around Delia's bed.

"Go on," he beckoned.

Guthrie stepped inside and peered at his wife. The gag had been removed and a different mask placed over Delia's mouth, one that was held in place with straps around her neck and head. The tube that led from the mask was thicker and opaque and led to a machine that hadn't been there before. The blanket still lay over her body, but from the throat up, she looked pale but unscratched. That, at least, was a hopeful sign.

"Mr Guthrie?"

"Yes."

"Your wife was involved in a nasty traffic accident. She's lucky to be alive. The paramedics placed a tube in her throat to help her breathe, and she was transported here like that. That tube's now connected to a mechanical ventilator to help her breathe. She's been given medications to elevate her blood pressure and IV fluids for hydration. We're also monitoring her heart. She has some broken ribs, a fractured tibia, some cuts and grazes and extensive bruising, of course."

"OK," said Guthrie. From the doctor's tone, he knew there was more.

"The main concern is a serious head injury. The paramedics said she was initially responsive. She was able to give her name and some personal details. But soon after that, her condition deteriorated. SWe've taken bloods and she's about to go for a CT scan, and from that we'll know more about the extent of the trauma to the brain. For the moment, we're monitoring her, and we'll have to wait and see what happens."

"I understand."

"At the moment, she's not responding at all. Frankly, that's a worry. She may recover quite quickly but it's also possible that she could be severely injured."

"No, she can't be," said Guthrie. The words came out before he had a chance to stop them. "She looks fit as a fiddle."

As soon as he'd spoken, he thought how foolish he must sound, an ignorant old man arguing with a medical expert. But when he looked at the doctor's face, he read not irritation but pity.

"It looks serious, I'm afraid." said the man. "She's getting the treatment she needs, that's the good news. But we suspect there's been some substantial trauma. We're running tests and the scan will tell us more. In the meantime, please go back to the waiting room. We'll come and find you when we have more news."

"Yes," said Guthrie, rising to his feet. "Thank you."

The hundred-and-one questions that were to follow still remained unformed, even as he re-took his place opposite the shaven-headed man and his wife. Of course, in the weeks to come, he was to learn more than he cared to about traumatic brain injuries. About the Glasgow Coma Scale, and intracranial pressure, fluids and swelling, and the damage caused by blood passage to tissue. About subdural haematoma and subarachnoid haemorrhage. About neurochemical problems that disrupt normal brain functions.

One night, a fortnight into his new hell, Guthrie sat in front of his PC and gave his fears free rein. He'd been unable to sleep, a regular occurrence these days, and he read a page from an NHS website on serious head injury titled *TBI and Altered Consciousness*. He took in the section headed *Coma*, but began to stall at the one marked *Vegetative State*. By the time he'd scanned *Minimally Conscious State* and *Brain Death*, he found that he was weeping soundlessly. From that episode he learned a valuable lesson. While ignorance might not be blissful, it was certainly preferable to full disclosure.

There were doctors and nurses, pamphlets and the World Wide Web, and what he learned he only half-absorbed, as if to know the precise details was to admit the seriousness of Delia's condition. Instead, he chose to filter in only the more palatable details. The natural plasticity of the brain, its dynamism and ability to create new neural pathways when established ones were destroyed. In addition there were the past cases that he read and heard of, miraculous recoveries from horrendous injuries, all brought about by a combination of love and hope and patience. All of that was to come, though. For now, he sat in the waiting room and watched the second hand of his watch tick by.

It was hours before they let him see her again. She was lying in a ward bed, still wired up and ventilated and unconsciousness, and all he could do was reach over and touch her hand. It was cool and dry, and he stroked her knuckles with his fingertips.

Later they told him to go home and sleep. It was a doctor who spoke to him, a tall thin man with wiry eyebrows, stooped shoulders and the kind of shrivelled face that reminded Guthrie of a lizard. He talked first about the medical issues, sentences that Guthrie struggled to take in. He picked up only fragments. *Haemorrhage* and *coma* and *lucky to be alive*.

"I know it's difficult, but we have to be patient," the doctor told him. He explained just how different one head injury was from the next, both in its immediate effects, and in terms of long-term prognosis. "Whatever the damage, it's important to begin the rehabilitation programme as soon as your wife is able."

Guthrie sensed that the man chose his words carefully. A positive message, no talk of damage or disability, no focus on permanence. And in his vulnerable state, Guthrie noted all this with gratitude.

He kissed his wife on her cheek before he left. It was pale and soft.

"Goodbye, love," he said. "Back in the morning. And don't you worry. We'll have you back on your feet in no time."

He slept badly, of course. At half-past two in the morning, he got up and opened a tin of oxtail soup, as much for something to occupy himself with than out of hunger. The piece of toast that he cut got stuck on the toaster and burnt, and the smoke set off the fire alarm. He struggled for a minute to switch it off. Then, succumbing to a growing rage, he pulled the gadget from the ceiling, taking with it a chunk of plaster.

"Ah, Christ," he whispered, sank down on the chair and laid his forehead on the kitchen table. It was cool and slightly sticky. He thought for a moment that he might cry. That hadn't happened for as long as he could remember, but would become something of a habit in the weeks that followed. On this occasion, no tears came, and presently he poured the soup into a bowl and dabbed at it with his blackened toast.

At dawn he dressed and wondered when he could return to the hospital. He'd forgotten to ask the night before, and despite his anxiety, he still felt an old-school respect for the medical profession that made him wary of earning its disapproval. To kill time, he attacked the bindweed in the garden for an hour, then polished his black lace-ups and prepared a bag for Delia.

He'd not seen anything of the bag she'd packed for Sheffield, so he found a new toothbrush and paste and face cream, a hairbrush, two nighties, her old slippers, her spare reading glasses, the latest copy of *Take a Break* magazine, and a paperback he thought she hadn't yet read. She liked historical romances. The colour of a by-gone age, the lowly woman finding love against all odds. Victorian scullery maids, Tudor wenches, nannies in the Raj. The cover of this novel showed the back of a woman in nursing uniform gazing up at a spitfire.

At eight a taxi took him to the hospital, and an hour later he was sitting on a chair beside Delia's bed. The nurses' station was empty, and he'd slipped in without anyone noticing. Delia was still unconscious. A nurse appeared and he asked her for news.

"She's been stable," said the woman. She was a short, black, pear-shaped woman with close-cropped hair, thoughtful eyes and an accent that Guthrie supposed was African. "You shouldn't really be here yet." He peered up at her and she must have seen something in his eyes for her expression softened. "Well, I suppose it can't do any harm."

"Thank you," he said. He wanted to know more, but didn't know what to ask. Besides, he was afraid she'd think him a nuisance and shoo him away. As if sensing his vulnerability, the nurse said,

"The head injury was haemorrhagic. That means there was some bleeding from an artery in the brain. The bleeding has gathered between the brain and the skull. That's increased the pressure and caused swelling. She's in a coma now. The doctor will-"

"What does that mean?"

"It means she's stable but poorly. Look, you're welcome to stay, my dear," she said. "But it may be a while yet before she wakes up."

"And when she does, she'll be alright?"

"We don't know. The doctors will have more of an idea. They'll have seen the scans. But for the moment, we can't say how she'll be. I'm sorry."

"Thank you for explaining."

"Dr Sumander will be doing her rounds mid-morning," said the nurse as she headed for the door. "She may have more news."

More news. If he'd known then that three weeks later, he'd be sitting in the same chair with no more answers than now, he'd not have unpacked Delia's bag and tidied her bedside table with such calm sanguinity.

Guthrie 2

The days that followed, he tried his best to remain positive, and for the most part he succeeded. It wasn't too hard, as any less hopeful outlook was too frightening to contemplate. He visited every day, and by and by the ebb-and-flow of the ward became familiar. Mealtimes, the doctors' rounds, the orderlies with their mop-buckets, the comings and goings of nurses checking machines and making notes.

He arrived upbeat and left frustrated, though not yet at this stage despondent. The craving for some sign - a twitching finger, a raised eyebrow - was all-consuming. He'd think, Patience, my old son. Maybe next time.

It was hard carrying the burden alone. When he'd first spoken to Eric, his son announced that he'd take the next plane home.

"Hold your horses," Guthrie had told him. "The doctors say she's stable. Wait a while until we get a clearer picture of what we're dealing with."

Though he'd have loved to have his son at his side, Guthrie knew Eric could ill afford the airfare, nor the time away from his job. He'd recently set himself up as a building contractor, had picked up a couple of jobs but this was a crucial time for the business, and there was no one to hand things over to. Still, Eric had ignored his father's plea and arrived four days later.

He'd only stayed a week, the most he felt he could be away from the job. But it was a relief for Guthrie to have someone close to lean on.

Things must have taken a turn for the worse back in New Zealand, because a month later, it was Eric who was making excuses.

"I'm so sorry, I feel I ought to be back there with you but there are too many balls in the air. If I leave now, the business will fold. I've put everything into it, the house and all the savings. I just can't get away for a few months. Not unless it's, you know... ." He left the sentence unfinished. "I promise I'll get over as soon as I can."

"That's OK, son," said Guthrie. They'd taken to phoning each other at times when Guthrie was at Delia's bedside, so he could put the call on speakerphone, and Eric could tell his mother his news from afar. "Just keep calling. I know that means a lot to your mother."

The most approachable of the nurses remained the one with the cropped hair. Guthrie wondered whether she was as competent as the British nurses, but decided not to dwell too much on that. Her name was Gloria and she had a five-year-old son called Nathaniel. Guthrie's first proper conversation with her hadn't started well.

"Where are you from?" he'd asked.

"Kidlington," she'd answered.

"No, you know. Which foreign country? Jamaica? Africa?"

"Africa's not a country," she said. "But yes, I was born and raised in South Africa."

If he'd listened carefully, he might have picked up the trace of tension in her tone, but he didn't.

"I've read a few books about the history of South Africa," he said. "It must have been a relief to come here."

"A relief? Why do you say that?"

"Well, you know. All the violence. The poverty."

There was a long pause while she studied his face.

"A relief? I don't know. It was scary coming here. And lonely. I gave up my life back there. The first two years I had to leave Nathaniel at home with my mother. I haven't seen my family since I went back to fetch him. A relief, you say? It must be a relief to have a qualified and experienced nurse looking after your wife, Mr Guthrie."

"Yes, well, of course," he said. He had a distinct sense of having said something wrong, though he wasn't quite sure what. "I'm sorry. I didn't mean to offend you. I'm very grateful for your care. Delia is too, I'm sure. That goes without saying."

That seemed to placate the woman, but he was careful not to probe too personally after that. Instead, he took to asking her for help with Delia's crossword puzzles, having discovered in the first month that she too enjoyed solving them.

"Australia's capital," he'd call out as she passed by. "Eight letters."

"Canberra, man," she'd reply. "Is that the hardest you can come up with?"

And so a friendship of sorts grew between them, and with that came trust. One day, she said,

"You don't have to act, you know. Putting up a cheerful front. It's hard to keep that up all the time."

It was Gloria who explained to Guthrie any changes in procedure or treatment. The insertion of a nasogastric tube to provide nutrition. The purpose of a craniotomy, and why the decision was made not to go ahead with the planned procedure. The danger of pressure sores, and how to prevent them. And in between the explanations, the everyday chatter was just as much of a balm for Guthrie.

Sometime during the first month, Gloria mentioned that her husband had walked out on her in 2016.

"Bringing up a child on your own, that can't be easy," he said, when she told him.

"Easier than when he was around," she answered.

"Ah, like that, was it?"

When Guthrie wasn't at his wife's bedside, he began to organise the house for Delia's return. After Dr Sumander had examined the scans and other tests, she'd told Guthrie that when Delia regained consciousness, there'd most likely be some brain damage, at least temporarily, that might well manifest itself as physical disabilities.

In fact Dr Sumander had actually said, *if and when Delia regains consciousness*, though Guthrie had edited her words. The way she'd couched the rest of the prognosis, those terms like *might well* manifest, *most likely* be, that was the language Guthrie would encounter whenever he talked to doctors henceforth. A hedging of bets, a covering of backs. And Guthrie, unable yet to face a future without hope, was happy to let the language go unchallenged.

Physical disabilities, she'd said. That stuck with Guthrie, and he began to research what they would entail and how he could prepare for them. It was a relief to find distraction in practical matters. Through leaflets and the internet, he set about turning his house into a disability-friendly environment. Slip-mats and shower stools, grab rails and handi-reachers.

To-ing and fro-ing from hospital, ferrying things that she liked. Hairspray and a silk headscarf she liked to wear, a warmer dressing gown and slippers. Also a CD player and some Elvis Presley CDs she liked. *Love Me Tender, Can't Help Falling In Love*.

Long days at the hospital, evenings at home putting up handrails or staring blankly at the TV screen. The hospital had his mobile number in case Delia's condition changed, but his phone remained silent on the mantelpiece. Guthrie's only other distraction was the research into his family ancestry.

He'd developed the interest in his late forties following his discovery, amongst his father's effects, of a number of letters written by his great-great-grandfather, a Belfast plumber who'd emigrated to Canada. This had piqued Guthrie's curiosity.

He loved it when he was able to connect his own flesh-and-blood with world history, and took the greatest pleasure when his research took him back to the British Empire. In his mind this had been a force for good, a benevolent entity nominally tarnished by one or two black marks such as the slave trade. But you don't make an omelette without cracking a few eggs. And besides, you only had to look at the benefits to the ex-colonies. Imperial measures and railways and impartial judiciaries. Civilization, in a word.

Guthrie tended to work mostly at night, it was better than lying awake in bed stewing over his troubles. His focus at present was on Corporal William Bremner, an ancestor on his mother's side of the family. She'd died in the early 1990s, but her sister, Guthrie's aunt, had passed away more recently, and Guthrie had been given a trunk of her personal effects.

Amongst the photo albums and old school certificates, he'd come across several volumes of Bremner's hand-written journal. By the end of the third paragraph, he was hooked.

According to Bremner's account, he'd served under a certain Major Robert Rollo Gillespie, a veteran of imperial campaigns. This sent Guthrie off on another trail, and he'd soon learned from Wikipedia that as a young man, Gillespie killed a rival in a duel in northern Ireland, then joined the army rather than take up a place at Cambridge University.

According to Guthrie's reading, Gillespie had earned his spurs putting down revolts and uprisings in the West Indies during the 1790s. There was resistance from the Caribs, the original inhabitants of the islands, and there were slave revolts, and attacks by Maroons, the descendants of runaway slaves who lived in the mountains of Jamaica. On one occasion, Gillespie beat off an attack on his house in St Domingo, killing six of the eight burglars armed only with a sword.

Gillespie then travelled to Asia by ship and road. There was a near-miss with pirates, only avoided by forcing the ship's captain at gunpoint to set a course for Constantinople. From there he travelled further east, taking up his army post in India.

Bremner's journal traced his own soldiering, from his enlistment in Oxford to his posting in India, where he first served under Gillespie. They both arrived in 1806, and the newly-promoted Colonel took up the post of Governor of Arcot. Guthrie read a thrilling account of Gillespie's heroism, and imagined Bremner at his side.

One story struck home with particular intensity. Gillespie was out riding before breakfast one day when news came of a mutiny of sepoys at Vellore. A band of fifteen hundred local troops had turned on less than four hundred European soldiers, penning them into a section of the fortress. Gillespie (with Bremner at his side, in Guthrie's imagination), raced to the fortress with soldiers from the 69th Light Dragoons. They snuck inside the fortress and held off the sepoy attack until artillery arrived from Arcot. The mutiny was put down, and its leaders executed.

And there was more. Although the trail became sketchier, it appeared that Gillespie and Bremner travelled to the Far East as part of the troops assembled for the conquest of Java, then sailed to northern India. By now promotion meant that Bremner's commanding officer was General Sir Rollo Gillespie. They advanced into Nepal, but Gillespie was killed by Bulbhadar Singh and his force of twelve thousand Ghurkas at Kalanga fort in 1814.

Though Gillespie had perished, Bremner's adventures continued. For a while he seemed to have left the army, joining a government-funded scheme to send settlers to South Africa. Its aim, Guthrie read, was to provide a counter to the Dutcher settler influence.

It was a frightening time for civilian farmers, facing continuous attacks by aggressive Xhosa warriors intent on curbing the settler expansion. Militia were set up in the 1820s to deal with these indigenous attacks, culminating in the battle of Mbholompho, where Bremner fought alongside regular soldiers under Colonel Henry Somerset.

It was during the first weeks after Delia's stroke that Guthrie uncovered the final pieces of the Bremner puzzle. The man had sailed to Australia after Mbholompho, again to try his hand at farming, on this occasion in Bathurst. But once again he became embroiled in fighting, this time against the local tribesmen, who resented the white settlers' incursions.

In 1826 he returned to Britain. He was fifty-six years old and seemed to have found employment as a manservant to a military gentleman he'd served under in India. The man lived in the Oxfordshire countryside, and Bremner remained there until his retirement. A last postscript. Bremner married late and had a son. He retired to a cottage in Iffley village, outside Oxford, and died there in 1841.

By the time Guthrie had pieced together the details of his ancestor's life, he was gripped by a peculiar nostalgia for that distant era. Oh, to have been born a hundred and fifty years before! Wouldn't that have been a fine life? To be sent to the colonies to make your fortune, to feel yourself transformed from milksop to man. He loved the sound of those old places. The New World, the Antipodes, the Raj, the Heart of Darkness.

It was while he was working on a Bremner synopsis, a condensed two-page account typed with a single finger on his old PC, that he learned that Delia had come out of her coma. He'd slept fitfully, woken at six, then made a mug of tea. He was sipping it as he checked his mobile phone. There it was, a text from Gloria:

Hey Mr G weve been trying to call your wife out of coma come at once.

It was the second Tuesday of October, the day after Guthrie had picked up his replacement car, a second-hand Nissan Micra.

The hunt for the car keys, the crawl through Oxford congestion, the scramble through the corridors to Delia's ward. Yes, her eyes were open. A miracle. And yet it soon became apparent that the world Delia came round to would not be kind to her. Though she was awake, of sorts, she was also profoundly diminished.

It took a week of tests to assess the extent of the damage. No signs of speech, no displays of mobility. At times she made a groaning sound, and at others her fingers twitched and her mouth opened. She could breathe unaided. But she was doubly incontinent, incapable of feeding herself, and her eyes were open but unseeing.

With Gloria's prompting, Guthrie tried to converse with her, encouraging her to use a crude system of blinking, one for yes, two for no. It was hard to know whether it failed because she was unable to answer, or deliberately chose not to. Either way, the exercise was frustrating.

"Come on, love," he'd urge her on. "One small step at a time, and we'll get there in the end."

Each day he told her the same thing, but on his own at night, the doubts crept in. Was this new Delia a permanent one?

Days to weeks, and weeks to months. Mornings when he read to her, afternoons when she lay in bed and he called out the crossword clues from the magazine he continued to buy for her. Her expression remained impassive, her body stubbornly unresponsive.

Worse was to come. A cold, miserable Christmas. He'd finished adapting the house for Delia's return and had begun to wonder whether he'd been wasting his time. The couple in the house opposite, the Cartertons, invited him round on Christmas Day, but they'd never been close friends, and he couldn't face the thought of their pity, so he made an excuse. He had phone calls from Eric in New Zealand, from a nephew in Aberdeen, and Barry in Yorkshire, and from one or two of Delia's relatives, a niece and a cousin. He bought Delia some bed socks and a digital radio, and a large tin of Quality Streets for Gloria.

"For your lad," he explained.

Then, on Boxing Day, another call from the hospital. Delia had picked up an infection, it'd gone to her chest. They were treating her with antibiotics but her breathing had deteriorated and she was back on a ventilator.

Over the course of that week, Delia struggled to cling on. When the pneumonia settled in both lungs, they induced a coma. Days by her bedside, nights battling his own demons. A bleak new year beckoned.

Eric flew in again, this time just for five days. Guthrie begged him not to, but his son must have suspected that the end was approaching. It was a sweet pleasure to be with Eric at the hospital, even more so to have him back in his childhood bedroom, the spare one beside the study. But the pleasure was mixed in with guilt at the thought of what it was costing his son, in air fare and the damage to his fledgling business. The visit came and went in a flash, and before Guthrie knew it, he was back on his own.

The one spark of comfort was that he'd taken to holding imaginary conversations with Delia, often late at night or in the early hours of the morning. Often it felt as if she was the instigator.

"Alright, love?" she might begin. "You seem a bit down in the dumps."

"I'm alright," he said. "Just, you know… ."

"You need to look after yourself, Oswald," she went on. She was the only person who called him by his first name. "Hot meals, exercise, keeping the brain ticking over. I'll be out of hospital soon enough, and you'll be no good to me an invalid."

"I know, love. I'm doing my best."

"A tin of soup? Sardines on toast? Call that doing your best?"

"You're right. I'll get in a nice lamb chop for my tea tomorrow. I'll walk up to the shops and back."

"That's the ticket, love."

Apart from the inert body of his wife, Gloria was the only consistent landmark in the hospital. A series of doctors took charge of Delia's treatment. Guthrie, who held traditional views of what constituted acceptable medical expertise, had mixed feelings about the team. The first registrar was Asian and female, almost beyond the pale. The next, a young Welshman scarcely out of his teens, had an angry rash on his oversized Adam's apple, and was prone to blushing. The third one, a consultant, was reassuringly middle-aged and white and male, with a good speaking voice. It was Dr Lawton that helped Guthrie see that his old life was gone for good.

Months had passed. Where had the time gone? The antibiotics had chased off Delia's pneumonia, her condition was stable, but she was still ventilated and unresponsive. The nasogastric tube had been removed and an operation had been performed to fit a PEG feeding tube into her stomach to provide artificial nutrition and hydration.

It was Guthrie who first brought up the possibility of taking Delia back home. Dr Lawton's message was clear.

"Frankly, we've been a little disappointed with your wife's progress," he began, as if Delia had been somehow at fault. He began to talk about the tests they'd been doing on Delia, something called SMART assessments. "There's no prospect for the time being of a return home, I'm afraid. I think we need to consider our options for residential care. Somewhere where she can get the right specialist treatment."

They were sitting in Mr Lawton's office, Guthrie and Lawton and a woman called Maggie Khan, who Lawton introduced as Mrs Guthrie's social worker.

"Can she not stay here until she gets better?" Guthrie asked. It wasn't that he relished his visits to the hospital. Rather, he pictured a nursing home as a forgotten corner of abandonment and neglect. As he spoke, he knew what was coming. He'd read about the pressure on hospitals to clear their wards of the long-term infirm, and he understand at once that Delia's turn had come.

"Look, this isn't the right place for her. Your wife's condition is delicate. It's impossible to tell how long she'll remain like that. She needs to be somewhere designed for long term residence, somewhere that has the appropriate care and equipment."

"Yes, I understand."

"Mrs Khan here can help you work through the procedures." He glanced at his watch. "I've got to go. But I'll leave you two here to talk."

Guthrie looked at her properly for the first time and thought, Another foreigner.

Maggie Khan, approaching middle-age, had a round face, shoulder length hair and plump lips. Did the whites of her large eyes stand out against the darkness of her complexion, or was it the other way round? Her expression at rest, dour and unsmiling, carried with it the air of an unpopular headmistress. He looked at her doubtfully and thought, What does she know of my life?

The woman launched straight into an explanation of the system, and how it applied to Delia.

"Basically we need to assess your wife's medical needs," she began. Guthrie heard, *Basically ve need to assess your vife's medical needs*, and thought, How can she help my wife if she can't even speak proper English?

And then she smiled and the effect was instant. There was a warmth in her eyes. It wasn't a stern demeanour that he'd noted, but a no-nonsense determination. He thought, I should at least hear her out.

Maggie Khan was still talking, and Guthrie forced himself to concentrate. She was explaining what they were working towards, but as with the medical updates he'd received from nurses and doctors, a lot of it passed over him without settling. She spoke of *Decision Support Tools* and *local authority involvement* and *priority weighting*. The abbreviations were particularly confusing, though he managed to pick up a couple of them. CCGs were *clinical commissioning groups,* and PHBs were *personal health budgets* and MDTs were *multidisciplinary teams.*

"We need to consider how complex and intense your wife's medical needs are, and how predictable they are too," she continued. "We don't want to set Delia up with a package and then find that her needs have changed and her health is threatened. There's a checklist we use. We look at things like mobility, cognition, continence and states of consciousness, and we use a scale that runs from 'priority' to 'no need'.

She stopped and peered at Guthrie to check that he was following. He nodded to show that he was.

"In a nutshell, if the assessment shows that your wife has genuine medical needs, then the NHS is obliged to provide care, and to cover the cost of that."

"I see," Guthrie said. He'd slept poorly the night before. He was tired and his head felt muzzy, but he was doing his best to keep up.

"If the assessment concludes that her care needs are non-medical, then provision falls to the local authority. In this case, the cost of care is means-tested. They take into account the patient's assets, particularly capital. That means your savings. Then they work out how much they'll contribute, and what the patient will have to cover."

"Right," he said, though he was struggling. A thought struck him. "Are we going to lose the house?"

Maggie shook her head.

"No. It's complicated, and of course the government might decide to change the law at any time. But to put it simply, in some cases property can be viewed as capital after a certain amount of time has passed, but if a spouse is living in the property, then it doesn't count as such. Do you understand? That means your house is safe."

Guthrie nodded and forced a smile.

"Whatever the result of the assessment, it's only valid for a certain amount of time, usually twelve months. After that, the process is repeated to check that circumstances haven't changed."

"OK."

"Anyway, the point is, we're confident that Mrs Guthrie will be granted full continuing healthcare. That means the NHS will cover the costs."

Maggie stopped speaking for a long moment to allow Guthrie to process the information.

"The second issue is where she should live once her care package has been finalised."

"I heard what the doctor said, but I want her back home," Guthrie answered at once. He stared at Maggie with a look of defiance. Then, aware of his belligerent tone, he added, "Please."

"At the end of the day, you're the next of kin, so your voice will be heard above all else," she answered. "But if the patient cannot be cared for effectively at home, then the other options would be to remain in hospital or to move into a nursing home."

"You heard what Dr Lawton said. Everyone knows the hospitals are desperate to free up beds. Won't they want her out as soon as possible?"

"Well I take your point," Maggie answered, nodding. "But they wouldn't discharge her to a nursing home or private residence unless they were sure the care would be appropriate."

"So she could come home?"

"At the moment, the doctors have told me she's in a stable enough condition to transfer to a nursing home. But her needs are still too complex to consider a return home. She needs a trained health practitioner at hand, not to mention the specialist equipment. You don't have the resources to cope at home, even with twenty-four hour support."

Guthrie swallowed his disappointment as he contemplated her words.

"But when her condition improves?" he began.

"Then we'd reconsider the decision, of course," she finished for him. Then she added, "It's all about getting the best possible care for your wife, Mr Guthrie."

Guthrie was still not convinced that a return home was not the best option, and said so to Eric the next time they spoke on the phone.

"Dad, I know you want what's best for mum. I know it'll hurt to see her in a home. But I'm begging you not to think about getting her back to the house for the moment. The social worker's right about needing expert care and the right equipment. But it's not just that."

"What do you mean? What is it, then?"

"You've got to think about your own care. You're no spring chicken, Dad. And if you're going to avoid going crazy, you'll need to create some distance between what's happened to mum and the rest of your life."

"I'm fine."

"You're fine for the moment, but she's not at home with you, is she? You don't know how long this is going to go on."

"But she's my wife."

"I was talking to my GP about it last week. He-."

"What were you doing at your GP, son? Are you ill?" Guthrie interrupted.

"No, no, just a routine check-up, a thing for my insurance. Anyway, he was talking about people in long-term relationships. He was saying that when one of the pair gets ill, like really ill, and the other takes care of them, then the relationship changes. You know, for years they're equal loving partners. Then all of a sudden it changes to something else, a new relationship, like patient and nurse. You can be loving husband and wife, and you can be carer and patient, but you can't be both. If you become her carer, the old relationship will die."

"I'm not going to stop loving her."

"I know, Dad. That's not what I'm saying."

They talked for an hour, and it was Eric's arguments that prevailed in the end.

"Alright, you win," said Guthrie at last. "A nursing home it is, but it's got to be a good one. And it's just for a while."

It was Eric, the long-distance angel, who worked with Maggie Khan to organise Delia's transfer. He quizzed Guthrie in minute detail about his personal finances, a full inventory of pension and savings and other assets. He liaised with Maggie over the NHS Continuing Healthcare assessment, dealt with all the paperwork, set up Guthrie's visit to several homes they'd selected for his wife, and all that from the other side of the globe. As always, Eric was apologetic for not being by his father's side.

"I've had to re-mortgage the house, Dad. I'm hanging on by a thread. I feel rotten, but I can't see my children lose their home. I swear I'll be back as soon as I can."

Guthrie tried to reassure him.

"You're doing so much already. I couldn't have dealt with all the bureaucracy," he told his son. "I can't thank you enough."

"Even with the full continuing healthcare thing," said Eric, "I'd still think about tightening your belt. You never know what's around the corner, Dad."

After the call ended, Guthrie ran through his finances, something he'd taken to doing regularly since the accident. He'd paid into a private pension scheme all his working life, but the contributions had been limited and it didn't amount to much, more a topping-up of the state pension. They had little in the way of savings to fall back on. The house was paid for, that was something. They'd looked forward to a retirement without major financial worries, not because they were flush, but because they had few needs beyond weekly supermarket costs and utility bills. They'd never holidayed abroad and there were no other significant expenses, though they'd always hoped to save up one day for a trip to New Zealand. If their retirement life seemed austere to some, it hadn't felt so to Guthrie and Delia. After all, they'd had each other. Still, Eric's advice made Guthrie wonder what else he might do to strengthen his finances.

It was Delia who came up with the solution during one of their imaginary conversations.

"Look, Oswald," she said. "Whatever happens, you mustn't mope. You've never been much good at socialising, you've always relied on me for that. But while I'm out of the picture, you must find other strategies to keep from getting lonely."

"Don't worry about me, love. I'll be-"

"Now, I've got an idea, love," Delia continued, ignoring the interruption. "You may not like it, but I think it's for the best. Plus it'll earn you a few quid, and you never know when that'll come in handy."

"What are you talking about, love?" he asked.

"Lodgers," she said. "Think about it. We've got two spare bedrooms that are sitting empty. Having someone around'll be good for you."

He'd put it to the back of his mind, but now that he needed money, he gave it more serious thought. A quick google showed he could charge a few hundred quid a month for each room. He'd put the money aside in case the next NHS assessment went badly.

Guthrie put aside his ancestral research and launched into a study of property rentals. He read about legal responsibilities and tenancy agreements, about references and deposits. On 11th January he posted an ad on the local *Daily Info* website. It took two hours to draft. He wanted to include a number of details that he considered significant but struggled to put them into words. They included matters pertaining to cooking smells, use of foreign languages, acceptable jobs, sexual behaviour and many other topics. It was Eric who edited the initial drafts into a shorter, more diplomatic message. The final advert read:

Two rooms available in Rose Hill house. GCH, shared bathroom. Use of garden. Applicants should be professional non-smokers. No pets.

It was followed by the monthly rent, a figure suggested by Eric, and by Guthrie's email address. He uploaded the advert to the accommodation website and waited.

On the first day, he had three responses. He rejected them all without contacting the applicants. He'd worked out from the start that he could see the email addresses of those replying to the advert, and deleted the first reply without even reading the message because the address was *ali9761abdulla@gmail.com*.

The second message was rejected on linguistic grounds. *Hey is the room still avalible when can I come 2 see it plz.* Perhaps his own lack of formal education had given him a heightened respect for good grammar, but when he took in the casual tone, the mangling of punctuation, the deliberate misspellings and abbreviations, he summoned in his mind a picture of someone capable of these abuses, and found that he couldn't contemplate co-habiting with such a creature.

The third applicant was more hopeful, and Guthrie invited him to view the house. But the individual who appeared at his door was a pigeon-chested, limp-wristed young man called Jonathan, a lad barely out of his teens with an explosion of curly black hair and a suspiciously-Jewish nose. When Guthrie quizzed him about his employment, the boy mentioned a part-time course he was studying in aromatherapy, and an ambition to become an essential oil practitioner. The final straw was his announcement that he was vegan and lactose-intolerant. Could part of the kitchen be set aside and kept untainted, please? Guthrie improvised a story about a pair of nephews having first dibs on the rooms, but promised to contact Jonathan if the tenancy didn't work out, then ushered him out as swiftly as he could. He thought, Oh Lord, what am I letting myself in for?

Salvation came on day three, in the shape of *abi.palmer3296@hotmail.co.uk*. Abigail Palmer was the eighth respondent to the advert. She wrote a short query in plain but grammatical English asking if a room was still available, and whether the rent would include council tax and bills. Guthrie invited her round and began the interrogation almost at once.

"You local, love?" he asked, as she climbed the staircase to inspect the first bedroom. He followed behind, looking up at her mop of shoulder-length ginger hair.

"Pangbourne," she answered. "Berkshire."

"You got some Irish blood in you?"

"Not as far as I know. English through-and-through."

"That's alright. It's the hair, that's all. I've got nothing against the Irish. The wife's got Irish in her on her father's side. I've got some too."

"Right."

She paused at the top of the stairs, and he got a good look at her face. He was poor at guessing the age of young folk.

This one could be a teenager, or she could be pushing thirty. Probably she was somewhere in between. She was short and slim with flinty eyes, and pale skin, slightly greasy and flecked with a few spots on both cheeks. Her clothing looked as if it hadn't been near an iron for a long while, but she was well-spoken and friendly, and she'd offered to take off her shoes when she first came in. He'd liked that touch, it showed respect.

"What d'you do for a living?"

She explained that she'd just started work in the admin department of the Nuffield Hospital. He nodded in approval. She began to tell him a little of her circumstances, the move to Oxford, the job-hunting, the first weeks in a hostel, and the present need to find her own place.

"Have you got a boyfriend?" he asked. It was the thought of strangers staying in his house that prompted the question. After he'd spoken, he peered at the girl, and saw that she was eyeing him carefully. He watched her open her mouth to speak, then close it, then take a deep breath. Her answer caught him by surprise.

"I'm not sure if you're supposed to ask that sort of question, Mr Guthrie," she said. "I mean, have *you*?"

"Have I what?"

"Got a boyfriend?"

He stared at her face, half-expecting to read signs of aggression or defiance, but she was smiling. He began to chuckle.

"I see what you mean," he said. "And no, I don't. Do I look like one of them?"

"I don't know," she said. She seemed to be enjoying the exchange. "What's one of them look like?"

"Well, you know," he began. But he was faltering, the conversation was winding away in a direction he hadn't planned, so he attempted to rein it in.

"I'll need a letter from your employer and a copy of your passport. And a month's deposit too, along with the first month's rent, if that's alright."

It was, and a day later Abi Palmer moved in.

Abigail 1

Abi Palmer, twenty-three years old, left home one September morning following an argument with her mother and step-father. She filled her old gap-year backpack with clothes and shoes, two swimsuits, her running gear, a bathbag, her laptop, passport and a copy of Richard Mabey's *Food for Free* that she'd recently found in a local charity shop. She'd taken to wandering outdoors, anything to escape the house, and had grown curious about the possibility of sourcing food through countryside foraging.

Two days' before, she'd picked a pocketful of hazelnuts, and half a bucket of rosehips and hawthorn berries that she planned to turn into jam. Roger, her step-father, had spotted the fruit on the kitchen table as he helped himself to a mini pork pie from the fridge. Linda, Abi's mother, was upstairs having a nap.

"Living off nuts and berries now, are we?" he'd scoffed. His mood today was mocking good cheer, preferable to the acidic sneer when his frame of mind turned frostier, or worse still the slick lechery when he'd had a drink or two. Six months ago, when he'd first appeared on the scene, he'd made an effort to ingratiate himself with Abi, though she hadn't been fooled.

"I'm very fond of your mother," he'd said to her in the pub, when Linda had disappeared to the ladies. "I want us to be friends, me and you."

Linda seemed content to have found someone to carry the burden of life for her. The realisation that her mother was an alcoholic had dawned on Abi in stages. At first there were only suspicions. After all, Abi was away at university, so it was hard to gauge the slide. Since her return home, though, the clues had built up steadily. The morning jitters, the pre-first-drink funk. The afternoons resting, the dull eyes and sour breath. The assembly line motion turning the full bottles of Sauvignon Blanc kept hidden beneath the sink into those empties that filled the wheelie bin.

The transformation from tippler to drunk had begun at the time of Abi's father's departure. Of course, the revelation of Tim Palmer's affair was a landmark in all of their lives. Twenty years teaching English at the posh school up the road, a life of quiet routine, a plateaued existence with neither peaks nor troughs. Then the announcement that he'd fallen in love with Emily Kenton, the new Biology teacher, closer to Abi's age than Linda's. His resignation from his school post, the lovers' departure up North, the pieces to be picked up by Abi and her mother.

They coped in their own ways. Abi was in her final year of university. She turned in on herself, lost some friends, took to solitary pursuits. The long walks, the river swimming and ten-mile runs. Linda, it turned out, took to the bottle.

Those early days of Roger's appearance, soon after Abi graduated and came home, she was happy to give him the benefit. True, he gave her the creeps. His scrawny body, the neat paunch, the pencil moustache and weasel face. His wardrobe, too. Mustard trousers and tweed jackets and a flat cap he wore to hide his thinning crown. He worked as a salesman in one of the luxury car showrooms in Pangbourne, and cultivated the image of a leisured gent.

Abi learned more of his background through her mother's boozy blabbering. There were working class roots that Roger preferred not to talk about. His father collected scrap metal, and later opened his own breaker's yard. He'd narrowly avoided prison once for some kind of tax fraud. Roger fancied himself as a political animal. He'd toyed with the idea of standing as a UKIP councillor in local elections. All this, Abi felt sure, Roger had told her mother in confidence, unaware yet how thoroughly alcohol dissolved the filter of Linda's chatter.

What prompted Abi's departure that September morning was not a spat about Roger's past, nor some drunken squabble with Linda. Rather it was her step-father's outing of Abi, or rather the manner of his action.

She was eleven when she first became aware that she preferred girls to boys. Her deputy head teacher, a girl in the year above, one of the characters on Hollyoaks, they all stirred in her a certain urge that confused her. She studied her best friends, Mindy and Ellie, and felt sure that neither would be able to understand or share these feelings.

She passed through school celibate, hobbled through fear and ignorance. The first taste of what she was missing was a gap-year fumble during an Inter-rail trip. She was travelling with a school mate, Libby, and at the end of the second week, Libby fell in love with the barman in an Irish theme pub in Lisbon, an Aussie named Gerry. When she announced that she was going to stay on there with him, Abi travelled on alone to Barcelona.

She met Bettina-from-Frankfurt in a bar. They drank a string of rum-and-cokes and went back to the girl's hotel room. Something may have happened during the night, though Abi could remember little. In the morning, Abi spent an hour retching into the toilet while the German snored. As soon as she felt strong enough, Abi fled in shame.

At University in Bath, Abi continued to curb her inclinations, hoping that if she waited long enough the feelings would disappear. She had three relationships before she graduated. There was a term-long thing in her first year with a boy who claimed to be bisexual. Then a four-week one in her second year with a Brummie at catering college who gave her more pleasure in the kitchen than the bedroom. The sporty Mancunian in her final year slept with her every night for two weeks, then announced that she was frigid. With all of them she found comfort in the human touch, a sating of curiosity, but no more satisfaction than she got from a successful teeth-floss or toe-clipping.

She returned home after she graduated because she had nowhere better to go. Six months before, her father had revealed his affair, so when Abi came back, there were only two of them left in the family home, a daughter dreaming of new love, and a mother drinking to forget the old.

The year in Pangbourne passed slowly. The roots of her mother's drinking habit took hold, and Abi's initial jokes were replaced by gentle advice to cut down, then pleas to seek help. Sometimes Linda grew tearful and begged her daughter to give her more time. It was a phase, she said. Be patient. She needed to get Abi's father out of her system. At other times she took umbrage at Abi's concerns, told her to mind her own business. There was never an admission that things were not under control.

It was hard for Abi to point a finger, as her own life was no crowning success. She found a series of part-time jobs, bar work in the pub, nights at the petrol garage, chambermaid at a local hotel. The few old school friends she kept in touch with had moved away. Her mother was dry and angsty one day, wet and leaky the next. To escape, Abi went running along the Thames towpath or swimming off the boat ramps at Pangbourne Meadows.

Summer came. She had no close friends and so no holiday plans, but she told herself she was staying on in Pangbourne to save money. Luckily there was no one who cared enough to ask her what for. She was drifting, like the twigs she watched pass her as she lay on her back in the Thames current and gazed off towards the distant Chilterns.

Occasionally, when driven to despair by her hometown tedium, she'd head off to Reading, two stops on the train, on a Friday or Saturday night for some unidentified adventure. Some internet snooping had given her the names of a few gay-friendly venues, and she'd convince herself that she'd find the courage to explore these places. She'd even walked past a pub that held

LGBT-friendly nights. Walked past but hadn't managed to go inside.

Any excuse to get out of the house. By now, Roger had arrived on the scene and was courting Linda. At the end of the second month, he told her, over breakfast,

"I suppose you'll be planning to move out soon. A young girl like you should be away having all sorts of fun."

It was an innocuous comment, but there was something in his tone she didn't like, the wandering eye as she sat in her dressing gown nursing the day's first cup of tea.

Then, towards the end of August, she came across an online article announcing that Reading Pride would take place the following weekend. There'd be a parade and food stalls and several pubs offering an LGBT-friendly club night.

When the weekend came, Abi took the train on Saturday morning. She told her mother she was going to Reading, but not why. It was a bright day, the tail-end of summer, a last hurrah before the season's death. Down at Kings Meadow, stallholders were unfolding trestle tables and hanging awnings. She felt, as she wandered the streets, at one moment a lightness of heart, at the next a clawing dread.

When the crowds began to gather, she wanted to feel as if she was part of something bigger, but found herself wondering what a casual passer-by would make of her. A random bystander? A ballsy activist? Or a sad no-mates loner?

She bought a tepid can of Red Stripe at a stall and that helped a little. As she finished the first can and contemplated buying a second, a young woman tapped her on the shoulder and held out a placard.

"There you go," she said. "You look like you need a bit of company."

Abi stared at the placard, a black poster glued to cardboard and nailed to a baton. The meassage read *Some chicks shag chicks – get over it!* She looked up at the woman. She saw someone her own age, petite, dressed in jeans and sleeveless tee shirt. Short brown hair, hazel eyes, small teeth, pale skin. The woman smiled and Abi felt her face flush.

The parade took them through the centre of town. They passed a zebra crossing, the black-and-white stripes painted over in rainbow colours. There was a sound system and drag queens and a lot of hugging and shouting and blowing of whistles. The two women marched side-by-side, and Abi tried to peer at her new friend out of the corner of her eye.

Back at Kings Meadow, the woman disappeared for a few minutes and came back with two more beers and two wrapped burritos.

"Let's sit," said the girl, as she sank down onto the grass. "I'm Paisley." She had a nice voice, confident and neutral like a TV presenter. She handed over a beer and one of the burritos. "It's veggie," she said, taking a bite of her food. "Christ, I love Mexican food. If I was on Death Row, this is what I'd order for my last meal."

They both ate for a minute.

"What about you? What'd be your Death Row meal?"

"North African, probably," said Abi. "Tagine, couscous, that kind of thing. Or maybe Thai."

The sun was hot and Abi was sweating, and she drank too much too quickly as the afternoon drifted towards dusk. A blurred memory of walking back through the streets to the shared house where Paisley lived. The kitchen was simple but comfortable, a scratched-up wooden table, mugs hanging from hooks. Above the sink, a rainbow flag taped to the wall. Abi drank a tall glass of cold water to sober up, then a cup of milky tea. There was an awkward silence as she and Paisley sat in the kitchen playing with their empty mugs.

"Do you get on with your housemates?" Abi asked, for something to say. "Are they all, you know... ."

"Lesbian? Yeah," said Paisley. Then, meeting Abi's eyes, she said, "Come on. Let's go to bed."

The first time, properly. The first proper orgasm. Nothing short of an awakening. The next morning, all through breakfast, Abi wondered how to start a conversation, the one where they talk about whether the night meant anything. At last, when she could bear it no longer, she blurted,

"I'd like to see you again. If you want to, that is."

Paisley smiled a little sadly.

"I'm actually seeing someone at the moment. She's in London. It's … complicated."

"Oh right. Sure. No problem," Abi blustered. She was reddening again. She left soon after. On the train journey home, she tried to focus on the positives. She may have lost out on a proper relationship, but she'd found a little part of herself in Paisley's bed.

As autumn closed in, Abi continued to work her jobs and save her money. In September, Linda announced that Roger was moving in with them. More revelations followed. Roger, it appeared, was in the throws of a divorce. Part of the settlement called for the selling of the house he'd lived in with his wife.

"It makes sense to pool our resources," was how Linda explained it. Abi wondered how Roger had sold it to her mother. She was sure she hadn't needed much persuasion. She continued to lead a life of stealthy, numbing inebriation. Still, Abi found herself playing devil's advocate.

"Are you sure that's a good idea, mum? How well do you really know him? Maybe you should spend a bit of time on your own. You were with dad for years. It might do you good to stay independent for a while. You know, put yourself first. Be kind to yourself. Cut down on the booze. Maybe think about –."

But Abi had pushed the wrong button. Linda, already half-cut, heard only the booze comment and snapped,

"You just don't want me to be happy, do you?"

After that, Abi gave up trying. Worse, Linda's tongue must have loosened soon after. It was clear that word had got back to Roger.

"Are you trying to come between me and your mother?" he hissed, the next time they found themselves alone together.

"Just because you can't find anyone yourself. Let your mother be happy. Stick your nose out of our business."

Then the bombshell in mid-September. Roger could have come across the old copy of the *Reading Chronicle* anywhere. There was a front-page photo of the Pride parade. A background of smiling faces and placards. And near the front, arm-in-arm, Paisley and Abi.

He announced his find when he got home from work. Abi, dressed in running gear, was cooking a stir-fry. Linda sat at the table sipping a glass of white wine. Early evening was the best time of the day for her. It was acceptable to take a glass or two at that time, but she wasn't yet slurry and uncoordinated. Roger thrust the newspaper in front of Linda's face.

"I knew it," he announced. "I knew there was something odd about her. Look, your daughter's a star," he said with faux cheer.

Abi, at the stove, looked round to see what he was showing her mother. Linda tried to focus on the photo.

"A star among the who's-who of lesbian Reading," he continued, his voice light and measured. Then he turned to Abi. "Isn't that right?"

Abi stepped over to the paper and peered down at the photo. Linda now held the paper up to her face and peered. Her hands shook slightly.

"Lesbian?" said Linda. "What's he talking about, Abi?" She looked up into the pale face of her daughter.

"He's right," Abi whispered. "I'm gay."

A moment of silence as Linda poured herself another drink and took a healthy swallow. She set down the glass and shook her head.

"Nonsense. You're not gay. You can't be."

"I am."

"What about the boy at university? You slept with him, didn't you?"

Abi had mentioned the second-year Brummie once. She was surprised her mother even remembered.

"What's that got to do with anything?"

Abi found that anger was replacing the shame she'd felt at the start of the conversation. The tipsy mother was bad enough, but Roger's presence was the last straw.

"Perhaps you're just lonely," Linda said. She reached for the bottle.

"Perhaps she just needs a good seeing-to," said Roger.

A long stunned silence. Abi thought, How dare he? She waited for her mother to come to her defence. To her astonishment, Linda took another sip and laughed.

"You can't say that, Roger! It's not politically what's-it-called."

Trembling with anger, Abi turned off the hob and walked out of the kitchen. In her bedroom she took the backpack down from the top of her wardrobe and began to fill it. She was folding tee shirts when she heard someone at the bedroom door. She turned, expecting to see her mother's face, flushed but frowning with concern. Instead, it was Roger who stepped inside and stood before her.

"This is for the best," he said quietly.

"For you, yeah."

"And for you mother. A fresh start, that's what she needs."

"Piss off."

She continued with her packing, refusing to look at him. She hoped he'd turn around and leave, right up to the moment he reached over, grabbed a handful of her hair and yanked back her head.

"Ow."

"Sshh," he said, pulling her face up close to his. "Shut your mouth, bitch."

He was breathing heavily now. There were flecks of spit on his lips, and the skin of his face was mottled. Then she felt his hand reach down inside her running shorts. Probing fingers. She closed her eyes, frozen with shock.

"You and me, there's a weird chemistry between us. But I'm not sure how healthy it is. You could hang around and we could find out. Or you could, you know, spread your wings. I know what I think would be best for you. See if you can work it out."

And with that, he withdrew the groping hand from between her legs, let go of her hair with the other, and walked out of the bedroom.

She spent the night wracking her brains for her best escape plan. She could go back to Bath. She didn't know anyone there anymore, but at least the city was familiar. There was London, too. One or two university friends were now living there, but she knew she'd find the metropolis grim. Mindy from school had moved up to Manchester, Ellie to Guildford, but she'd lost touch with both of them.

In the earlier hours, still furious with Roger, even more so with her traitorous mother, Abi played the kitchen scene back in her mind and found herself thinking about that front-page photo. Her and Paisley, arm-in-arm, smiling yet fierce. She remembered the strength she'd got from her friend, from all those people around her that day. Oh, to feel as brave as that now!

It was this train of thought that led to her decision to head for Reading. She knew the town well enough, there'd be no fear of the unknown. But that wasn't it, was it? Who was she kidding? Paisley was there, that was the real draw. But would she have the courage to seek her out?

She left the house before Linda and Roger stirred. She walked to the railway station. Sitting on the Reading train, she set off on a mental inventory of her current situation. True, her possessions didn't amount to much. But she had her health, her education and several thousand pounds in savings. She'd be alright.

The sky clouded over early afternoon, and the breeze that had earlier been pleasant now cut through her flimsy jacket. She realised she was still in summer mode and wished she'd taken her thicker coat. Eventually, as the sun sank lower in the sky, she found herself in the street where Paisley lived. It was fear, not courage, that pushed her to the doorstep.

"Is Paisley there?" she said to the woman who opened the door. She was tall, mixed-race, with a nose ring and headscarf.

"Paisley? No, she was before my time," the woman said, her accent a gentle Irish lilt. "I think I've got her old room. Wait now, I'll ask."

She disappeared and after a minute or two, another woman came to the door. This one was large and round, with short curly hair and hard eyes. She stood, one hand on the doorframe, her hip cocked, looking Abi up and down.

"You're after Paisley?"

"Yes."

"She's a friend of yours?"

"Yes. Well, sort of."

"Well, you can't be that close, or you'd know she moved to London. Streatham, I think. Or Tooting."

"Oh."

The woman took in the backpack on Abi's shoulders.

"Were you expecting to stay?"

"Well... ."

"You got anywhere else to go?"

Abi shook her head.

For a long moment the woman fixed Abi with a penetrating stare. Then she shrugged.

"Well, you'd better come in. I'll make you a hot drink. I'm Teddy, by the way."

The kitchen was just as Abi remembered it, the same rainbow flag and battered table, only now that high summer had made way for autumn, the lighting felt gloomier and there was a faint tang of damp beneath the scent of spices and frying.

Teddy served Abi instant coffee in a mug marked PUTTING THE TEA BACK INTO LGBT. Later she announced that it was her turn to cook for the house.

"You can stay and eat, if you like. I'm doing something Moroccan," she announced. "We're all lefty lesbo vegans. Walking clichés, eh?"

She winked at Abi.

"Can I help?" Abi asked.

Teddy opened a bottle of wine while Abi diced onions and peeled carrots, opened tins of chickpeas and sliced up a cabbage. By the time the stew was simmering and the couscous steamed, it was dark outside and the kitchen, warmed by pungent cooking, felt safe and comfortable.

"Hungry?" Teddy asked, as she took plates from the cupboard, and cutlery from the drawer.

"Where are the others?" Abi asked. "Aren't we going to wait for them?"

"Naomi's gone out and Theresa's working. They won't be home til late. They can help themselves when they get back. I think Jackie and Bibi are away this weekend. Looks like it's just the two of us."

They ate slowly, and the food was delicious, and the wine smoothed away Abi's nerves. Teddy did most of the talking, about her work on a psychiatric ward, her love of martial arts and early nineties techno. She struck Abi as no-nonsense, sharp, a little hard-nosed perhaps, the way she talked about the patients at work, her friends, the other housemates. Still, it was better to be here, inside, with this tough cookie, than outside on her own.

That night Abi slept in Teddy's bed. There was nowhere else to go apart from the floor.

"You better keep your hands to yourself," said Teddy, up in her bedroom, as she wagged a warning finger, then spoiled the effect with a leering wink.

The events of the last two days had left Abi exhausted and she fell asleep almost at once, woke an hour or so later to feel a hand on her thigh. A moment's panic, the instinct to retreat, but then she thought, Well why not? She felt no particular attraction to Teddy, but didn't she owe her something for her hospitality?

The next three days passed in a pattern of routine. Teddy was working days that week, so they woke and ate breakfast together, along with Bibi and Jackie. She felt awkward hanging around the house while Teddy was away, even though her new friend pressed a house key into her palm when she left for work that first morning.

Abi spent the days walking the streets of Reading, trying desperately to make some plans for her life. The big decision she couldn't bring herself to make was whether to stay in Reading or not. If she chose to stay, she ought to be job-hunting, so that she could find her own place and begin to make roots. But if she decided to move further afield, she needed to choose where to go, and make rapid tracks. And yet the first day passed, and then the second, and Abi found herself stranded, unable to take the plunge either way.

Back in the house, Abi watched the group dynamics and saw how Teddy dominated the others. True, she was thirty-one, the oldest tenant in the house by a good five years. She made the rota for cooking and shopping and cleaning, drew up shopping lists and ordered housemates to put the bins out. She called a meeting on the second day to discuss whether to change the house broadband contract that was coming up for renewal, but the gathering was less a discussion than a relaying of her decision. Abi observed the interaction with interest. She thought, They're all so busy. It must be good to have someone in charge, sorting things out.

For Abi and Teddy, the intimacy in bed continued, though Abi felt no great pleasure. If anything, she felt more attraction towards Bibi, or Theresa, who'd come back from the trip to see her parents in Widnes. Still, Teddy was very kind to her, and she felt, what was word... *looked-after*? By the third day, it struck Abi that she might now be in a relationship, of sorts.

The change came towards the end of the first week in the house. There was no sudden transformation, just a gentle nudge up the scale each day. It began in the morning, as Teddy made to leave for work.

"Make sure you have your phone with you today," she said, on the doorstep.

Abi opened her mouth to ask why, then a car alarm went off in the street and she was distracted. But twice during the day, Teddy called, both times it seemed, without any particular reason. The second time, Abi was in the local library, using a PC to polish up her CV.

"Hiya, doll," said Teddy. "Just checking in."

"Hi."

"Thought we might have a takeaway this evening. Fancy that?"

"Sure."

"OK, we can decide what food when I get home."

"OK."

A long pause.

"What're you up to?"

Abi explained about the CV.

"So you're in the library?"

"Yes."

"How come you're talking, then? Aren't you supposed to stay silent?"

"They have quiet zones for silent working. I'm in the normal part. It's cool to talk quietly."

As she spoke, Abi wondered whether she'd detected a hint of accusation in Teddy's questioning. She thought, Am I imagining it? What's she suspect me of?

After that, Teddy took to random calls during the day, then a string of faux-casual questions in the evening. Where'd she been? Who'd she talk to? Abi chose not to confront the older woman. After all, where would she be without Teddy's kindness?

One evening, they went to the pub. Teddy drank pints and Abi gin, and somewhere in the hazy maze of the conversation Abi asked after Paisley.

"Paisley? She was a slag and a bitch," said Teddy. "Pure poison."

She drained her pint and got up to buy another round. By the time she returned with the drinks, Abi had forgotten the conversation.

"Why'd you want to know anyway?" Teddy asked, after a long pull on her pint.

"Know what?" Abi asked.

"About Paisely. Come on, don't play Little Miss Innocent."

"I don't know what you mean."

"You still fancy her?" Teddy said. "Well, she's out of your league, babe."

Abi stared at Teddy, confused by the sudden switch in tone. Her face must have dropped.

"Hey, just joking," said Teddy, but her smile was bogus and her stare probing.

Two days later, a similar scene at the pub, another conversation flipped from casual to wired in the blink of an eye. This time Abi was asking about Reading Pride.

"Is there a big scene in Reading?" she asked. "I've looked online, but all the places mentioned on the chats are from conversations that are like three or four years old."

Abi watched Teddy stiffen and thought, Uh-oh.

"A big scene? Why'd you want to know?"

"I just-," Abi began. Teddy's smile had turned cold.

"You looking for fresh meat, bitch?"

"No, no," Abi backtracked. "Just interested. You know, Pride was a great vibe. I just wondered where people go the rest of the year."

A long drawn-out pause. Abi found herself holding her breath. Then Teddy shrugged.

"Hey, I'm only kidding around," she said. "Can't you take a joke?"

From that evening onwards, Abi began to feel trapped. The temperature had dropped, and the weather was damp and wet. By the end of October, it became harder to stay outside all day, though she still felt awkward hanging around the house. She began to see that Teddy's bossiness was based on a need for control, and that what she'd mistaken amongst the other housemates for respect for the woman, was actually something closer to fear.

A pattern began to emerge. Three or four days of domestic fair weather between Abi and Teddy, then a single intense storm. The trigger was always a chance remark made by the younger woman, anything that could light the fuse of jealousy and suspicion. Meanwhile Abi remained paralysed by indecision, leaning one day towards planting roots in Reading, the next towards a new start elsewhere. Bath, Liverpool, Edinburgh, Birmingham.

She'd begun to toy with the idea of applying for a master's, though she changed her mind each day about what she'd study. Her first degree in sociology had been interesting, but she didn't see how it could lead anywhere. No, she wanted to do something more practical. Sport's Therapy? Horticulture? Nursing? Conservation? She spent hours on the PC in the library, but felt like she was going round in circles.

A big argument in November after she left her phone at home and went out for the day. A rat-a-tat of accusations like fists slammed on the table. At the end, Teddy smashed a mug against the kitchen wall.

Before each spat, and after, they shared many pleasant hours together. Teddy, at her best, had a dry smart sense of humour, a fierce loyalty, a generosity of spirit. At other times, though, Abi realised how insecure she could be. She kept the house on edge. All the housemates were aware who the firework was, but no one ever knew whether today was the day that the rocket would explode.

Every couple of months, one of the women would move out and another would take her place. Bibi left for London, then Jackie for Manchester. By the end of November Abi was not sleeping well. She felt hemmed in, scared of Teddy, but too weak to escape.

The situation reached its climax on the morning of the first of December. A Welsh housemate called Georgia had just left for work. She'd stayed on in Reading after University and now worked in a printing shop. The other housemates were either asleep or away. As Abi stood at the sink washing up the breakfast things, Teddy asked her what she thought of Georgia. Distracted by her chores, Abi didn't sense the danger.

"She seems cool," she answered.

How it moved from there to the accusations of flirting, the allegations of betrayal, Abi could not remember. There was a to-and-fro of conversation, but Abi's mind was on the day she planned to spend running through post-graduate courses in the public library. One moment, she was drying up the mugs, the next Teddy had grabbed a handful of her hair and was dragging her towards the front door. In the kitchen doorway, Teddy stopped and bent low, her face inches from Abi's.

"Fucking bitch," Teddy hissed. She was breathing heavily and her face was screwy and flushed. Abi flinched as flecks of spittle splattered across her cheeks and lips.

Slap! The back of Teddy's hand across Abi's face, the shock as painful as the sting. Then they were in the hallway. Teddy pushed her hard against the wall. Abi felt the wind knocked from her lungs. She said nothing as the older woman flung open the door and shoved her outside.

"Back on the streets where you belong, you slag."

And then the door was slammed on Abi's face and she stood there, in jeans and a sweatshirt and trainers, trembling with fear as a woman pushing a buggy passed by on the pavement, shot her a curious glance, then moved on.

Eight thirty in the morning. Abi had neither phone nor money, just the change in her pocket. She thought about ringing the doorbell and pleading with Teddy, but she was afraid. Perhaps she could wait until the older woman had gone to work, then let herself in. She searched her pockets for the key. Damn, she could picture it on the bedside table where she'd left it the night before.

A blue sky, crisp and bright, sunshine without warmth. A grim morning walking the pavements of Reading, shivering in doorways, squeezing all the heat out of a sweet milky coffee.

At noon she thought one of the housemates might have returned. Instead she found, on the doorstep, her hastily-packed bag. She checked through. Her passport was there, her purse and phone. Well, that was something. She hauled the backpack onto her shoulders and looked around. Though she was relieved to have escaped Teddy's madness, a new reality now appeared before her. She was homeless and alone.

Where to go? The sky had clouded over and now hung low and heavy. If the morning's wanderings had taught her one thing, it was that Reading now felt foreign, so alien indeed that she soon got lost amongst the streets that had so recently felt familiar. She wandered through a park, watched a mother and daughter feed bread crusts to the mallards at the pond, felt the beginning of a soft drizzle on her cheeks. In the distance, a young woman was walking away from Abi, her hand pressing a phone to her ear. For a moment Abi thought it was Paisley, felt a frisson of excitement, then the woman turned and Abi saw that it was not her.

On the other side of the park the residential streets narrowed. She walked on, her mind racing as she tried to decide what to do. It was mid-afternoon and the first suggestions of panic began to whisper in her ear.

At the end of the next street she turned right, then came out on a busier road. She passed a betting shop, an Oxfam, a nail bar. Up ahead a road sign pointed left for the railway station. It felt like an omen.

The train station was quiet. A line of taxis idled outside. On the forecourt a quartet of pigeons were working through an abandoned baguette. Inside the station café, a fruit machine flashed urgent reds. Abi gazed up at the departures board. The next train was going to London. No, she couldn't face the city, that was too great a challenge. She peered up again. The one after that was the 15.15 to Banbury, leaving from platform 8B, stopping at Oxford.

Oxford. She'd been there on school trips. There was a museum with mummies and a McDonalds, and a lot of old buildings. But it wasn't the architecture that drove her to buy the one-way ticket, but rather the growing panic at the thought of a night on the streets.

The journey was short and she found a backpacker's hostel close to the train station. There were cheery Australians and loud Italians, but the excited chatter only made her feel more alone. She slept fitfully, and as soon as she woke, she set about finding her own room and a job.

That first day in Oxford, she signed up to four employment agencies. She used the hostel address for the forms she filled, and once she'd done that, she realised she might as well stay there until she started work. She hadn't ditched her idea of further studies, but they'd have to be put on hold for the time being.

The admin job at the Nuffield hospital felt like a great step forward. For the fortnight before, she felt lonely and fragile. She lay awake for hours, and when sleep came, her dreams alternated between the final scenes with Roger and Teddy so that in time they merged into a single episode of horror. The close-up face, the grimace of hatred. The flecks of spit, the probing fingers, the slap and sting. The thud of her back hitting the wall. The slam of the door in her face.

The job was easy, though she knew she'd get bored sooner rather than later. Still, it gave her what she needed for the time being: an income, a distraction, some social interaction.

Christmas in the hostel was a grim affair, and then it was Boxing Day, another day off, and she was scrolling through her phone alone in a Costa when she saw the Daily Info advertisement.

Two rooms available in Rose Hill house. GCH, shared bathroom. Use of garden. Applicants should be professional non-smokers. No pets.

She read it through twice, looking for warning signs, but found none. She opened her email app and began to compose a reply.

Garai 1

One sunny day in September, Garai Hove, and his two schoolboy friends were arrested by a host of baton-wielding ZRP cops. One moment he was standing beside Tafadzwa Mahanya watching Ted Watt-Leakey shoot pictures with his Nikon, his life journey set and mapped. The next moment he was off-course and rudderless, bound for a destination he could never have imagined.

It was three o'clock in the afternoon and they were standing outside the Harare Central Police Station on the corner of Inez Terrace and Kenneth Kaunda Avenue. They'd been there half an hour, Ted taking photos while Tafadzwa used his digital recorder to grab on-the-cuff interviews with some of the protesters gathered in front of the building.

The plan was to head back to the boarding school in Borrowdale afterwards to put together the latest post of the blog they'd been secretly writing for the past two years. It was a running commentary on the state of the nation, on the corruption and mismanagement of the Zimbabwean government under Edison Mnangagwa. The aim from the start had been to highlight the various forms of opposition to the state, and the authorities' reaction to the protests.

Today's demonstrators seemed to have set their sights on several targets. Some were demanding the release of those arrested the previous month during anti-Government demonstrations, others protesting the abduction of some human rights activists who had recently disappeared from their homes. Garai and his friends had got what they needed for the post when the police appeared in riot gear from both ends of the street and charged the protestors.

Garai watched Ted put up his hands in surrender as two police officers closed in on him. Then Ted turned round to let them cuff his hands. Tafadzwa was less fortunate. He followed the same manoeuvre, his arms held aloft to show that he offered no resistance, but the approaching thug in uniform lifted his club, swung it in an arc and brought it down hard on the boy's skull. From some ten metres away, and even above the crowd's hubbub, Garai heard the crack, and felt a sickening spasm in his gut.

A few moments later, it was Garai's turn. A barked command from a policeman with bloodshot eyes and chapped lips. The man looked scarcely older than Garai's seventeen years.

"*Gara pasi!*"

Sit on the ground.

Garai shoved his notebook inside his jacket and squatted down. He turned to stare at his fallen friend. Tafadzwa was lying on the tarmac of the road, his face turned away from Garai, his body motionless. The digital recorder had spilled from his hand and lay a metre away. Around them, the police had gained the upper hand, a dozen or so protesters arrested, the rest dispersed.

"Taf!"

That was Ted shouting. He was closer to their friend, and had a view of his face from the angle he was sitting. Garai took one look at Ted and read nothing good in his wide eyes and pallor.

"Is he OK?" Garai called.

Ted looked over at Garai, opened his mouth to speak, but just then the arresting officer hauled the boy to his feet and pulled him towards the entrance to the police station. An instant later, two uniformed constables reached down and hooked their arms beneath Tafadzwa's armpits. They half-dragged, half-carried the unconscious boy in Ted's wake, his heels scraping along the tarmac, over the curb, across the pavement and up the steps into the building. Now an officer was tapping Garai's shoulders.

He stood before Garai and gestured for the boy to get up and follow him.

"*Simuka*," he commanded. "*Nditevere*."

It was random luck that saved Garai. Two dozen new protestors appeared behind the police officers. A rock was thrown, it hit Garai's arresting officer on the shoulder and the man cursed in anger.

The officer turned to face the surging newcomers, and with his captor distracted, Garai needed no prompting. He was on his feet and running like a spring hare. He headed away from the fight, expecting at any moment to hear the crack of a rifle, to feel the thud as the round slammed into his back. At the end of the street, he turned left and put his head down. He didn't stop until he reached the taxi rank on Seke Road.

All around him ordinary citizens were going about their everyday lives. People on their phones, buying peanuts from a street vendor, or waving, or hailing a cab. It would have been easy to believe he'd imagined what he'd witnessed just minutes before The raised fists and chanted slogans. The arc of the baton on Tafadzwa's head. The sickening snap.

Where were his friends now? What was happening to them?

*

At the taxi rank, Garai stopped to catch his breath. His flight instinct, overwhelming in the face of the police violence, was replaced now by a cooler line of reasoning. He thought, OK, what are my options?

He could return to school and pretend nothing was wrong. But he'd been seen at the demonstration, and Tafadzwa and Ted were in police custody, and links would be made between him and them. Sooner or later, the hunt would begin, and the police would be paying St George's a visit.

He could go back home to his parents' house. The security forces would be going there too, though perhaps not right away. When his mother and father found out what had happened, they would be distraught, their dreams for their only son shattered. He felt an instinctive wish to put off that moment for as long as possible.

So that left the most dangerous option. To return to the police station, find a safe surveillance spot outside, then watch and wait for signs of his schoolmates. The thought was terrifying, but in his state of disorientation, it seemed the least worst plan. Reluctantly, he retraced his steps.

As he headed back, he thought of his two friends.

Ted Watt-Leakey would not have to wait long at the police station, not with his family connections. Once the officer had asked him his name, he'd be placed in a cell while calls were made to his father. They'd take his camera, but otherwise he'd be released unscathed.

There'd been a few close shaves with the blog over the past two years, but this was the first time Ted had been arrested. His parents would be furious, of course. Not that they didn't know about his political views. He'd described to Garai the sort of arguments that took place in the Watt-Leakey house. Ted liked to wind his parents up, it was good sport. But they had no idea that his beliefs had translated into concrete action.

Garai already knew the broad facts about the Watt-Leakeys from hearsay, and Ted had added to this with personal detail. For years his father's haulier firm was instrumental in bolstering Zimbabwe's fragile economy. As the man liked to boast, it was *his* fleet of trucks bringing foodstuffs up from South Africa, filling the wholesale warehouses in Harare, and keeping the supermarkets and restaurants stocked.

What else had Garai gathered? The Watt-Leakey name had held sway in these parts for almost a hundred and thirty years, ever since Ted's ancestor, Albert, had ridden alongside

Rhodes on the Pioneer Column. Hadn't he fought with Rhodes to annex Mashonaland, the first step towards the creation of Rhodesia? Watt-Leakeys had been the cornerstone of the old country, establishing a chain of farms that helped feed the whole of southern Africa, his maize flour sent as far as Lilongwe and Lüderitz, the tobacco raising vital foreign currency when the Smith regime became *persona non grata*.

And it was Ted's grandfather, Edward Watt-Leakey, who'd had the foresight to sell up the Zimbabwe interests in the mid-eighties, when Mugabe was still the honeymoon bride, and the economy was strong, and the troubles to come – the seizure of white farms, the hyperinflation, the violent suppression of all opposition – were on nobody's mind.

Edward Watt-Leakey sold all the farms bar one. He sold the two hotels and the three restaurants, the wholesale business and agricultural supplies network. He transferred most of his wealth to South Africa, expanded the haulier business, purchased the beautiful Cape Town villa in Constancia and the vineyard in Stellenbosch. He bought a townhouse in Kensington and a loft apartment in Manhattan, just in case. And by running his food trucks back and forth so that Zimbabwe didn't starve, he showed the Mugabe regime that it would pay to leave alone what interests remained. That was crucial for Edward, and for his son William, Ted's father, when he took over the business. Because though these were tricky times in Zimbabwe for a white man, and even more so for a *rooinek* Rhodie, neither father nor son could live with the thought of cutting their ties completely. As William told anyone who cared to listen,

"Say what you like, I'm a son of the soil. I may have white skin, but cut me and I'll bleed African blood."

That was why they maintained the farm in Marondera, the house in Chisipite. And why they insisted that Ted should go to boarding school in Harare. They themselves had boarded at Prince Edward's School, and that's where Ted had started. Only a run-in with the head over an incident involving *mbanje* and a bottle of Bols brandy had ended his school career there. The

Head had agreed to hush up the incident, but only on condition that Ted would voluntarily withdraw.

St George's was the compromise. St George's College, Borrowdale, founded in 1896 by a French Jesuit, Father Marc Barthélemy. Once a symbol of Colonial rule, now catering to the post-independence elite. Ted had promised to behave himself, and perhaps would have done so, had he not met Tafadzwa Mahanya in his first week at the new institution. All this, Ted had disclosed to Garai in drips and drabs starting with their first conversation after Debating Club.

It was early in the term and Ted knew no one in his dorm, so he'd joined the club out of boredom, at least that's what he'd told Garai. The debate itself had been anodyne. *This House believes* blah blah blah. Something about the electoral system, proportional representation vs first-past-the-post perhaps, though Ted had scarcely listened to the debate. The speakers had been pedants, and Ted wished all the way through that he'd signed up for chess or jazz band or the photography club, anything but this drivel.

Halfway back to the dorms, Ted realised that two other boys were making the same short walk. Garai and Tafadzwa. He knew their names but they hadn't spoken much so far. They were all in the same house, Hartmann, named after the chaplain to the 1890 Pioneer Column.

"Howzit?" he said, and they nodded back.

"Man, that was shit," said Tafadzwa. "Halfway through, I'd have paid you to shoot me."

"Ya, and I'd have done it for you, if I hadn't already hanged myself," Ted answered. They both laughed, and Garai smiled along with them.

The dorm was empty and Garai watched Ted look around awkwardly.

"Hey," he said at last. "Do either of you smoke *mbanje?*"

Garai had never tried, and didn't want to either. Before he could answer, Tafadzwa shook his head.

"Oh very good, let's all get stoned and stop worrying about the real world. Opium is the religion of the masses, right?"

"Hey, I was only-" Ted began, but Tafadzwa cut him off, beginning the tirade that would seal their bond.

"What's the point worrying about PR or first-past-the-post or house of fucking representatives? It's all bullshit if we don't have a real democracy. Open your mouth and the CIO will have you gagged before you get the first sentence out. Sit down in protest and they'll stamp your head to pulp. Pick up a placard and they'll shove it up your arse."

Garai stared at Ted's bewildered face and almost smiled. He loved the effect of Tafadzwa's rhetoric on newcomers.

"ZANU-PF may have once been the party of liberation, but now it's a putrid swamp of venal corruption," he continued. Garai watched Ted's eyes widen. "It'd be better to put the Party out of its misery. Shoot it and stuff it and keep it in a glass case on the shelf next to your TV. We know there'd have been no Chimurenga victory without those old men who founded the Party, but what it's become today, that gang of thieves has no part to play in Zimbabwe's future."

Garai continued to watch Ted's face. Yes, he could see that the *murungu* liked what he was hearing. And why not? Tafadzwa had a way of rousing the spirit. Garai could almost feel the heat of the fire stirring in Ted's belly.

"Look what it's done, the Party. Turned an independent judiciary into a yes-man tool through strategic appointments. And the other institutions of government have just become cogs in the Party machinery. The police are nothing more than ZANU's private militia. And don't talk about the Army. Let's be honest, it runs the country. Mnangagwa may be a psychopathic dictator, but when push comes to shove, he's the Army's puppet, just like Mugabe was at the end."

A pause as the young man gathered steam.

"The Army creates policy to benefit itself, not the wellbeing of the *povo*. Take its involvement in the war in DRC. That was just a ploy so that the Generals could fill their pockets with Congolese diamonds. Nowadays it doesn't need to wage proxy wars in other countries, it's got its own diamond business at Marange. It's a business, only it's not accountable to any shareholders, and profits go straight into the Generals' bank accounts."

"So what's the answer?"

That was Ted, little more than a whisper, the first time he'd spoken.

"Well, don't get me started on the opposition. MDC-T, MDC-M, MDC-B-for-bullshit. There's nothing there to *inspire*, man. What's the point of democracy, if there's no real *choice*? Where's our Thomas Sankara? Our Bobi Wine? We don't need PR or a different parliamentary system. We need to start *afresh*."

There was more along the same lines, a venting, and when he'd finished, they sat together in silence. When they did eventually open their mouths, it was to start a conversation that would lead to the setting up of the blog, to the political activism that fed it, and to one of those magnesium friendships of youth, a fierce conflagration that burned at a furious pace, then was extinguished at a single stroke that September day when their paths diverged so brutally.

From the start, they each had their roles. Ted was the joker and the rebel, all who-dares-wins and devil-may-care. He was the IT-savvy one too. He set up the blog and found out about VPNs to render the blog untraceable to what he called the CIO dinosaurs. He also owned a top-of-the-range Nikon digital SLR.

Tafadzwa was the orator and writer, the theorist and strategist. He was street-smart, a scholarship boy, born and bred in Mbare, the original black township back when Harare was Salisbury. Ever since those early days, Mbare had been a hotbed of dissent.

His father worked as a driver for a hotel in town, ferrying the manager or VIP guests to the airport or business meetings around town. His mother was a teacher, but she'd been arrested at an MDC rally, and the school had fired her. Now she worked in the informal sector, buying vegetables outside Harare, selling them in town at a roadside stall.

Tafadzwa had a close, extended family. He was the youngest of seven. His aunt ran a shebeen on Chatima Road. Tafadzwa sometimes helped out during the holidays. His uncle sold soapstone carvings, knobkerries and other tourist tat at Mbare Musika open market. The whole family were politically active.

It was Tafadzwa who decided the grand themes of each post, then where to go, who to see and talk to. Then he turned what they'd discovered into those piercing angry diatribes that called for resistance and revolution.

Garai, quiet and watchful, let Tafadzwa take care of the bigger picture while he concentrated on detail. He designed the blog, edited Tafadzwa's words and brought them to life through the careful employment of Ted's images.

They tried, in the blog, to offer a snapshot of contemporary politics, using interview and image to produce oral histories of their time. They researched their stories using independent Zimbabwean and foreign media sites, backed up by local social media. Over the months, their readership grew steadily.

One early post looked at Mugabe's 2017 fall from power. There were interviews with people who'd witnessed the appearance of rolling tanks in Harare, the tens of thousands who poured onto the streets to celebrate. Recorded in words and images was a nation's hope.

A second post looked at the first post-coup violence, the shooting of innocent civilians during opposition protests in Harare in August 2018, and the subsequent Motlanthe Commission of Inquiry. They interviewed families of some of the deceased and pointed out that the Inquiry's recommendations - to hold the perpetrators to account and compensate the victims - had been ignored.

Tafadzwa also wrote a piece describing how Mugabe had promised to establish an Independent Complaints Mechanism to investigate wrong-doings by members of the security forces, and that Mnangagwa had buried the plan.

Further articles looked at the government campaign of harassment and intimidation against independent national media. The detention of Violet Gonda and Pauline Chateuka, Gilbert Nyambavhu and Idah Mhetu. The administration's failure to amend or repeal Mugabe's draconian anti-media laws such as the Access to Information and Protection of Privacy Act (AIPPA), the Criminal Law (Codification and Reform) Act, and the Public Order and Security Act (POSA).

Not all the posts were overtly political. Tafadwa shared a Human Rights Watch document with the others. It described the eviction of widows from their homes and the confiscation of their property by in-laws due to traditional laws governing ownership in marriage. They travelled out to a homestead near Masvingo during the school holidays, their only trip outside the capital, to interview a woman who'd been chased from her home by her brothers-in-law after her husband died.

Soon after that article, Tafadzwa wrote another one about institutional homophobia and anti-LGBT persecution. It focused on the resignation of a teacher at St John's College in Harare after he received death threats because of his sexual orientation. For the piece, Tafadzwa also interviewed several members of GALZ, the national pressure group.

Many of the posts sought to publicise the scale of protests against the government, and the crackdown that inevitably followed. Interviews with the victims of the state-sponsored torture and rape, family members whose loved ones had disappeared or were killed. Some of the protests were carried out in the name of the official opposition, the rival factions of the MDC, but often the victims of the backlash were non-affiliated anti-government activists, or non-political civilians attacked for protesting about fuel hikes or inflation or wage stagnation.

There was a series of articles that narrowed in on random civilian deaths, innocent folk swept up in strikes or stay-away protests, caught out in the wrong place at the wrong time. Elvis Nyoni, Solomon Nyaruwa, Kelvin Tinashe Choto.

A parallel series looked at the effect of the economic crisis on ordinary people. Not the drama of a public shooting, but the squeezing of life by starvation or lack of health facilities, or by preventable diseases like cholera. A different kind of demise: the death of hope.

The blogs were spearheaded by Tafadzwa, but it was Ted's photography that brought them to life. And as the months passed, Garai watched Ted's interest grow as he mastered the techniques of his art . He'd never match Tafadzwa's ideological passion, nor Garai's steady political commitment. But he was nevertheless a key link in the chain.

That day in September marked the end of their underground blog. This Garai considered as he stood behind a street vendor selling salted groundnuts served in twists of old newspaper. Garai watched the entrance and waited, and slowly the minutes passed.

Police vehicles came and went, but the first car to park itself was a luxury Mercedes, silver and sleek, that arrived over an hour after Garai had begun his vigil. Five minutes passed, then ten. Finally the building entrance opened and Garai saw his friend Ted emerge, blinking in the bright sunshine. He looked around, caught sight of the Merc and walked towards it. At the same moment, Garai stepped forward and hurried towards the vehicle.

Ted arrived first, opened the back door and slid inside. The motor revved but before it could move away, Garai was up at the passenger window, rapping on the glass.

Ted opened the door and slid across the seat to make space.

"Hey, man. I thought they got you. Get in." Then, as the car moved off, he added, "This is Ncube, my father's driver."

The man was squat and heavy, a bull-neck and shaved head. He looked at Garai through the rear-view mirror and nodded.

"Did you see Tafadzwa?" Garai asked at once.

"Only outside. It looked... ."

He didn't finish the sentence, and no one spoke for a while. Garai noticed that the car was heading south, through the high-density townships, not north towards Ted's family home and St George's. Ted must have noticed too, because he asked Ncube,

"Where are we going?"

The driver glanced into the rear-view mirror.

"Airport, Mr Edward," he said.

"Airport?"

"There's a flight to Jo'burg in two hours."

"What? Are you serious? This is what my dad ordered?"

"Yes, Mr Edward."

A minute passed while Ted digested the news.

"What about my passport?"

"In the glove compartment, Mr Edward."

"Clothes? Shoes?"

"Your suitcase is in the boot, Mr Edward."

A long silence followed. Garai looked at Ted and saw something that could have been fear. He realised then what should have been obvious to him. That whatever would happen next, the repercussions of the demonstration and of the violence that followed, would not affect Ted. That he had a sort of immunity. And that Garai himself was not so blessed. That he would have to deal with the aftermath alone.

"Stop the car," he said. "I need to go home."

Ncube glanced at him again through the rear-view mirror, and slowed the car. Garai looked at his friend, but Ted wouldn't meet his eye. Instead, he carried on gazing out of the window.

Garai got out.

"Thank you," he said to the driver. To Ted he said,

"Good luck, man."

Ted met his eye now and nodded.

"You too."

Back on the street, Garai took a moment to get his bearings. Was this Simon Mazorodze Road? Yes, there was the Total service station up ahead. He'd hail a taxi and head back into town. He needed to see his parents, however painful that may be.

He stood on the curbside and wondered how badly Tafadzwa was injured. He imagined Ted on the way to the airport. He pictured him outside Departures, Ncube handing over Ted's suitcase, ticket and passport, along with a wad of South African currency.

"Someone will meet you in Jo'burg," Ncube would say before he headed for the exit ramp. Ted would gaze at the cloudless sky, pick up his suitcase and walk through the terminal doors. Garai wondered whether his friend would ever again see the Zimbabwe sun.

And then a strange feeling came over Garai, a kind of divergence. An unbonding of friendship that had recently seemed unbreakable. There was Ted at the airport about to board a plane, a new life awaiting him. There was Tafadzwa, gravely wounded, perhaps still at the police station, perhaps already on his way to Parirenyatwa hospital in the back of a police car. And here he was, Garai, standing by the side of the road, dreading his return to the family home in Mabelreign where he would, no doubt, break his parents' heart.

Returning for a home visit was a rare term-time occasion, not because he felt estranged from his parents, but because they insisted that any distraction from St George's curriculum could be risky. After all, they were investing every cent they had in their only child. They couldn't afford to diminish the dividend.

Garai's father worked as chief finance officer for a private firm. The owner's brother was a minister in the current Government, and so the company always contributed generously to ZANU-PF Party funds. The connection was lucrative, it meant a number of state contracts always went its way.

Garai's mother worked as senior nurse at Parirenyatwa, when the medical staff were not on strike. Together with her husband, she'd succeeded in alienating the entire extended family on both sides by investing all that they had in their son. By refusing to contribute to the financial wellbeing of their poorer rural nieces and nephews, they'd gone against a fundamental principle of their culture. It was a tough choice to make, but once they'd decided that Garai should attend one of the most prestigious schools in Zimbabwe, all their resources were needed to pay for the fees and books and endless sundries. The price was high in another way too: the Mabelreign household was shunned by its relatives back home in Gweru.

Garai stood for a while, hoping that the ebb and flow of passers-by would soothe his agitation. He was now south of the city centre, miles from his home north-west of the hub. The thought of standing still left him antsy, so to put off the moment of arrival, he decided to walk. He would head directly back into town up along Rotten Row, then skirt the western edge of the city centre. Perhaps by the time he got home, his head would have cleared.

Before he set off, he took out his phone and messaged Tafadzwa. Perhaps he was panicking over nothing. He imagined his friend reading the message back in the dorms where he was nursing a sore head. They'd meet up again this evening to plan the next blog post and chuckle over the near-miss of this adventure. That would lead to the re-telling of old tales, the other scrapes they'd got into in the past. They were warrior-brothers fighting for truth, and they'd remain so for the rest of their lives.

All the long dusty walk home, his mood swung between hope and fear. It was late afternoon by the time he appeared at the top of his street. As he opened his garden gate, he glanced once again at the screen of his phone. No message from Tafadzwa.

His father was home on leave. He was weeding the small plot of rape and tomatoes that he nurtured round the back of the house. When Garai called out, he appeared wiping the sweat from his brow with a grubby handkerchief. His face wore a frown of concern.

"Everything OK, son?"

"Yes, sure. I was just passing," Garai said, though he knew this sounded lame.

"Really?"

"Yes. Well, no, I wasn't passing. We had the afternoon off. I don't have to be back until eight. I was dreaming of mum's *sadza ne huku*. I just followed my nose."

His joke broke the ice and now his father was smiling.

"Well come in, come in. Your mother's still at the hospital. She'll be home in an hour or so. You can help me finish in the garden, then I'll make a jug of Mazoe. How does that sound?"

"Good."

Garai was glad to be working alongside his father. Conversation was limited to gardening matters, so he was spared the usual inquisition about school and his academic progress, until Mr Hove asked,

"How are those friends of yours?"

Both Ted and Tafadzwa had visited several times over the past couple of years, either out of curiosity to see where Garai had grown up, or on their way to or from a blog assignment. Of course, Garai's parents knew nothing of their investigative journalism. They'd have been terrified of the repercussions and would have demanded that he quit at once.

"They're fine," Garai answered. And then, to distract his father, he said, "The tomatoes are looking healthy. You got rid of the what's-it-called."

"Red spider mite? Yes, they won't be showing their faces round here for a while."

Mr Hove chuckled. The garden was his great passion, he loved to talk about it.

Afterwards, they made orange squash and drank it in the lounge. Garai's father put on one of his old records, Devera Ngwena Jazz Band singing *Svika Fair Fair*. They talked about Garai's latest test results in maths, and university course choices.

Garai sneaked glances at his phone, and wondered how he was going to break the news to his parents.

It was half-past six when Mrs Hove walked through the door. One look at her face told Garai that something terrible had happened. Could she know about the demonstration? As soon as she opened her mouth, he saw that she did.

"Thank God you're alive," she said. "Oh Lord, I was certain they'd killed you too."

"Killed?" said Garai, his voice a whisper.

"What are you talking about, Brenda?" said Garai's father. "Who's killing who?"

Mrs Hove, face stiff with fear, stared into Garai's eyes.

"I saw him. Your friend, Tafadzwa. The police brought his body in." She began to sob. "He's just a child. How can you do that to a child?"

"What are you talking about?" Mr Hove said. "Speak clearly now, woman."

"Just tell me one thing, *mwana wangu*, and tell me the truth" said Garai's mother. "Were you there at the protest?"

Garai hesitated for a moment. It was enough to confirm his mother's worst fears. Her sobs multiplied.

"Will somebody tell me what the hell's going on?" Mr Hove said, his voice rising. His tone brought his wife back from the brink. Between spluttered sobs, she described the arrival of the police with the boy's body, the call for a doctor to sign a death certificate, the constables' claim that the deceased was a troublemaker who'd fallen and banged his head while attempting to escape from an arresting officer.

"The moment I caught sight of the body, I recognised the face," she went on. "My Lord, I was so afraid, I couldn't think straight. My phone battery was dead. I didn't know your number by heart so I borrowed a friend's phone and called St George's."

The receptionist had put her through to the head teacher. No, Garai Hove was not on the school premises, he'd last been seen in the morning. Then the head said,

"Look, I shouldn't be telling you this, but the police have just left. They took away Tafadzwa Mahanya's possessions and a laptop that belongs to Edward Watt-Leakey. They asked questions about his friendship group. I didn't mention your son, but they'll find out one way or another."

They sat together in the lounge as night fell. Mrs Hove cooked *sadza* but no one ate more than a mouthful or two. Garai told them about the blog, the events leading up to the visit to the police station that day. As he spoke, he realised that he was living on borrowed time. He could imagine the police connecting Tafadzwa to Ted, to himself. If they managed to hack into Ted's laptop, they'd find the folders of photos and filed blog pages. And there was hard evidence in the school lockers, Tafadzwa's memory sticks that held dozens of interviews, Garai's own notebooks crammed with edited text and blog ideas. The more he spoke, the more misery he saw etched on the faces of his parents. At a single stroke, the events of the day had laid waste to their hopes.

"He cannot stay here," Mr Hove said after the conversation had lapsed into silence for a minute or so. "They will come and take him."

It was night, now, and the mealie porridge lay stiffening on their plates.

Garai expected his mother to object. She'd say, There must be another way. She'd snap her fingers and come up with a plan, a strategy, a way-out from the looming nightmare. Instead she nodded.

"As soon as the police connect Garai to this house, they'll pay us a visit," Mr Hove said. Garai noticed that they were addressing him in the third person, as if he was no longer present.

"I have a friend in Bulawayo," said Garai's mother. "You remember Joyce? We did our nurses' training together. We'll send him there."

"Yes. From there he can get the train to Francistown," Mr Hove continued. "From Botswana he will travel to South Africa, and from there to Britain."

"He'll need papers. A passport. Your boss must have connections. The whole world knows he's a crook."

"It's an idea, Brenda, but I wouldn't trust him," said Mr Hove as he scratched his chin thoughtfully. "Now wait, there's another guy who comes to the office. He works for the boss. He's a snake, but they say he can fix anything for the right money. I have his number."

"Well, what are you waiting for? Call him, man!"

While Mr Hove went off to make the call, his wife disappeared into their bedroom and returned with a cashbox. She opened it with a key. Inside was a large bundle of US dollars. She began to count it slowly.

"Where did you get that?" Garai asked.

Mrs Hove gave him a look as if she'd forgotten he was there.

"Our savings. It was for your education. To finish school and start at university. Now it's your way out."

Garai met his mother's eyes and read a pain he'd never seen before. It was a before-and-after moment. For months to come he would feel like a butterfly caught up in a great sweeping sandstorm that blinded him and deafened him and left him a stupefied zombie.

There were a few more hours in the house as his father made arrangements for transport to Bulawayo, and for the papers he needed to proceed further. After that, things became blurred. There was a wordless journey in a car with a stranger, a week in someone's spare bedroom in Bulawayo. A man with gold teeth came to take his photo, and a few days later a South African passport appeared, and a train ticket, and soon after that he found himself in a foreign country. He made his way to Gaborone and from there took a bus to Jo'burg. He travelled in a daze, felt neither hunger nor thirst, only the loneliness of an outsider. Once every few days he emailed home. His parents had warned him not to phone, in case the call was traced. They were brief, guarded messages, updates on his progress.

In Jo'burg, Garai's father sent him an address of someone who could arrange the visa and ticket. The money Garai's mother had given him was almost gone, but his father assured him that he'd take care of the cost of the ticket from home. Garai could only guess the sacrifices his parents were making to help him escape, the debt they were acquiring. Garai met a man with mirrored sunglasses and handed over his passport. There was a week sleeping rough, in bus and train stations. And then the call came, and a meeting, and the passport was handed back, now stamped with a visa. Two days later, he caught the flight to London.

Memories like fragments of a broken mirror. The bucket seats in the departure lounge, a mother with long braids and hooped earrings soothing a screaming baby in the next row. The click of his seatbelt, the lurch and sway as the plane became airborne. The sweat of the red-faced man sitting next to him, an odour of raw meat ripe and pungent. The tang of orange juice brought by the flight attendant. The fur on his teeth when he woke up for his breakfast tray.

He knew what to do when the plane landed, the man in Jo'burg had coached him. Find a toilet before you go through immigration. Tear the passport to pieces and flush it down the pan. Claim asylum from the first person in uniform you meet. Give your real date of birth, that way you'll be treated as an unaccompanied minor. Say nothing more until you know the UK authorities are processing your claim. Whatever happens, you need to make sure they don't put you on the next plane back to Africa.

He arrived in UK in early October. The first two months were the hardest. They called it a detention centre, but it was really a prison. The first night, an Eritrean boy in the dorm next door slashed his wrists with a razor. A week later, an Afghani named Hassan tried to hang himself in the shower room. An Arab boy went crazy one day at breakfast. He was screaming and shouting and when the guards came too close, he threw chairs at them. Eventually they dragged him off. When he returned, his face was so swollen it looked as if he'd had a stroke.

Garai kept his head down. Around him, the conversations centred around how best to navigate the intricacies of the asylum process in Britain. He listened carefully. It surprised him to hear how arbitrary the outcome seemed for so many cases. This one was allowed to stay, that one was deported, yet their stories were almost identical. Life, it seemed, really was a lottery.

When he wasn't eavesdropping, Garai found his mind returning to Tafadzwa, as if he'd put his grieving on temporary hold during his escape, but was now ready to face the hideous loss.

It was during these days that Garai began to understand the debt he owed his deceased friend. Before their friendship, Garai had given little thought to the state of his own country and how it came to be so. It was Tafadzwa who provided his awakening, who made him see the bigger picture, the journey that a country such as theirs had been through.

They'd been given neighbouring beds in the dorm at school, and the first time Garai saw Tafadzwa he was lying on his back reading a copy of Fanon's *The Wretched of the Earth*. He looked soft and slight, the only sign of resistance the determination in his eyes. Fast forward to the morning of his death, and Tafadzwa was describing the latest book he was reading, *Natives* by Akala. He looked no different, just the hint of bum-fluff on his upper lip and chin. In between those two meetings, Garai received from his friend a first-class education in the politics and sociology of oppression.

Through their conversations, and the books Tafadzwa pressed on him to read, Garai began to see that his country's journey was shared by many Commonwealth nations: the initial contact with Europeans; resistance leading to violent conflict leading to forced absorption into the British Empire; the influence of the colonial mentality on social development; the liberation movement. Then, at the far end of the journey, lay independence, and a new freedom shaped by what had come before. Shaped, or as Tafadzwa used to say, *poisoned*.

One debate they never quite resolved was to what degree the colonial past could account for the toxic state of politics in the ex-colonies.

"Of course, each country has its peculiarities," Tafadzwa once told Garai. "In Zimbabwe's case, there was the particular disaster of the Lancaster House Agreement in '79. Disaster, because the land reform issue was swept under the carpet."

Tafadzwa went on to explain the pledge the British had made, to pull together funds from the international community to pay for land redistribution. As so often happened, Garai sat back and listened as his friend, in full swing now, detailed the political machinations with every date and name and figure at his fingertips.

"The seeds were sown right there for all the shit that followed," Tafadzwa concluded. "That agreement was a ticking time-bomb."

It was Tafadzwa who taught Garai that there were post-colonial ills that Zimbabwe shared with many of Britain's ex-colonies. A failure of good governance. A lack of political authenticity, of an independent judiciary and impartial state security forces. Poor infrastructure and economic investment. A drain of resources to wealthier countries.

"Would Zimbabwe be a fine example of democracy now if there had been no British Empire?" Tafadzwa once asked rhetorically. Of course it was impossible to say. But when they talked about such matters, he always concluded,

"Well, things couldn't be any worse than they are now, right?"

It was hard to argue with that.

All this Garai thought about for those two months in detention, as he listened and watched and waited. He understood from the solicitor appointed to deal with his case that his age gave him protection, but that once he turned eighteen, he'd be more vulnerable to deportation. For the time being, he believed himself to be in a kind of bureaucratic limbo. It was something of a shock, then, when one day in early January he was told that he was to be released into the care of a children's home.

The home was less of a prison than the detention centre, but it housed its own dangers. There were half a dozen asylum seekers amongst the residents, all of whom looked wary and said little. The other youngsters were British. The quieter souls amongst them were dominated by others who were loud and brash and fearless, the girls as much as the boys. They cursed the staff, and drank and smoked *mbanje,* and there were flare-ups of temper a dozen times a day. One evening a big fight erupted between two boys in the kitchen. A knife appeared, and when the care worker intervened, there was a scuffle and a scream, and then the adult was on the floor clutching his arm.

After that, it was bedlam. Screaming voices, crashing doors, splintering wood, and then the faint smell of smoke. Someone must have broken the glass on the fire alarm, but Garai could not guess how serious the fire was, because by then he'd retired to the bedroom he shared with an Eritrean boy named Kidane. He was tall, with the beginnings of an afro, and scatterings of acne. He'd been kind to Garai on several occasions, sharing with him his deodorant and stash of instant noodles, and in so doing had earned Garai's trust.

"This is madness," said Kidane, as the hubbub continued from the corridor outside. "Look, I have a friend in Oxford. A cousin I met in Calais. I'm leaving this madhouse. Are you coming?"

Garai sat paralysed by indecision.

"Brother, this place is on fire. If we get caught, no one can blame us. We'll say we were fleeing from a house fire. We were traumatised. We're only children, remember?"

Garai found himself nodding.

It was only out on the street, as Kidane led him towards the train station, that it struck Garai that he had no idea where he was.

"Which place are we in?" he asked.

Kidane glanced at him and laughed.

"You're in heaven," he said. "Welcome to Slough."

Kidane's cousin-friend, Dawit, lived in a room off a courtyard that lay behind a betting shop in east Oxford. He was working as delivery driver for a Chinese takeaway, cash-in-hand. His asylum case had been rejected and he was waiting for his appeal. Knowing that if that went against him, he could be deported at any moment, he went about his day in a state of simmering agitation. For a fortnight, Kidane slept on his sofa while Garai made do with the floor.

One afternoon Kidane and Garai were at home playing *Call of Duty* on the games console when Kidane's phone rang. A hurried conversation in a language Garai could not follow. The Eritrean boy hung up and turned to Garai.

"That was Dawit. He lost the appeal. He's going underground. He's waiting for me at the train station. We're going to London. It'll be easier to get lost there."

"OK."

"I'm sorry, but he says you can't come. He's worried about drawing attention. You understand, bruv? I guess you can stay here until the landlord kicks you out."

Together they looked around the dingy bedsit. There was a flimsy wardrobe with some of the cousin's clothes, a TV, a Playstation, a microwave beside the sink, and a bicycle leaning against the wall.

"I'm sorry to leave you like this," said Kidane. "You're welcome to anything in the flat. Maybe you can sell it."

Five minutes later, the young Zimbabwean was alone. He looked around at the four walls and wondered if or when the police would come looking for Dawit. Should he too flee this place? But where would he go? He remembered Kidane's comments about being innocent children and thought, Well I have nowhere else to live, so I might as well stay here.

The next day, Garai sold the TV and console at a place on Cowley Road called PX Korner. Among the clutter on a shelf in the flat, he found an A-to-Z of Oxford, and that gave him an idea. In the evening, he parked his new bike outside the takeaway where Kidane's cousin had worked, and walked inside.

"Dawit can't make it," he told the Chinese man behind the counter. "I can fill in for him."

The man frowned and peered at him for a long moment. Garai held his breath. Then the man shrugged and pointed at the plastic bag that lay on the counter. He glanced at the receipt stapled to the back.

"OK. You must work fast. First delivery, Howard Street. Address on invoice. All paid for."

"Yes, sir," said Garai, unhitching the back pack he'd taken from Dawit's flat and placing the food bag inside.

"Be quick," said the man. "Two more deliveries waiting."

For the first three weeks, Garai never refused a shift. There were two or three other delivery guys that worked for the restaurant, but they had cars. One of them, a Sudanese man, was kind to him. He sometimes offered to swap his shorter deliveries for some of Garai's out near the ring road. He asked no questions about Garai's background, and so the Zimbabwean was not forced to lie. He made sure Garai was paid the going rate, and was happy to let the young man pick his brain when he had questions about life in Britain. The Chinese owner paid them weekly in cash, precious banknotes that Garai added to the money he'd got for the TV and console.

One Monday morning, Garai was woken by loud banging on the door. He'd been expecting a visit from the police at some time, either in search of Dawit, or on his own trail. He thought, Oh Lord, this is it. It was a relief to see a short, paunchy man standing before him. He looked old to Garai, fifty or sixty. A scattering of grey hair on the bald pate, black leather lace-ups, a baggy grey suit.

"Who are you?" said the man, frowning.

"I'm a friend of Dawit."

"I'm the landlord. The rent is four days late, and he still owes me for last month. Where is he?"

"He's out," Garai said. "He'll be back soon."

"Well, tell him I called. Tell him he has until Friday to pay. After that, I send round my sons. I told him when he moved in, with me there's no games with bailiffs and courts. I have my own legal system, you get me?"

"Yes, sir."

Four days to get a new home. When he asked his Sudanese friend the best way to find cheap accommodation, the man gave him the name of a local media website.

"A room in a shared house or a lodger in someone's home, that's the cheapest way," he advised. The site's called *Daily Info*. It's better than going directly to a letting agency. They'll ask you to provide references, and proof of stable employment. For some people, that can be tricky," he added, eyeing Garai knowingly.

For three days Garai checked the website from an internet café on Cowley Road. He answered a few ads but the landlords he spoke to wanted to see references and other proofs up front. Then, on Thursday afternoon, he saw the ad.

Two rooms available in Rose Hill house. GCH, shared bathroom. Use of garden. Applicants should be professional non-smokers. No pets.

He took his time writing his response, trying as best he could to strike a plausible, confident and reliable tone. When he'd finally settled on a draft, he clicked 'send'. And then he waited.

Guthrie 3

As the weeks passed, there was no change in Delia's condition, and though Guthrie felt she was in good hands, she still remained a closed book. The only distraction in his life was Abi's arrival.

It wasn't so much an immediate bonding between landlord and lodger that Guthrie felt, more just the presence of another human in his home. Sometimes it was not even that, just traces of her presence. Her shoes in the hallway, a new toothbrush in the bathroom, a washed-up mug on the draining board. He was away at the hospital most days, while she worked. Often she went out in the evening, while he pottered in the kitchen or read his history books in the lounge. When she returned, she'd head to her room, and he'd face the long sleepless hours on his own.

Breakfasts were the only occasions when their timetables merged. She liked to take her time over two or three cups of tea and several rounds of buttered toast. He didn't usually linger at the table, but the opportunity for fresh company made him take his time with his own tea and cereal. Like that, he learned a little of her background. There was a childhood in Pangbourne, a family who still lived there, a schoolteacher father, a mother who sang in the church choir. There was an interest in nature, an ambition to train as an environmentalist, a passion for running and swimming in the river. Most importantly, there was, he believed, a kind disposition and a tolerant ear for his wittering.

The hardest part of his hospital life was the pretence with the doctors and nurses that all was well. Even with Gloria and Sumander and Lawton, the only familiar faces amongst the strangers who came and went, he forced a faux good cheer. Each day he carried out a new performance of his one-man show, *The Optimist*. Yes, Doctor, I believe she's looking a bit better today. Yes, Nurse, I have been playing a bit of music for her. *Heartbreak Hotel. Jailhouse Rock. Are You Lonesome Tonight?* I know deep down she's listening.

Perhaps it was a wish to avoid this bruising pretence that kept Guthrie from revealing Delia's situation to Abi. Once, early on, she'd picked up a framed photo of Delia and asked if that was his wife. He'd said yes, of course, but didn't add more and she hadn't pressed. He supposed she thought him widowed or divorced.

The daily hospital trips were a little harder to disguise. He'd told her early on that he was retired, so he couldn't say he was away at work each day. Besides, he didn't want to tell an outright lie.

"Off out again?" she'd asked once, early on, when they'd crossed paths in the hallway one morning.

"Hospital visiting again," he'd said, as vaguely as he could.

"Oh, you volunteer. That's nice," she's announced.

He hadn't corrected her, and so the story stuck.

His friendship with Gloria remained steadfast. For Christmas, she bought a brush and comb set for Delia out of her own money. For a moment Guthrie felt himself welling up, and wondered why this of all things should set him off. Of course it was a generous act. But it was something else that brought the pain, a wretchedness as he wondered whether Delia would ever be able to acknowledge the gift. He swallowed hard as he assumed his role of optimist.

"Look, Delia, love, isn't it lovely? What a nice gift," he said, holding it up to his wife's still face. Then, to the nurse, he added, "She'll tell you herself as soon as she's better. Thanks so much, Gloria."

Gloria was such a familiar presence that Guthrie had even begun to forget the doubts he'd felt as to her medical credentials. Indeed it was Gloria who he turned to when he had medical questions.

"Is Delia brain dead?" he asked before Christmas.

"No, brain dead means the brain stem isn't functioning. It means the person cannot survive without life support machines to help her heart beat and her breathing. It means there's no hope. But the brain stem governs breathing, and your wife can breathe on her own, right?"

"So, what is she?"

"I'm a nurse, not a consultant. I can't give a definitive diagnosis. But from what I understand, you could say she's in a *prolonged vegetative state*. That means she's been like this for more than a month."

"A vegetable?"

"It's a medical term, not a very nice one. I can understand people find it upsetting. Some prefer to call it *unresponsive wakefulness syndrome*. That's a bit of a mouthful, though."

One day, Gloria mentioned that she'd got mould growing in the kitchen of her Kidlington home, and when Guthrie began to run through the possible causes - condensation, poor ventilation, a failed damp-proof course, a leaking pipe - she'd looked at him so helplessly that he found himself offering to go round and take a look.

The next day, a Sunday, Gloria wasn't working, so he drove round before his hospital visit. It didn't take long to spot the culprit, a cracked pipe fitting.

"Get the pipe fixed and then let me know. I'll give your kitchen a lick of paint with some anti-fungal stuff. I can still get it trade price at the builders' merchants I used to use."

A fortnight later, he spent another Sunday slapping on two coats right through the kitchen. It felt good to be using some muscles that hadn't seen service in months. Gloria asked him if her son Nathaniel could help out, and Guthrie enjoyed teaching the youngster how to use a paintbrush. Gloria went to the trouble of cooking a hot meal for lunch. At the end of the day, when she offered to pay for the work, he shook his head.

"You've gone above and beyond with Delia. It's the least I can do."

By now Delia's lungs were clear, the crisis was over, and her condition was stable. At times there was eye movement, some jerking of her hand in response to touch, and something that seemed to mimic a sleep/wake cycle. But Guthrie still struggled to tell where reflex ended and cognition began. There were days when Guthrie read hope into the tics and twitches, but at other times, they felt like a cruel joke.

Occasionally, Delia's demeanour displayed all the appearances of pain. She might writhe and sweat through gritted teeth, as if she was engaged in some inner fight. At other times she grimaced and yawned and pulled faces he'd never seen before. These mannerisms, along with twisted arm movements that Gloria called dystonia, never failed to torment Guthrie, despite the doctor's assurances that Delia could not feel pain.

"A stimulus like a pinch sends a signal to the receptors in the brain, which may recognise the signal and send back confirmation, but Delia as a consciousness being is not involved. Think of it as an echo of pain, not the real thing."

Guthrie tried to understand, but could not shake the 'what if' question. He raised it at every meeting until eventually Dr Sumander prescribed pain relief for the patient. Guthrie was certain that he could see the visible change in Delia, a relaxing that brought as much comfort to husband as it did to wife.

As those first few months of the new year passed, it was the minute day-to-day changes that allowed Guthrie to pronounce, on any given visit, that she looked good today or a bit peaky, those rolling eyes and twitches that gave Guthrie hope.

If someone at that stage had described the person in the bed as a voided shell, he'd have given them short shrift, all the more vociferous for the fear that lurked in the back of his mind, fermenting but as yet unacknowledged.

Were her eyes watering or was she crying? Was she enjoying the Beatles CD or were the smiles coincidental? Was that emotional agitation or a physiological spasm when Guthrie held the phone to her ear and Eric began to talk?

Every week the ward seemed to grow more crowded, the medical staff ever busier. It was hard for Guthrie to watch the nurses deal with Delia in such a frenzy. It was not neglect, but still he had to work hard not to resent it. He'd voted this Conservative government into power, and he vaguely recalled the Prime Minister's election promises. The man had pledged extra NHS funding, the recruitment and training of tens of thousands of new nurses, the building of more hospitals. Well, Guthrie thought, as he changed Delia's nightie, washed her hair and clipped her nails. Not much sign of that!

On Delia's birthday in March, Guthrie mentioned to Gloria that he'd like to buy his wife some new clothes. It was the first time he'd ever done such a thing, and the prospect was intimidating. Gloria came straight to the rescue.

"I'll come with you. That is, if you want some help choosing."

They spent an hour in the Westgate mall and ended up with a plum-red bed jacket and a bottle of Delia's favourite perfume, then picked up a new nightie from Marks and Spencers. On the day itself, Gloria produced an Elvis Presley CD, a compilation of his greatest hits. Of course Delia already had all the songs on it, but Guthrie didn't mention that.

"That's very kind of you, Gloria," he said. "It's got her favourite, *Always On My Mind*. She'll be chuffed to hear it."

Though Delia no longer required a ventilator to breathe, she suffered another poor chest that spring. They gave her IV antibiotics and kept an oxygen mask to hand. Guthrie found it distressing to watch his wife's body battle the infection. At times she grunted and moaned and ground her teeth, and one day she bit her lip and it bled profusely. For a week the phlegm got caught in her throat. She'd cough and cough until he cleared her mouth with a suction pump the nurse produced. Then for days, there were no signs of life. She lay like a dummy, kept alive by the PEG tube that fed nutrition straight into her stomach.

Through all of this, he sat by her bedside, rarely missing a day, never for less than four or five hours at a time. He washed the greasy hair, and bathed the body that smelled faintly of damp mushrooms. He sat beside her, reading her historical romances and working his way through her crossword puzzles. He brought a tablet that he propped up on her sliding table so that she could watch her favourite TV programmes, *Bake Off* and *Britain's Got Talent*, and the sewing competition with the camp presenter. He detailed to her the minutiae of his daily life. When the weather improved, he described the state of his garden, the crocus bulbs coming up, the buds on the branches of the cherry trees. Sometimes he swore he saw signs of animation in her eyes, but mostly they remained blank, unassailable walls.

The first weeks after Abi moved in, his breakfast interactions with her were fleeting.

"Off out?" she'd say, munching on a piece of toast. He'd have washed up his corn flakes bowl and would be buttoning up his coat.

"Yes," he'd answer. "See you later."

Later, once they'd established a greater intimacy, he still maintained the secret of his other life. After the initial falsehood had been accepted, it felt too awkward to correct it. Perhaps, too, he didn't want the pity. It was a relief to have a sphere of his life that did not revolve around the tragedy that had befallen him. After all, when he wasn't actually face-to-face with Delia, his wife's condition consumed not only his private thoughts but the little other social interaction he took part in, the fortnightly Skype conversations with Eric in New Zealand, the well-meant enquiries from the Cartertons and Barry, phone calls from the other relatives. That was why he kept Delia a secret from the lodgers, first Abi and then the second newcomer, Garai.

After Abi moved in, Guthrie forgot to renew the online ad, and so a few weeks passed before Guthrie remembered to re-post the ad. Garai was the first person to respond. He'd sent a short email as *g.hove@gmail.com*, a polite note in impeccable English asking if he could view the room. He signed the email *Mr G. Hove.*

"He spelled 'accommodation' right," Guthrie told Delia on a visit. "That takes some doing."

Guthrie was a stickler for such things, and the message made enough of a positive impression for him to follow up, so he offered a viewing the next morning. In truth, he was getting a little tired of the whole process of looking for a lodger. Once Abi moved in, he'd found no one suitable before the ad had expired despite receiving a dozen or so emails. The others who came to view the property had either found fault with Guthrie and his room, or else the old man had identified one reason or another to exclude them.

Here was a chance to end this tedious business, but the following day the appointment slipped Guthrie's mind entirely, and he upped and left the house straight after breakfast. It was only when he got home that evening that Abi told him what had happened.

"This dratted memory of mine," he said as he busied himself with the kettle and mugs. Abi had accepted his offer of a hot drink and was sitting at the kitchen table. "Well, what did you make of him?"

He brought over the two cups of tea, sat down opposite her and helped himself to milk and sugar, and then a biscuit from the tin he kept on the table.

It was nice having a bit of company in the house when he got home, and so far, Abi had proved herself an easy housemate to have around. She wasn't Delia, of course. But still, she was better than silence.

"Yeah, he seemed OK. I showed him around and he liked the room. He said he'd take it, if it was still available."

Guthrie looked at her and wondered how best to ease from her the information he sought before he committed himself to this newcomer.

"Can you describe him?" he managed, after a few moments' thought. "What does he do?"

"Erm, I don't know exactly. He said he was working in catering logistics. That he was hoping to go to university soon."

"That's good."

"He was young, well-spoken, you know. Like he'd been to a posh school."

"Sounds promising. Anything iffy, if you know what I mean?"

"Not that I can think of."

"Unpleasant habits? Spicy cooking? Religious nut? Anything skew-whiff?"

"Skew-what?"

"You know. Anything dodgy."

Abi laughed, then took a sip of her tea.

"He seemed like a nice guy."

Guthrie peered at her.

"Got a soft spot for him, have we? Handsome fellow?"

"Not my type, Mister G," she answered, her tone neutral.

"Sorry," he said. "Just my little joke. But you'd say he was alright? A good addition to our little household?"

She shrugged and nodded.

"Sure. He was interested in your book."

"Which one?"

"The one in the lounge. About the British Empire."

"Really? Well, that's a good sign. He takes an interest in history, then?"

"I suppose so."

A pause as he savoured his tea.

"What did you say his name was?"

"Garai," she said.

Guthrie, intent on taking a hobnob from the tin, misheard her answer.

"Gary," he repeated. "Gary Hove. I had an uncle used to live in Hove, down near the seafront. Well, Gary Hove, I think we've found the missing piece of the puzzle."

That evening, after his tea, Guthrie emailed the young man. He apologised for having missed their appointment, offered him the room, and invited him to move in as soon as he wished. He checked his email messages before bed.

Dear Mr Guthrie,
Thanks so much for your offer. If it's OK with you, I'd like to move in as soon as possible. Can I come round tomorrow at eight-thirty?
All the best,
Garai.

Guthrie replied straightaway: *See you at 8.30.* As he put on his pyjamas, he thought, Garai? That's an odd spelling of Gary. Perhaps he's Welsh.

*

That night Guthrie slept badly, his rest disturbed by dark thoughts. He woke late to the sound of voices from the kitchen, pulled on his dressing gown and went down to investigate. It was only at the foot of the staircase when he caught sight of the cheap backpack that he remembered Gary's arrival. That'll be nice, he thought. We'll have some breakfast together. He opened the door to the kitchen and stepped inside.

He stopped dead in his tracks at the sight that met him. He took in the figure of the young man seated at the kitchen table, the slender build, the round face, the close-cropped curly hair, the skin dark as tar. He stood there blinking. He opened his mouth, closed it, opened it again like a drowning fish.

"But... ," was all he could manage.

"Hey, Mister G. This is Garai Hove," said Abi, standing up to fetch a mug for the old man. She pronounced the surname in an unexpectedly exotic manner. *Ho-vey*.

"I didn't … I mean, I don't … ," he spluttered.

"Tea, Mister G?" Abi asked.

"Yes," he said.

Inside, Guthrie was floundering. A coloured boy for a lodger? He had nothing against the idea on principal. After all, he wasn't a racist. You could look at his friendship with Gloria if you didn't believe him. It was just that given a choice between someone reassuringly white and British, and someone who didn't fit this profile, he'd prefer the former. It just made things *easier*, didn't it? And as far as he understood it, he was supposed to have had a choice. But here he was, railroaded into a decision he hadn't made. Was it too late to wriggle out?

He took his mug and smiled, a rather sickly attempt as his mind ran through his options. His usual get-out clauses wouldn't work at this late stage. He couldn't delete the email, couldn't claim that the room was already taken, that he was waiting on someone else's decision, someone he'd offered first dibs to. No, the most he could do was to play for time and look for a loophole.

"Are you a local lad, Gary?" he began.

"No, sir" the boy answered. Guthrie waited for more.

"Where did you grow up?" he tried again.

"Zimbabwe," the boy replied.

"Ah, Rhodesia. And what are you doing in Britain?"

"I live here now, Mr Guthrie. I'm working at the moment. Hoping to study."

Guthrie peered carefully at the young man. He thought, Abi was right, he's well-spoken. A bit shabby-looking, sort of down-at-heel. But not unimpressive. Narrow shoulders, calm in his demeanour, nothing cocky or loud, kind of *clean*-looking.

Guthrie gazed at the young man and thought, Who does he remind me of? Hmm. Wait a minute, that's it, the black comedian, the one who started off on *New Faces* all those years ago. Yes, that's it, Lenny Henry. He looks like Lenny Henry did on *New Faces*.

The young man was talking now and Guthrie studied his manner. He kept his tone level, and when he spoke, he made eye contact with Guthrie. A steady gaze. Was there a hint of something else, an anxiety or fear? Guthrie thought, What's he hiding? Maybe he's unemployed, a sponger. Maybe he's hoping I'll be a soft touch. Guthrie's expression hardened. He thought, Perhaps it's not too late.

"You know the deposit's a month's rent?" he asked, to test the water. "And I'd like the first month's rent's in advance, if that's alright with you."

"Is cash alright?" the lad answered. He took out an envelope and passed it over. Guthrie took it and wondered whether it would be rude to count it. He went through the mental list he'd prepared for his lodgers.

"References?" he said. "I think I mentioned that in my email. A letter from your employer?"

"I talked to my boss," the boy replied. "He asked if you could call him. He could give you a verbal reference, if that's alright. I have his number."

That caught Guthrie unprepared. He didn't have a ready answer so he harrumphed, took a sip of his tea and returned to his mental list.

"And a copy of your passport, if you don't mind? We wouldn't want to be harbouring illegal aliens now, would we?"

He smiled to show he was joking, and took a biscuit from the tin he kept on the kitchen table. Then, remembering his manners, he pushed the tin over towards the young man.

"Help yourself, Gary."

"Actually, it's *Garai*," said the boy.

"Sorry?"

"Garai. My name. Not Gary."

"Ah, yes, sorry. Ga*rai*," he said, running his mouth around the word with an expression that seemed to suggest that he found it a strange fruit, novel and peculiar and not altogether pleasant, though not, as he'd first suspected, poisonous.

"About the passport," said the lad. He met Guthrie's stare and returned his smile. "I haven't had a chance to get to a photocopier yet, but I'll do it as soon as I have a day off. Is that OK?"

"Yes, I suppose so," said Guthrie. He'd just remembered Abi's comment about the boy's interest in his book. "I hear you're interested in British colonial history, Gary," he said.

"Yes, sort of," the boy answered. "And it's Garai, remember?"

"Oh, yes, of course. Garai. Sorry. I'll get the hang of it in a minute. I've got a fascinating book about Rhodesia, Garai. The Robert Blake one. Have you read it?"

"No, I haven't, Mr Guthrie."

"You can borrow it, if you like."

"Thank you, I'd like to."

Guthrie's enthusiasm had swept away his qualms. He began to tell the young man what he knew of Cecil Rhodes and his remarkable achievements. For the next five minutes, any reservations were swept away, and his demands for the reference and passport copy were forgotten.

He'd never again ask for either of them.

The next day, Maggie Khan was waiting for him at the hospital. A decision had been taken by the CCG about Delia's care provision. Due to her complex medical needs, she would receive NHS continuing healthcare. The situation would be reviewed on an annual basis.

"It's great news," she told Guthrie as they sat together by Delia's bedside. "The next step is to get your wife into a nursing home. Things will be less hectic there, the nursing staff will have more time to spend with her."

Guthrie looked at her doubtfully. He was tired of finding Delia neglected when he wasn't around to see to her grooming, yet he couldn't deny that this place had saved Delia's life. The thought of change was terrifying. Maggie must have been reading his thoughts.

"The place I'm thinking of is that one you visited in Headington, remember? It's an excellent facility and less than a mile away. You can go back for a second viewing, of course. But I'm certain you'll be impressed. It's not some brand-new bells-and-whistles place, but it's well managed and the staff are really caring and professional."

"Well, if you're sure," he said.

When Eric heard about the continuing healthcare, he was jubilant.

"Thank God for the NHS," he said. "But don't forget it could all change. Mum's going to get better, so they may end or cut the funding. The laws could change too. I wouldn't put it past that lot in charge."

Guthrie, a life-long Tory voter, frowned into his mobile phone. Eric had swallowed Labour's socialist tripe in his teens, and that had led to a thousand arguments between them that no one ever won. Before Guthrie could start a fresh squabble, Eric said,

"Remember what I said about your finances. No Caribbean holidays or fancy yachts, eh?"

"I remember. In fact I've already taken steps. I've got two lodgers in to help with the bills."

"What?" said Eric. This was the first he'd heard of it. "Really?"

"You told me to watch my finances. It was your idea, son."

"Yes, well, it's just... . I guess I worry about your safety. What are they like?"

"They seem alright. Young folk. I'll soon whip 'em into shape," Guthrie said.

"I'm sure you will, dad. You know how guilty I feel, being so far away. It's good you've got a bit of company at home, and knowing there are folks around in case of an emergency, that's a relief."

A week later, the meeting took place in the hospital to discuss Delia's transfer to the nursing home. Maggie Khan was there along with doctors and several men in suits. Guthrie was fog-headed after a poor night's sleep, so a lot that was said went over his head. He still had mixed feelings about the move. He feared being away from the high-tech equipment that had kept Delia alive, but it would be nice for his wife to have her own room. He'd miss Gloria, too, even though they'd agreed to keep in touch.

In fact there'd been a little frostiness between the two of them ever since he'd spent that day decorating her kitchen. It was sparked by a conversation they'd had over lunch. The meal had got off to an awkward start because Guthrie, fearing he might be offered something exotic, had made sure to pack a round of cheese-and-pickle sandwiches in his lunchbox. When Gloria announced that she'd cooked a special South African dish to say thank you, a chicken stew she called *umleqwa*, Guthrie pointed out that he'd brought his own provisions. She dismissed his protests with a shrug.

"No pale limp sandwiches for you. I won't hear of it," she said. "Of course the stew would taste better with a proper village fowl. The frozen chickens you buy in this country don't have any taste," she explained as she ladled stew over a mountain of rice.

Despite his misgivings, the stew did smell rich and meaty, so he gave in and ate a small portion, just to be polite. He finished as much as he could. After all, he didn't want to cause offence. But he thought, Odd seasoning, and far too spicy for my taste. This is going to play havoc with my digestion.

The awkwardness began after she'd cleared the plates and made tea to round off the meal. Guthrie asked Gloria about other patients she'd nursed who'd suffered similar levels of brain injury. He still found it distasteful to use the term 'vegetative'.

"What's the longest time you've ever seen someone stay unconscious?" he asked. "You know, like Delia?"

She looked at him and he saw that she'd switched from her jovial self to someone more cautious.

"Eight years," she said quietly.

"And then she woke up?" Guthrie asked.

"There were two cases. A middle-aged man. He had a stroke. Another, a teenage boy, he was knocked off his bike. And no, they both died."

"What happened? How did they die?" he asked. There were support groups Maggie had offered to link him up with, and websites she'd shown him where he could read about other cases that resembled his own. He'd never had the courage to investigate either.

"The man had a wife and kids. The boy had parents. In both cases, they stopped believing that the patients would get better. They decided they wanted to end their loved ones' suffering. They applied to the Court of Protection to remove the feeding tubes."

For a long time, Guthrie remained silent. Inside he felt a pressing on his chest, a sense of dread that made him wish he hadn't asked.

"You know, Delia may not come back, don't you?" said Gloria. It was almost a whisper. "The longer she stays unresponsive, the less likely it is. My job is to care for the patient, but it's the loved ones I feel most sorry for. I would never blame them if they made the same decision as those ones I was talking about."

"What?" he said, channelling his fear and grief into a cold fury. "If you think I'd ever... ."

He paused, as if he knew that to continue would threaten their relationship.

"I'm sorry," said Gloria. "I didn't mean ... ."

"I don't know what people do in your country," he said, his voice icy. "But we don't go around letting people die because we run out of patience. A life has a ... has a ... *value*."

"Of course it does," she said.

If Guthrie had looked carefully, he would have seen anger in Gloria's eyes to match his own. But he was looking down now at his empty mug of tea.

There was a long minute of silence and Guthrie felt himself calming. He looked up and met her eyes. They both managed a weak smile, and like that their friendship was brought back from the brink, bloodied but not broken.

*

The great distraction from it all remained Guthrie's interest in his family history.

His own Protestant Irish ancestry, on his grandfather's side, had always piqued his curiosity. The old man had long since passed away, but there was a cousin from Ballymena that Guthrie had met a decade ago at a funeral in London. The two men had hit it off, and when Guthrie mentioned his interest in ancestral research, the cousin had contacted him from time to time with titbits of various sorts, letters and birth certificates and photographs dug up from cleared-out attics.

Recently, the man had sent half a dozen photos from an album he'd discovered at the house of a deceased aunt. They were black-and-white, now sepia in tone, and showed a tall thin man in khaki shorts and shirt standing in what looked like a tropical garden, a backdrop of drooping blossoms and lush undergrowth. There was no writing on the back, nothing to offer clues as to the provenance, but the enclosed letter mentioned that among the effects found in the aunt's house were two Oriental puppets, and a framed picture of a river, stamped on the back with an address in Rangoon.

That's Rangoon in Burma, what they now call Yangon, Myanmar, wrote the cousin in the letter. *My guess is that's where the puppets are from, and the river could be the Irrawaddy, which makes me think maybe we have a relative that lived out there. Can't find a date anywhere, but the photos make me think after WWI. What do you think to that?*

It was an intriguing prospect, to trace back his links to this mysterious man and fill in the blanks from his past, but Guthrie had made little progress beyond buying a book on Burma's history. He'd been surprised to learn that the country fell within the boundaries of Britain's Indian Empire from 1886, and stayed a province until 1947.

He read several histories of the country, skipping the pre- and post-colonial sections, then got caught up in a book titled *Forgotten Voices of Burma: The Second World War's Forgotten Conflict*. This was Guthrie's cup of tea, a hundred tales of plucky English bravery. Chindit commandos swimming the Irrawaddy River to bring reinforcements to malaria-ravaged regulars. Royal Marines parachuted into enemy territory, cheered on by locals as they swept away the Jap invaders. Big-hearted troops going without rations so they could feed the starving children they'd rescued from the clutches of the Axis devils. By God, those stories helped fill the nights when sleep wouldn't come and all he had to look forward to was another day on the ward.

Soon the time came for Delia's transfer, and Guthrie was there to welcome her to her new home.

As Guthrie knew from his first visit, the building itself was nothing to write home about, a converted Victorian red-brick primary school not too far from the Manor Ground where he'd taken Eric to watch the Yellows all those years before.

It was the staff at the home who gave Guthrie the most doubts at first, there was scarcely a Brit amongst them. And yet at the same time, Guthrie could not doubt their professionalism. That and something else, a gentle compassion which he'd found had been drained at the hospital by staffing shortages and the hectic turnover of the wards.

The manager, Vicky from Canada, was a large plump woman with a rosy complexion. She wore wire-rimmed spectacles and kept her hair in a ponytail. One of her two deputies was Colin, a thin balding Trinidadian with an accent Guthrie could barely follow. The man had a tendency to mince when he walked in a way that Guthrie found more than off-putting. Guthrie was there when the man first came into Delia's new room to welcome her a few minutes after her arrival. He'd already greeted Guthrie, and now spoke directly to his wife.

"Hello, darling," he began. "Well, I think before we get too settled we need to give you a shower, my love. We'll wash your hair, and after that I'll call our hairdresser and make an appointment." He picked up Delia's left hand and peered at her fingers. "She can do your nails too, darling. We're going to make you look like a proper queen."

Guthrie was about to object at what felt like something of a liberty, but then peered down at his wife, lying flat in the bed, and noticed, as if for the first time, that her hair was greasy and unkempt.

He gazed up at Colin and saw that the man was staring down at the far end of the bed. He followed his line of sight, then saw that he was eyeing Delia's foot, which poked out from the blanket. A wave of shame passed through him as he noticed how gnarled her toenails had become. When had he last cut them? The indignation he'd felt a moment before was gone.

"Mr Guthrie," Colin said, meeting his eyes with a smile. "Would you like me to arrange for a chiropodist to come in and take a look at your wife's feet? They look like they'd appreciate a bit of pampering, eh?"

"Yes," said Guthrie. "That would be lovely."

The second deputy was Luisa from Brazil. She took Guthrie into Vicky's office for a welcome chat. The room was simply furnished, though the walls were lined with framed photos of smiling folk in dressing gowns that Guthrie took to be past residents of the home. The three of them sat down.

"Look, I'm going to be perfectly honest with you. I've seen quite a few people who've suffered major brain trauma like your wife. In my heart of hearts, I don't believe that they are aware in any meaningful way of who they are, and what's become of them," said Vicky. "Of course, we can't be a hundred percent certain, even of the most damaged of our residents. But it doesn't matter to us one way or the other, we'll always treat them as if they *were* conscious. We'll make them feel loved and cared for, as if they know exactly what's going on around them."

Vicky peered across at Guthrie as if looking for a response, so he nodded.

"No, we can't be sure about the level of awareness of the residents," Luisa said. "But we're certain that what their loved ones are going through is very tough. I'm sure there are moments of strength and hope, but there'll be other times when you feel pretty much alone and desperate. Am I right?"

"I suppose so."

"Between Luisa and Colin and myself, one of us will be on duty at any time of the day and night," Vicky continued. "What I'm telling you, it's what I tell the families of each new arrival. I want you to know that you can always give us a call, night or day, and one of us will be here to talk. It doesn't have to be about anything in particular, just the sound of a friendly voice. It's a policy we have. We might not be able to help, but sometimes it's just about letting off steam, right?"

"Thank you," said Guthrie. He felt, for a moment, as if he might cry. Just then Luisa stood up and asked,

"Would you like me to show you around?"

Colin had already given him a tour when he'd first visited, three weeks before, but the call to action was what he needed to control his emotional leakage.

"Yes, please," he said, getting to his feet. "That'd be great."

A week passed, and then another. Within a month his doubts about the move had passed. He'd got used to the routine here. The atmosphere was more relaxed, Delia's care more personal. Gone were the fears of neglect. Still, he never ceased to watch her like a hawk, every movement and response. Each time her eyes travelled round the room, each yawn, wince, each twitch and grimace and grunt. Everything he mined, minted and then banked in his treasury of hope.

Eric was still too busy to fly over, but occasionally one of Delia's friends or relatives would visit or write or call. Usually the messages attempted some note of optimism. The cousin sent links to stories of remarkable treatments, checklists of techniques to help the patients' recovery. The niece said that she'd read about a man in India who woke up right as rain after twenty-five years in a coma. Guthrie knew better than to believe in these miracles. And yet he couldn't help the tiny charge of hope detonated in his heart when he heard this, and then whenever he remembered it afterwards.

Abigail 2

At first Abi didn't take to Guthrie. She didn't trust him. It wasn't that he reminded her of Roger exactly. After all, her mother's partner was tall and stooped while her new landlord was short and round. No, it was just her suspicion that they were of the same *type*. It began with a comment Guthrie made in the first week about a young person interviewed on breakfast radio who identified as non-binary.

"We never had all this kerfuffle in my day. You knew what you were, and you didn't make a fuss about it."

He must have seen something in her expression, because he tried to explain himself.

"Of course we had the gays back then. I once did a bit of work for a couple in Summertown. They worked in publishing, I think. I did the whole house through in Damson. And I had a cousin too. We always knew he was a bit, you know." He made a limp-wrist gesture. "The thing is, they didn't shove it in your face in those days. They just got on with it quietly."

On another occasion, soon after Abi moved in, Guthrie complained to her about the neighbours' drains.

"It's all that foreign food they cook, it's dripping in grease and it all goes down the plughole. We never had any problems when the Batesbys lived next door."

And there were other passing comments that rankled. About eastern European tradesmen pricing locals out of business. About muslim taxi drivers preying on young girls. About women playing football. About immigrant children lowering standards at schools. About the lunacy of same-sex marriages, and gay couples adopting. And about the migrant drain on NHS and welfare resources. In the early days, Abi lacked the courage to challenge her landlord, and hated herself for her weakness. She hoped instead that her refusal to engage might be enough to shut him up.

And he wasn't all bad. Most of his talk was gentle, harmless nattering.

"I once worked for a man over in Eynsham. Name of Knowsley. A real one for the horses. He used to give me tips," he said one day over breakfast, after a feature on the radio about the upcoming Grand National. "Delia and me, we've always liked a little flutter from time to time. Don't get me wrong, I'm not talking the last of the big spenders. Fifty pee each way, never more."

He stopped to take a swallow of tea. Abi took in the round face, the thin veins around his bulbous nose, the sagging beneath his eyes. Her gaze travelled from the flap beneath his chin, to his unruly eyebrows and the shock of white hair, a thatch at the front, thinning on top.

"Anyway, this Knowsley, I did his whole house through in green. Denver Greengage for the walls, I remember. Fern for the woodwork . It was 1971, early April, the run up to Aintree, and he says to me, 'Guthrie, here's a tip if you fancy a flutter. Specify,' he said. 'Mark my words.' Well, he went on about it for days. Specify, Specify, blah blah blah. In the end I put a bet on just to shut him up. A pound each way. That was a lot of money in those days. Well, you'll never guess. The nag came in at thirty-three to one! We got a set of kitchen knives out of it, and Delia bought a new pair of shoes, and the rest paid for a pergola in the garden."

There seemed to be an endless supply of these sorts of stories, but Abi didn't mind. It was soothing prattle. He mentioned his wife a lot in the tales, and Abi wondered what she'd died of, but didn't feel it was appropriate to ask in case the death was recent and the wound still fresh. For his part, he asked her questions about her home, the family, her childhood, and she gave answers that were not lies, yet neither did they reveal anything beyond the anodyne. Memories of her first day at primary school, sobbing as her mother waved goodbye. Summer afternoons swimming in the Thames with her father while her mother laid out a picnic. Half-terms camping with the Brownies. She offered stone-cold facts and nothing more.

Her job at the Nuffield gave her weekends off, and she spent as much time as she could outdoors. She bought stout walking boots and a waterproof coat out of her first month's salary, and set out each Saturday morning armed with her copy of *Food for Free*, determined to discover all the wilderness of Oxford.

Closest to hand, there was Rose Hill's own small nature reserve at Rivermead, as well as Iffley Meadows. The Thames towpath from the lock took her north into the centre of Oxford or south out towards Kennington, Abingdon and, eventually, as far as London. On the way, she knew the river would pass her own Pangbourne. The thought was unsettling.

She started her meanderings with the better-known spaces of Oxford like Florence Park, Headington Hill, South Park, Bury Knowle, and University Parks. As the weeks turned to months, she discovered the Trap Grounds in Jericho, the expanse of Port Meadow, the treasure of the Kidneys in east Oxford. She explored the established woods like Shotover and Wytham, and the better-kept secrets such as Brasenose Woods and Lye Valley. And there were the Botanic Gardens and Christ Church Meadow, of course.

She discovered that some of the university colleges were open to the public at no cost. She bought a bird guide and a book of mammals to help identify what she saw. One cold morning in February she spotted three waxwing feeding on the berries of a rowan tree in St Catherine's, each creature an exquisite work of art. A week later she saw a kingfisher at the Head of the River, a blur of rust and electric blue. At Bagley

Woods she came across a pair of roe deer. She froze, watched transfixed as they stared back at her, their nostrils twitching, and then disappeared into the undergrowth. There were muntjac at Headington Quarry, and one early morning at Lady Margaret Hall, she saw an otter in the stretch of Cherwell that marked the border of the grounds, its body a single sleek muscle as it slid through the water.

In March, as the weather turned, she bought a bike and began to venture further afield. She rode out to Farmoor reservoir and watched the intricate mating rituals of the crested grebes. Somewhere on the road to Thame she looked up and saw a peregrine rise and rise, then turn and fall, a vertical stoop so mercurial she almost fell off her bike in wonder.

At Stanton Harcourt she discovered the remnants of a stone-age henge marked Devil's Quoits on her map. On an islet on one of the nearby gravel pits she counted fifteen cormorants drying their wings in the weak sun like wicked leathery vampires, and a single black swan, an escapee from some abandoned estate.

One Sunday in April, the first warm one of the year, Abi rode out to Otmoor reserve. The first hobbies of the year had arrived from Africa and were hunting dragonfly across the meadows. Marsh harriers were quartering the reed beds for prey. The warblers had arrived and were singing for their lives, and Abi heard her first cuckoo of the year.

At the far end of the reserve, close to the second screen, she saw a weasel scurry across the path ahead of her. Then, as she returned to the carpark where she'd locked up the bike, a middle-aged man in khakis and wellingtons beckoned to her and pointed into a ditch-side thicket.

"Grass snakes," he whispered. There were two of them intertwined, lazy lithe bands of mottled brown basking in the sun. "They come out of hibernation and start mating straight away."

When Abi wasn't spotting fauna, she concentrated on her foraging. On a February riverside walk, she came home with a handful of jelly ear taken from rotting elder, and two dozen scarlet elf cups that stood out from the mulchy ground like rubies. She sampled both but found neither appetising. Still, all the pleasure was in the hunt.

At home she cooked pots of pulses and vegetables that last several days at a time, ate in her room where she could read or browse the web. If Guthrie was in the kitchen when she was serving herself, she'd offer him a plate, but he made it clear he preferred his ready meals. Occasionally she'd meet him there again when grabbing a hot drink, and sometimes they'd chat. At these times, she found it hard to relax in his company. In truth, it was rare for him to offer one of his unsavoury remarks, mostly it was idle chatter, but she was always on her guard.

Nights were always harder than days. She'd close her eyes and sooner or later the bad thoughts returned. Pictures in her mind of her mother slurry with booze, of Roger's groping hand, of Teddy's violent lunge. And once she'd been visited by such unpleasant notions, there'd be no escape in slumber.

Most days Abi arrived at work befuddled by lack of sleep. She longed to lay her cheek against the cool surface of her desk and doze, but the office was open-plan, and her boss, Emma, sat facing her from her table by the window.

Each day was a performance. Inside Abi was jittery with nerves, weak from sleep-deprivation, desperate to project a cool and polished façade. It was a relief that the work was so unchallenging. There was endless data to enter, the phone to answer, the email account to monitor. In the months that followed, the boredom would be crushing.

Emma was a thirty-something local woman, overweight and obsessed with dieting, her day regulated by protein-shake breaks, her conversation governed by what she'd eaten, or hadn't. She set her phone with periodic alarms and would leave a meeting in mid-flow when it pipped to fetch a rice cake or handful of carrot sticks. Towards Abi, her manner was brisk and professional, without a hint of warmth.

There was a group of four women, all longer-term employees, who lunched together in one of the vacant meeting rooms. Each had their own conversation agenda and demanded their slot. Penny's husband was a disappointment and she needed to vent. Celia was preparing for her wedding, it was consuming her life. Tammy and her boyfriend belonged to a civil war re-enactment club, they had cats and liked camping, her conversation was an unlucky dip of all three. Antonella was a single mother and her talk was dominated by the ongoing war she fought with her ten-year old daughter. When Abi was first invited to join them, she was too polite to refuse, but she grew quickly to loathe this daily ritual.

She lasted two months before she made her first excuse when Celia stopped by at her desk to say it was dinner time.

"I'm sorry, I can't make it today. I've got work to finish. I'll have to take a late lunch," she said, trying hard to inject disappointment into her tone. The relief outweighed the guilt, and she took to making regular excuses, even though she suspected that the others felt slighted.

It was a joy to have a new routine. She'd wolf her sandwich, then walk around the grounds. She began to take her lunchbreak later and later, sometimes not until half past two or three. It made the afternoon go quicker. She wondered, Are trauma and boredom the only two options in life? She lay awake at night and felt her depression sitting heavy on her chest like one of Tammy's cats.

Garai's arrival eased the tension that Abi felt in the house. Guthrie was just a little much some days, and it was good to have another presence, even if the young man never seemed to say a lot. Still, Abi sensed a gentleness. A vulnerability too. A boyish face with a build to match. But when she looked into his eyes, she saw that he carried his own burden of worry. She realised after a month that she'd never seen him smile.

The first days after the young man's arrival, Abi did her best to put him at ease. She showed him how to use the washing machine, ran through the bin collection days, tried tactfully to prepare him for Guthrie

One morning they chatted while Abi made tea and toast. When conversation lapsed, she changed tack.

"How are you finding Mister G?" she asked.

"He's OK," said Garai cautiously.

"He means well. All those hours he spends volunteering at the hospital."

"Yes, that's important work."

"But he's, you know, old school," Abi continued. "His generation had their views on race and gender and suchlike, and he's no different. Sometimes he speaks before he thinks, but he's harmless enough."

A pause as they focused on their food.

"Have you noticed, he can't open his mouth without mentioning some work he carried out some time in the past?" Abi said, to kill the silence.

Garai looked up and for a moment she thought he was going to smile.

"I know what you mean. Everything begins with 'I did the woodwork in a Misty Lake gloss' or 'the bathroom was a Frosted Sapphire satin finish.' He has a photographic memory for those details."

"And yet he can never find his car keys," said Abi.

It was a moment of levity, but soon the conversation trailed into silence. Garai finished his porridge and announced he was going to the public library. His departure left Abi alone with her thoughts.

She still couldn't make her mind up about Guthrie. She'd think of his meandering tales and the charitable work and feel entirely sympathetic towards the man, right up until the next time he made some remark about the nurse he met today who couldn't speak a bloody word of English, or the other who was 'bent as a corkscrew'. Then she'd feel a poisonous anger towards him, and wonder, How can I live with a man like that?

The first moment of any intimacy between the young lodgers occurred a month or so after Garai had moved in. It was a Saturday night. For five days straight Abi's sleep had been poor, it was one in the morning and she was close to breaking. She'd gone downstairs to the kitchen to make herself a herbal tea, and was sitting at the table overcome with exhaustion. She thought, I can't take this much longer. When her face crumpled and the tears came, it was almost a relief.

She cried for a while, until she heard the front door open and heard footsteps in the hallway. She knew that Garai's delivery job could run late into the night, and hurried to wipe her eyes. She had the makings of a smile ready when he came into the kitchen.

"Hey," she said. "How was your night?"

"It was fine," he answered. He had a way of speaking, slow and solemn, like words were not to be taken lightly. He poured himself a glass of cold water from the sink and turned to look at her.

"And yours?"

She tried again to smile, but instead found the tears returning.

"Oh no," she gasped between sobs. "I'm sorry."

Garai, who'd been edging towards the door, stopped and returned to the kitchen table. He took a seat opposite Abi.

"Hey," he said. "It's OK."

He said nothing more, just sat with her while she cried herself dry. Only afterwards, as she composed herself, did she see the weariness writ large on his face.

"I'm sorry," she said. "You're tired. I'm keeping you up."

"It's no problem. I can't sleep when I get home from a shift. Too wired."

"I can't sleep at all these days."

"That's tough. My mother always used to say, 'Sleep is like money, you only know its value when you don't have it.' Those days, I slept like an innocent lamb. I didn't know what she meant until I came to Britain."

They sipped their drinks for a minute. Garai broke the silence.

"What keeps you awake?"

Abi didn't answer straight away.

"Family. Relationships. The usual stuff. I guess I feel a bit … lost at the moment."

An apologetic tone. When she looked up, she saw that he was looking at her, waiting.

She hadn't meant to unburden herself. She gave only a potted version. She talked about her father's adultery, her mother's alcoholism, Roger's cruelty, but glossed over the reason for her own departure.

"I'm sorry," he said, when she finished. "All that would have an effect on anybody. It's no wonder you have problems sleeping."

He'd said nothing of import, but it was the first time she'd opened up since leaving home, and the very act of being listened to was a balm.

"What about you?" she said. She smiled at Garai, and this time it came a little easier. "Tell me about your family."

But before he could open his mouth, they heard footsteps outside the door, and Guthrie appeared in dressing gown and slippers.

"Couldn't sleep," he announced. "Thought I'd try a mug of cocoa. Anyone care to join me?"

While Guthrie busied himself with his hot drink, Garai poured a second glass of water and Abi made another mug of tea. It was the first time they'd all sat together. Garai went to his food cupboard and produced a packet of custard creams.

"Oh, well done, Gary," said Guthrie, helping himself to one. "Let me see, I've got some chocolate digestives somewhere."

"It's Garai," said the young man. "Not Gary."

"Sorry, yes," said Guthrie. "I keep forgetting. Silly old fool, eh?"

"It's OK," said Garai.

For a while, the only sounds were the slurping of drink and the munching of biscuit.

"I had a cousin who worked in the chocolate digestives factory in London. Harlesden, it was. He told me when the biscuits come off the line, they're softer than from the packet. He hated the job, though. Got so sick of the sweet smell of baking, he quit. Ended up in a sewage works in Beckton. He said he'd take the smell of you-know-what over biscuits any day!"

It was after two in the morning when they finally went upstairs. Guthrie's blathering had put them all at ease. They left their cups in the sink.

"Up the wooden hill to Bedfordshire," said Guthrie in the hallway. "Delia always used to say that at bedtime."

On the landing, they paused awkwardly.

"I hope you sleep well," said Garai to Abi.

And to her surprise, she did.

*

One Friday night Abi plucked up courage and made her way to the city centre. She'd done some research on gay-friendly spots and started off in the Jolly Farmers, a cosy joint down a side road next to the big shopping mall. She bolted two pints of lager as she tried to steady her nerves. She thought, Why am I so anxious? What am I ashamed of?

Her plan was to go on to a gay club called Plush, tucked down an alley off Cornmarket. The lager's Dutch courage fuelled the walk to the club, but then she panicked at the entrance. She thought, What if I end up with another Teddy? Everyone seems OK when you first meet them. And by the time you find out the truth, it's too late and you're trapped.

And so she turned round and headed home, stopping off at a minimart to buy a half of vodka and a carton of cranberry juice. She drank it all before she went to bed, woke at half three dry-mouthed and nauseous, lay awake until morning loathing herself for her cowardice and stupidity.

The following Tuesday, bored with watching TV on her laptop, she opened a new Word document and began to write.

The weekend before, she'd been walking in Bagley Woods and had been struck by the peace of the forest, the beauty of the gnarly old oaks, the intensity of the colours, and had come away feeling as if for that brief time she'd been transported into some ancient mystical fairy tale. She'd walked home filled with a certainty that she'd experienced something profound. She thought, I want to put this into words. I want to say something *meaningful*.

In her childhood, she'd read fiction with pleasure, gone through the same books as her contemporaries, the Harry Potters, the *Twilight* series, everything by Malorie Blackman. She'd become a little obsessed by *Room*, the story of the five-year-old boy and his mother held captive by a cruel man.

What to write? She began by sketching out short stories. As she wrote, she found that the tales that started out for children soon developed a darker side. The nice new neighbours build a torture chamber in their basement. The birthday gift mobile phone sends messages that kill. The step-father has a hunger for fresh bone marrow.

Abi tried scaling up to teenage fiction. She shot off a couple of coming-of-age tales featuring an orphan heroine pitched against a cruel world. A few days later, a breakthrough. The protagonist falls in love with another girl. Yet once more, however hard she tried, the denouement remained twisted. The girl's feelings are always unreciprocated, the love betrayed. In the end, the fiction Abi came up with brought her more sadness than satisfaction, and soon she gave up.

For a week, she dabbled in lesbian erotica. It was hard to play out the scenes with so little experience, but the process brought momentary relief. Afterwards, though, a gloom returned, and she abandoned the genre with only a single story completed.

One night, lying in bed, she realised that the urge to write had come from an aching need to process the events that were poisoning her life. She sat up in the darkness and thought, Of course, it's not fiction I should be writing, but real-life events. I need to get it all down.

She switched on the light, fired up her laptop, and wrote for an hour, a helter-skelter splattering of thoughts and ideas. Achronological, half-formed sentences appeared from nowhere, an angry-sad stream of consciousness that filled page after page. She wrote all night, happy memories of her childhood, her parents. And painful ones too. The separation, Roger and Teddy. And her mother.

The next day, and those after, when Abi came back to her notes, she found herself unable to form them into anything more coherent. And so they remained as they were, a digital file on the computer waiting to be transformed.

When boredom from her job drove her to despair, Abi began once more to plan her return to university. She still couldn't make up her mind between conservation ecology, occupational therapy or something to do with sport and exercise. She discovered that Oxford Brookes University offered graduate courses in all three areas. She spent hours on her walks toying with her choices.

Now that the weather was turning, she began to run after work. Soon she'd settled on a five-mile circuit into town along Iffley Road, then back through Christ Church Meadow to the Head of the River, along the towpath to Iffley Lock and up to Rose Hill. Each weekend, she rode her bike outside the city, to Thame, Islip, Brill. Occasionally, she'd wonder how her mother was doing and resolve to get in touch. But then she'd remember how they parted, the rejection, and she'd shelve the idea.

One day after work, she was sitting at the kitchen table with a cup of tea. Garai was cooking pasta, his ritual before he went out to work. The landline rang and Guthrie came in to take the call. Though Abi's thoughts were elsewhere, she couldn't help but pick up snatches of the old man's conversation.

"I thought I'd try spinach this year," he said, early on. "You still got your allotment?"

Guthrie carried the cordless phone to the lounge and back as he spoke, so Abi missed a chunk of what followed. When Guthrie next returned, he was saying,

"She's alright. No change really." He filled the kettle with his spare hand, flicked it on and said, "How's Ted doing?"

There was silence as he listened to the caller's answer. Then he spluttered with laughter.

"Ha! That's old Teddy for you!"

The caller seemed to want some information, an address or phone number, and Abi heard Guthrie read out a string of numbers. After a while, the call ended. Guthrie hovered in the kitchen, a lingering smile on his face. Eventually, he said.

"That was Stevo. An old mate of mine. Me, him and his brother, we used to work together from time to time. The two of them, him and Ted, they were like a comedy act. One time, must have been nineteen ninety-seven or eight, we were doing an exterior job in Islip. Ted was sanding down the fascia boards. It was a council job, there was scaffolding up, and he slipped and fell. He fractured his shoulder blade. He was never the same after that. Couldn't lift his arm above his head. He packed it in and got a job with the Royal Mail instead."

Soon after that, Guthrie went upstairs, leaving Abi and Garai alone. The young man ate in silence. After a while, he said,

"Is Ted a common name in Britain?"

"I don't know. Not really. It's kind of old-fashioned."

"I used to know someone called Ted back home."

Abi waited for more, but Garai continued to eat.

"What was he like?" she asked at last.

Garai contemplated the question for so long that Abi thought he was ignoring her. At last he said,

"I don't know. I thought I knew him, but I didn't. I thought he was a friend. That we shared something."

He continued to eat. Abi broke the silence.

"I used to know someone called Ted too. Well, Teddy."

"And? What was *he* like?"

"*She* not he," she corrected. She thought about it. "I guess she wasn't so different from your Ted. I thought she was one thing. She turned out to be someone else."

Another long silence

"She hurt you?" he asked quietly.

"Yes. And you?"

"I don't know. Maybe."

They chewed that over. Then Abi chuckled.

"Well, we've got something in common. Wounded by a Ted!"

A weak smile shared.

The next day, Abi was cooking when Garai appeared in the kitchen. He took out a saucepan and a half-filled packet of pasta to begin his pre-shift meal.

"I'm cooking a kidney bean stew," she said. "I've made a ton and it's almost ready. You interested?"

He paused in his preparations.

"Are you sure?"

"Sure I'm sure. I don't like eating alone."

"Well, thanks. To tell you the truth, I'm sick of pasta. I wish I wasn't such a poor cook."

"Well, then. I'll make a bit of rice, you lay the table."

It was their first meal together. At first the conversation was a little stilted. She ran through the recipe and he confessed he'd never heard of half the spices. After that, the dialogue faltered. Abi knew Garai was about to go off to work, this was not a time for profound intimacies. And yet she couldn't think of anything less probing to talk about that didn't sound utterly trivial. For some reason she recalled at that moment the conversation she'd had with Paisley, the game they'd played as they ate their burritos.

"What would be your last meal if you were on Death Row?" she found herself asking.

"*Sadza ne nyama*," Garai answered straight away.

"What's that?"

"*Sadza*'s the staple food in my country," he explained. "It's like a thick porridge made from maize meal. *Nyama* means meat. Usually beef. But you don't eat meat, do you?"

"No. Are there many vegetarians in Zimbabwe?"

"Not many out of choice," he said solemnly. "But the country's full of *economic* vegetarians, if you know what I mean. These days only the rich can afford meat."

"I'm sorry," said Abi. She felt embarrassed at her ignorance. "I didn't mean-"

"It's OK," he said. "We eat vegetables too, especially green-leaved ones like *rape* and *covo*. I guess they are something like spinach. Sometimes we cook them in a home-made peanut sauce. We call it *dovi*. My mother makes the best *dovi* in the world."

He spoke, with utter conviction, and a fierce pride. Abi stared at him, and for a few seconds the years dropped away and he looked like a five-year old. She smiled.

"Can you cook it?"

"I don't know. I don't think so."

"We should try. I bet we can get a recipe off the internet."

She looked at him, expecting a gesture of encouragement, but his face had shut down and now he peered down at his plate and took a mouthful without speaking. When he finished his food, he said,

"I'll be late for work. I'd better go."

He carried his plate to the sink and washed it up. On the way out, he said,

"Thank you, Abi. That was good."

After he'd left, she washed, dried and put away all that she'd used for the meal, leaving the half-full pot of stew on the hob. She stood for a moment in the kitchen, and wondered what to do. Her phone told her it was six thirty. Guthrie was in the lounge. Soon he'd come into the kitchen to put one of his ready meals into the microwave. Upstairs the book she was reading, Alice Walker's *The Color Purple*, lay on her bed beside her laptop. Outside was the Jolly Farmers, the Plush nightclub, a world of other people. A moment's hesitation before she walked into the hallway and up the stairs.

She sat down on her bed and checked her messages on the laptop and phone. Nothing. It was strange to think that she was twenty-four years old today, that she'd almost come to the end of her birthday, and not a single person had acknowledged it. Not a single person, not even her mother.

Garai 2

Tafadzwa discoursing, expression sober, mouth moving, finger raised in emphasis. Tafadzwa chewing a maize cob, teeth grinding, lips smacking, eyes aglow with pleasure. Tafadzwa at the punchline of one of Ted's jokes, head thrown back, face split wide, the laughter a cascade of unrestrained joy. Tafadzwa on the morgue slab, torso birdlike, limbs stiff, eyes open in defiance and accusation. Dead or alive, Tafadzwa haunted Garai's nights.

It was a household giddy from lack of sleep. Sometimes when he returned late from a shift and dropped exhausted into bed, Garai lay awake and heard the stirrings of others. He could imagine their trains of thought. The old man traipsing back and forth to the toilet, hoping that if he could squeeze a few more drops from his bladder, then sleep would surely come. Abi's footsteps on the staircase as she made yet another of her bitter herbal teas, praying that this time the effect would be soporific.

Alone at night, when he did dispel the nightmares of his dead friend, they were replaced by thoughts of his parents. Aching love tainted by guilt and shame. All that they sacrificed for him, and how had he repaid them? He'd betrayed their trust, looted their bank account, and poisoned their hopes.

When he first came to UK, he'd gone to an internet café and sent an email to his father's account, a brief message to say he'd arrived and that all was well. Since then he hadn't allowed himself to check for their response. After all, he wasn't worthy of their love.

There were other reasons, too, for his reticence. He couldn't take the risk of maintaining contact in case the communication was traceable. As the parents of a political criminal, they were vulnerable back in Zimbabwe. And here in UK, as an immigrant without legal status, he needed to keep a low profile. No, he had to sort out his life here first before he could send a message of hope back home with news that his parents could be proud of.

Aside from legitimising his status in Britain, there was only one other resolution he could hope for: a revolution in Zimbabwe leading to regime change. In his fantasy he pictured people on the streets, Mnungagwa resigning, the army stepping aside, then a general election called to vote in a new government. It would be a democratic one based on those original ZANU PF principles that had long since been usurped by greed and fear and the hunger for power

He couldn't help but be drawn to news from back home, even though he knew his fantasy was just a pipedream. Garai felt certain that the only way Mnangagwa could go would be if the army removed him. He thought, If that happened, they'd just put someone else in as a puppet, and we'd be back to square one.

Nevertheless, he spend hours each week searching for news from home. Social media and independent local news sites proved the best sources, along with articles on the Al Jazeera and BBC sites, and reports from Amnesty International, Human Rights Watch and other independent watchdogs.

The news was unsettling, and yet he ate it up like a starving man.

On the one hand the continuing mismanagement of power by the Government. Ministers accused of massive corruption over tendered contracts or pocketed budgets. Understaffed hospitals empty of medicines. Cholera outbreaks caused by collapsing sewage infrastructure. Daily electricity cuts due to unpaid government bills. Tuberculosis and HIV rife amongst starving, lice-infested prisoners. And a collapsing economy: rising inflation and food prices, a failing manufacturing industry, falling exports, and foreign currency in short supply.

And on the other hand, the government's response. Journalists arrested and detained, sometimes for exposing the Ministers' corruption. Routine torture for those in detention. Crackdowns on opposition party activists, on civilian protestors, on anyone who happened to find themselves in the wrong place at the wrong time. Unresolved cases of abductions, usually critics of the government, sometimes tortured and dumped, sometimes still unaccounted for.

Garai needed a phone for work but was frightened to take out a monthly contract in case it exposed him, so he bought a pay-as-you-go phone instead, as it required no credit check. He had no money for a computer or tablet, so he borrowed Abi's laptop for his browsing. The first time he asked, she agreed at once. After that, she told him,

"If I'm not using it, just help yourself. It'll be in my bedroom, and there's no password to log on."

Abi, he supposed, was a friend of sorts. There was a neighbour back in Mabelreign, Mai Chikwanda, who took life very seriously. His mother always used to say, "That woman walks around like she's got the whole world on her shoulders." Garai thought of her when he looked at Abi and saw how troubled she seemed. Troubled and wary, like a scared mouse.

Something about the young woman confused him. Despite the slight frame and hangdog demeanour, he sensed a fire in the woman that had nothing to do with her red hair, nor the flint in her eyes. Rather it felt to Garai like smouldering embers half extinguished, biding their time, starved of what they needed to come to life. He wondered at times what she was missing, what spark was necessary to set her ablaze.

He could see the effort Abi made to put him at ease when he first moved in. She showed him the lay of the land, where the nearest shops and bus stops were located, how to use the household appliances, where to store his food. They crossed paths each afternoon in the window between her return from work and his preparations for his own job, and they'd swap stories of their day. And when their landlord started on about one of his pet topics, Abi would roll her eyes and wink at Garai.

"The OG's off on one," she'd whisper with a grin. From someone else, the remark may have sounded cruel or malicious, but Garai could sense a certain fondness for the old man in her tone.

Oswald Guthrie. Abi called him the OG, the Original Gangster, or just Mister G. Garai found it hard to address the old man with such familiarity. Respect the elderly, that's how he'd been brought up. Still, the joke was funny because no one could look less threatening than this little man, in his cheap velcro shoes and beige cardigans, saggy-faced and bulbous-nosed. There was something comical about his mien. Was it those hairy ears and bushy eyebrows or that - what did Abi call it? - that *comb-over*?

The first time Abi cracked the OG gag, Garai smiled in appreciation. She grinned back and it made her whole face soften. That's when he realised that she needed his friendship as much as he did hers. Still, he didn't fully trust her, how could he? He knew nothing of her life. But if she knew his secret, she'd have the power of life and death over him.

With Oswald, there was no question of intimacy. True, he seemed harmless, despite the nonsense he sometimes spouted. But Garai felt sure that Guthrie would not look kindly at an 'illegal' in his home, given the views on immigration he seemed so keen to share.

Deportation. It was his all-consuming fear, the one that drove him to the brink of madness, that kept him edgy all day, sleepless at night. A recurring nightmare began with a dawn raid by members of the Border Agency. He pictured their arrival, their barked orders to get out of bed and put on some clothes. The journey in the police van to the detention centre. Then in quick succession, the few grim days in prison, the transport to the airport, the flight home to Zimbabwe, and the police waiting for him at Robert Mugabe International Airport.

To ease his anxiety, he began to plan an emergency escape route. First he examined his bedroom window, its locking mechanism, the drop down to the back garden. After that, when he pictured the dawn raid, he saw himself springing into action. Throwing on his clothes, flicking open the window catch, scootering down the drainpipe. Then over the garden fence and down the neighbours' side return, out onto the street and away. He took to locking his bike up against a lamppost a few doors down, to checking his jacket pocket last thing at night to make sure it contained his money and the few valuables he could fit in its pockets.

The takeaway delivery job was not only his source of money, but a distraction to help fill his evenings. The other delivery guys came and went, and soon he realised he was the longest serving member of the team. Not that he'd become any more intimate with his boss. The man still called him David, the anglicised name Dawit had used before he fled to London. The anonymity suited Garai, just as the cash in hand did too.

When he wasn't working, Garai stayed in and around the house. He supposed he ought to get out more, but he felt exposed on the streets and in the shops. It was boring to stay cooped up, and he slept as much as he could to kill the mornings. Late afternoons with Abi, that was his favourite time of day. They'd settle in the kitchen while he cooked pasta to fuel his evening's work, and she'd tell him about her day in the office, or the latest goings-on with Guthrie.

One afternoon, the old man came in with two shopping bags stamped with the logo of a women's clothing brand.

"Been shopping, Mister G?" Abi asked, peering into one of the bags. Guthrie had put them down on the kitchen table while he filled the kettle. Now he reached over and snatched them up.

"Just a few bits," he said. "I'll take them upstairs."

As soon as he left the room, Abi said,

"Why would he be buying women's clothes?"

"Maybe they weren't women's clothes. Maybe he just put his shopping in those bags."

"No, I got a good look. There was a pink nightie and something like a dressing gown, all flowery with frills."

"Maybe he has a lady friend," said Garai as he drained the pasta and stirred the shop-bought sauce that he was heating on the hob.

"Maybe he's trans," said Abi.

"What's that?" said Garai.

"Someone whose personal identity and gender doesn't correspond to their birth sex."

"I don't understand."

"It's like, you come to realise that you were born in the wrong body."

"You mean gay?"

"No, it's not the same."

"And you think Guthrie's one of those?" Garai asked doubtfully.

"I don't know. Maybe he's just a cross-dresser. You know, he likes wearing women's clothes. But maybe there's more to it than that. He could be going through a profound existential crisis, the first step to a transition to Mrs G. The important thing is to be supportive," said Abi. Either way, it's a bit of excitement in the house, eh?"

Garai thought, Excitement? That's the last thing I'm looking for.

It was the guilt he felt for destroying his parents' dreams that pushed him to continue his studies. Of course, he couldn't enrol anywhere, not without Home Office status or money. But he decided early on that he'd read as if he were a student. That way, when the opportunity came, he'd be ready. When he told Abi of his plan, she suggested joining a public library. And so, three weeks after moving in, he went to register at Oxfordshire County Library in the city centre.

The process was straightforward, no ID required, just an email address. For safety's sake, he created a new email account.

Armed with his card, he headed for the history and politics sections, and spent a happy hour choosing half a dozen books about colonialism and imperialism and the British Empire.

The Chinese takeaway was closed on Mondays, so that was the time he read. His first choices were two books he picked in Tafadzwa's memory, Akala's *Natives* and Fanon's *The Wretched of the Earth*. His third selection was John Newsinger's *The Blood Never Dried*.

He found the process addictive. Though he was working six days a week, his books were soon filling the hours between his mid-morning awakening and late afternoon, when he began to prepare for work. He forced discipline on himself, partly for his future studies, and partly as a way of connecting with Tafadzwa. He felt as if he was honouring his friend, who'd never get to study again. He bought school exercise books and filled them with jottings from his reading. Soon he had half a dozen filled notebooks.

He realised early on that he was not the only one in the house carrying out historical research. From time to time, when they met in the kitchen, Guthrie would engage him in some history-related conversation, usually about the British Empire. And the old man often had a book he'd just finished that he'd want Garai to read. And that was how it came about that they began their book-swapping.

"You'll like this one," he'd begin, handing Garai a copy of Major Herbert H Austin's *With MacDonald in Uganda* or something of that ilk. "It's a smashing read."

Garai took the book and stared at the cover doubtfully.

"Alright, Mr Guthrie," said Garai. "But I've got one for you in return. I'll read yours but you've got to promise to try mine."

"It's a deal."

So that first week it was Major Austin's book for the Fanon, and George MacDonald Fraser's *Flashman and the Redskins* for Akala's *Natives*.

Once they began swapping books, the follow-up discussions were inevitable. Garai remembered an early one.

"You know what they said? The sun never set on the British Empire, it was that big," Guthrie began.

"The sun never set, *and the blood never dried*. You know who said that? It was Ernest Jones, a Chartist in the middle of the nineteenth century. Even then there were a few who recognised the British Empire for what it was. There's a book by Newsinger called *The Blood Never Dried*. I'll lend you it. It helped me understand one important thing about the British Empire."

"And what's that?" Guthrie asked.

"It can only be defended if you start with the premise that all the other people who lived on what became colonies, all of those different peoples, they were all inferior to the British. If you can swallow that, then their violent subjugation is justified. In other words, it begins with inherent racism."

"Oh, come on, Gary. It started with trade and commerce."

"What trade, Mr Guthrie? The slave trade? By the time it ended, they reckon between ten and fifteen million Africans had been shipped to the Americas. Around two million of those died on route. By the mid-eighteenth century, the British dominated the trade. You guys shipped around three million of those slaves single-handed."

"There was slavery in Africa long before we arrived."

"A different kind of slavery. Slaves were considered a valuable asset. It was forbidden to harm them. The life expectancy of the slaves who survived the voyage to America was between seven and ten years, Mr Guthrie. They were treated like expendable livestock. Less than livestock."

"Well, it was us Brits who came to our senses and put an end to the slave trade. You can't deny that, Gary."

"It's *Garai*, Mr Guthrie. And yes, I can deny it. The end of the slave trade was triggered by slave revolution in the Caribbean, not British government benevolence. The government got out while the going was good, then took the moral high ground."

"You make it sound like we were a nation of brutes. Of course there were a few bad eggs in the colonies amongst the thousands who went out. But most of them were there to serve their country and make a new life for themselves. And don't forget, they weren't the only ones taking liberties. It takes two to tango."

"What do you mean, Mr Guthrie?"

"I'm talking about provocation. I've just been reading about Cawnpore in India. June 1857. General Wheeler's force had negotiated a ceasefire and were evacuating when the Indian rebels began firing on them. That's not cricket. And then in July the hundred and eighty survivors - men, women and children - were massacred by the rebels. That's what I call treachery, son. No wonder the army got a bit hot under the collar after that. You can't blame a man for getting a little heavy-handed when he's dealing with that sort of betrayal."

"Heavy-handed? Mr Guthrie, right from the start British policy in India was ruthless. The East India Company printed its Blue Book as a manual for torture techniques to be used by its officials in their tax collecting work. You can't count the episodes of brutality, atrocity and ritual humiliation carried out by the British in the name of civilization. I'll give you one example, but there are thousands. The massacre at Sikander Bagh in 1857. Two thousand rebels were slaughtered in cold blood. Prisoners were bayonetted in batches. Back home, the action was seen as heroic. Eight Victoria Crosses were awarded to the participants. It's all in that Newsinger book."

"I don't know about that. Perhaps the soldiers had gone a bit stir-crazy out there in the Tropics. All that heat and dust, it can send you a bit doolally."

"Britain acted no better towards its Irish colony. There was no tropical heat and dust there. The British Government knew that the potato harvest had failed long before the first Irish peasants began dying of starvation. The Irish Famine could have easily been avoided, but the Government refused to ban the export of food from Ireland and insisted that the principles of free trade should be allowed to prevail. A million dead, another million fleeing their homeland as refugees from this crime instigated by the British Government and the landlords in Ireland."

"You can't blame a person for a harvest failure. That's an act of God."

Garai wanted to say, You're not listening, Mr Guthrie. The peasants were deliberately sacrificed in the name of free trade. But he hesitated, worn down by Guthrie's resistance to argument and evidence. And so he shrugged and Guthrie smiled, and soon the old man was off on another anecdote from his past.

Another time, Guthrie was reading an article in the paper about the Hebridean island of Lewis.

"Look at that, Garai," he said, holding up the paper to show a photo of an impressive stone castle. "Stornaway Castle. Beautiful, eh? Nothing like that at home, I bet."

Garai took a deep breath before he began to speak. He described the monument at Great Zimbabwe, what was left of the capital of the vast Mwenemutapa Empire that existed in southern Africa in the late Iron Age.

"At its peak, scientists believe the city housed a population of 18,000," he went on. "There's nothing comparable in Britain at that time."

"Really? I'm not sure about–"

"Besides," Garai continued, interrupting the older man, "Did you know Stornaway Castle was built with drug money?"

"What? Give over. Don't tell me, a Mexican cartel?"

"No, opium in the nineteenth century. James Matheson was a partner in a company that exported opium from India to China in the 1840s. He got very rich. He used his money to become an MP. He bought the island of Lewis, and built Stornaway Castle. In the process, he cleared five hundred families off the land, forced them onto a boat bound for Canada. Later he become chairman of the P&O shipping line, Governor of the

Bank of England and the second largest landowner in Britain. All from opium."

"Well, I never. Are you sure?"

"Opium financed British rule in India. By forcing the trade on China, the British created twelve million local addicts. No wonder the Manchu emperor was not a fan."

"There must have been folk at home who wouldn't stand for it?"

"Not really. The only real anti-opium movement was inside China. Have you heard of the Taiping rebellion? It was a popular uprising of Chinese Christians who took up arms against the emperor. They fought to ban opium. They also wanted to ban prostitution, infanticide, slavery, and the binding of women's feet."

"That's sounds just the ticket. How did they get on?"

"Historians say that before World War One the Taiping Rebellion was the most bloody war in history. Up to twenty million Chinese were killed. Guess whose side the British joined? They didn't want to lose the opium revenue, so they fought against the rebels. And when it was over, the British turned on the Emperor, their ally, and carried on fighting against him. It was only after the Second Opium War in 1858 that the British got what they wanted. They forced the Emperor to accept the legalisation of opium in China."

As so often happened, the argument went back and forth for a while, until Guthrie harrumphed and said something like, "Well, say what you like, a lot of good men laid down their lives to make the world a better place," and Garai sighed and shrugged and thought, This is getting us nowhere.

"How about a cup of tea, Mr Guthrie?"

"Smashing, Gary. Oh sorry, I mean *Garai*."

Which Garai took as the real step forward.

Grim news from Zimbabwe coupled with gruesome reading from the colonial past. The combination began to affect Garai's wellbeing, exacerbating the insomnia. What with Guthrie's and Abi's sleep problems, it felt sometimes as if no one in the house ever slept, or if they did, it was in a kind of rota, a desperate shift system that was loathsome to all.

Every week brought Garai closer to his birthday, the moment he hit eighteen and lost his unaccompanied-minor status in the eyes of the Home Office. After that, he knew he'd be living on borrowed time.

He sustained himself on dreams. He'd finish his A Levels and apply to university. He'd study Politics or History, more precisely Black History. He'd help re-write the distortions of the colonial narrative. He began to research undergraduate courses. There was Black History, Black Humanities, African Studies. He found courses at Birmingham University, Goldsmiths, SOAS, Bristol and Brighton.

The book-swapping with Guthrie continued. He borrowed Richard Gott's *Britain's Empire: Resistance, Repression and Revolt* from the library, read it in two sittings, then exchanged it with Guthrie for Lieut. Vivian Dering Majendie's *Up Among The Pandies, or A Year's Service in India*.

The latest argument between the two centred on the one-sided nature of violence between the colonial oppressors and the locals.

"It was spears against guns, Mr Guthrie. By the end of the nineteenth century European technology was producing new weapons like the Maxim gun. It made any military confrontations out-and-out carnage, like the slaughtering at an abattoir. Every time I read of an episode of colonial conflict, the death toll is just so unbalanced. And that's according to British records, which often tried to underplay the nature of the massacre. At Tel-el-Kebir in 1882, the British lost fifty-seven, the Egyptian army somewhere between two and ten thousand. Over sixteen thousand Sudanese were killed at Omdurman in 1898. The British lost forty-eight soldiers."

"You can't blame us for being more technologically advanced."

It was exasperating at times, and so Garai buried himself in his own research, filling notebook after notebook with his writing. It still had no clear purpose, just something between therapy and the laying of an as-yet unspecified foundation.

With Abi, Garai could have a more nuanced conversation. He admired her enquiring mind, the way it probed into areas Guthrie would never have visited.

"The way you describe Britain during that time, it makes us sound like the school bully, helping ourselves to what tickled our fancy."

"You know how George Orwell described imperialism? A soldier and a policeman holding down a native, while a businessman went through his pockets."

"Right, so the rich and powerful benefited from the British Empire," she went on after a pause. "What about working class people in Britain? How did it affect them?"

Garai hadn't considered this question before.

"I guess they benefited from the natural resources brought from the colonies," Garai answered. "A better diet with more meat and tea and sugar. Copper piping instead of lead for the water supply. Cotton and wool clothing, and rubber and tin and so on. And there were other less concrete benefits. I was just reading about that in the Sanghera book."

"Like what?"

"When the Second Boer War kicked off, around half the recruits for the British Army were deemed unfit and turned down. It was a wake-up call for the Government. It led to Rowntree's 'Poverty, A Study of Town Life' report and the decision to offer free school meals and a programme of medical examinations for the general public. You could say that your welfare state came about on the back of colonialism. Of course, no similar services were offered to natives in the colonies."

"That doesn't surprise me."

Guthrie, hovering at the sink, piped in at that point.

"I did a job for a George Orwell once. It wasn't him, of course. A different one. Nice detached house in Shotover. I did the exterior. Oxford blue for the windows and the front door, and the garden gate to match. I fell off the ladder on the last day, brought down the whole length of guttering and broke my ankle. I was off work for two months. I said to Delia, 'It could have been a lot worse.' She said, 'It could have been a lot better too. If you'd landed on your head, no one would have known the difference.' Ah, a wicked tongue on her. Mind you, she was probably right."

Books and work and conversations, anything to fill the day. And then, always, came the setting of the sun, and the sleep-starved nights, waiting for the knock on the door. Terror-filled dreams replaying the crack of the baton, Tafadzwa's knees buckling, his body crumpled on the ground. Or lying awake, thoughts of his mother and father. The acid burn of guilt, that he'd wasted their savings, that he'd slayed their dreams.

Guthrie 4

It took a while after Garai moved in for Guthrie to notice any change at home. After all, these days it was a place he came and went from, where he tried to sleep, but he spent more waking hours at the nursing home than his own.

True, he'd had to make some domestic adjustments. He'd shifted the contents of his kitchen cupboards around so that both lodgers had their own storage space. Likewise, the shelves of the fridge were divvied up. The bathroom cabinets were more cluttered than before, and he had to remember to clean up after himself.

There were some minor inconveniences to the new arrangements. Sometimes he had to queue for the bathroom in the mornings, and the washing machine was not always free when he needed it. But he was banking the extra money every month, so he had to expect to pay a price.

Rose Hill was the place where he returned each evening to eat and sleep, but the nursing home consumed his life. Though it was a relief not to have to worry about Delia's basic personal care anymore, he still insisted on doing his bit of nail-clipping and hair-brushing. Partly he wanted to keep other people's hands off Delia, partly he needed the intimacy to remain connected to her.

Mostly, though, he passed the time at her bedside talking about the things he thought she'd like. He'd told her about the lodgers moving in, so these days he might start with a titbit or two about them, what they'd cooked in the kitchen or scraps he picked up in passing conversation. Then he'd get down to news of Eric and his family, of the other relatives. When he ran out of gossip, there were the Beatles and Elvis CDs to play, and her crossword magazines.

He'd tell her about his previous evening, what he'd watched on the telly or read in the paper. He paid particular attention to local news. She'd always preferred browsing the *Oxford Mail* to a national paper. There was the new housing estate to be built down towards Radley. The Cutteslowe grandmothers raising a thousand pounds with a sponsored knit for a cot death charity. The new playpark in Barton opened by the Mayor. The Cowley kebab shop closed due to a rat infestation. He read out the articles and scanned his wife's face intently for signs of comprehension. He still wanted to believe, and so every flicker, every gurgle was evidence that the old Delia, though buried somewhere deep, was nevertheless a receptive presence.

One day Guthrie found a message on his phone from Gloria, asking whether she could come and visit Delia on her day off. It was a pleasure to see his old friend again. He gave her a tour of the premises and then they sat by Delia's bedside with cups of tea, and Guthrie listened to the nurse's news. Nathaniel was turning into something of a bookworm, his teacher spoke highly of him. Life on the ward was busier than ever. Her mother was ill with diabetes and high blood pressure, she needed to go back and see her, so she'd bought two plane tickets to Jo'burg for July.

"And you?" Gloria asked. "You look tired."

"I'm OK," he said.

"You need to look after yourself, you know. You'll be no use to Delia if you end up getting sick."

"I know."

"Are you visiting every day?"

"More or less."

Gloria looked around.

"This place is good. Your wife's safe here. Well looked after. You can give yourself a few days off a week. To start living your own life again."

"I don't mind coming. This feels like how I want to spend my time."

Gloria looked at Guthrie sadly.

"What about your gardening? Isn't spring the season to get busy?"

"I suppose so. I haven't thought much about it, if I'm honest."

"Look, I could pop in here once a week. That could be a day you give over to the garden."

Guthrie was shaking his head before she finished speaking.

"I can't relax unless I know she's alright."

"Exactly. And it shows. You're frazzled, man. Look, don't say no outright. Think about it. The offer stands. We'll have a good time together, me and Delia. We'll talk and play music together, and do the crossword puzzles. You do your thing in the garden. When you visit the next day, you'll feel refreshed, and that'll help Delia too."

"I don't know."

"Just promise me you'll think about it."

"Alright," he said, after a pause. "And don't think I'm not grateful. Thank you for the offer, Gloria. I appreciate it. We both do."

Of the staff at the nursing home, it seemed as if Colin had overall responsibility for Delia's care, so Guthrie spoke to him most days. His initial misgivings about the deputy manager were soon forgotten. True, he still had problems with Colin's thick Trinidadian accent, and he still found the man's air of camp somewhat distasteful, but he couldn't fault Delia's care, particularly Colin's attention to detail. He never mixed up her shampoo with one of the other patients' stuff, brushed her hair and dressed her just the way Guthrie had shown him, and made sure that the auxiliary staff beneath him did the same.

What Guthrie appreciated most about the nursing home was that there was none of the hospital frenzy. He himself was too old to rush around like a headless chicken, and it pained him to see others around him doing the same. He came to visit his wife, but in truth it was a lonely endeavour. What he hungered for was company, a person to nod and smile at his chatter, an ear to bend. And it was Colin more than any of the others who showed the tolerance and patience that Guthrie sought. Guthrie suspected that he repeated his stories, that Colin was too polite to say anything, and for that he was grateful.

"I always said she looked like Barbara Windsor," he'd say, gesturing towards his wife. "The same bubbly personality. And the same figure, if you know what I mean. Christ I couldn't keep my hands off her when we were younger."

"You were a passionate couple then, Mr Guthrie?"

"Yes, I suppose we were."

Or else there were tales of his decorating past.

"I once did a bit of work for a West Indian family over in Blackbird Leys, Colin. They wanted it papered all the way through with anaglypta, Ivory gloss for the woodwork. It looked like a palace at the end."

"Nice one. The flat needs freshening up. You fancy coming round to price it up, Mr Guthrie?"

"Ah no, I've packed it in. It's a young man's game."

The real bonding came later, though, when Colin mentioned his allotment.

"I booked the whole weekend off to work on the raised beds," he announced one Monday morning in early spring. "Got a delivery of manure on Saturday, to give the soil a treat. Just about ready to sow. Just need to get re-potting."

"You got a greenhouse?" Guthrie asked.

Now Colin was checking Delia's charts.

"I got no greenhouse so my house is full to bursting with little pots of seeds. I pot 'em up, keep them nice and moist, wrapped in clingfilm. I put them on the radiators or the window sills, they like a bit of warmth. It drives Tracy crazy."

"I know all about that," said Guthrie, warming to the topic. "I used to do the same thing, and Delia never liked it. I used to say, 'Well, you don't complain about the vases full of flowers, or the carrots and cabbages on the table.' She couldn't argue with that. You should try the same argument with Tracy and see what she says."

"*He*," Colin corrected. "Tracy's my husband."

"Oh," said Guthrie, and thought, Well, that explains a lot.

Shortly afterwards, the conversation faltered.

It wasn't the only uncomfortable conversation they shared. When Colin mentioned his childhood in Trinidad, it prompted Guthrie to reveal his interest in colonial history. He'd recently read an account of the West Indies Campaign of 1804-1810.

"One of my ancestors went out to the Caribbean," he added, after he'd finished recounting what he'd learned.

"Is that right?" Colin said, his tone flat.

"Yes, he was in the army. I suppose he was there to protect you lot from the French."

"I expect so," Colin said drily.

When Guthrie began to tell him about the Jamaican Slave Revolt of 1831-2, Colin said he had a lot of paperwork to catch up on and left.

It was soon after this conversation that Guthrie fell sick. It was a bout of flu that lasted the best part of three weeks. At the time, it was just a grotty inconvenience. Later on, he looked back on the illness as a watershed moment.

When he first felt unwell, he phoned the nursing home and spoke to Luisa.

"Delia will be in safe hands," she told him. "You just concentrate on getting better."

He also called Gloria and she promised to visit his wife as often as she could until he was back on his feet.

The flu hit him for six. For a week he could do little more than stagger to and from the bathroom whenever nature called. He told Garai and Abi to say he was out whenever Eric phoned, so as not to worry him. The only calls he made were to the nursing home whenever he could manage to check on Delia.

Abi picked up on his condition by the end of the second day and brought him cereal and toast, paracetamol and a jug of cold water each morning before she went to work. He refused her offer to call a doctor, and her invitation to share her vegan sausage casserole for three days in a row. When his appetite finally returned on day four, he asked meekly whether she wouldn't mind heating up a mug of tinned soup. By day seven, she was leaving him cheese-and-pickle sandwiches for his lunch.

Even after the fever left, the flu left him weak as a baby for days afterwards, too sick to leave the house. Days of maddening frustration. He read a little, listened to the radio, and worried about Delia, until finally he was well enough to recommence his visits to the nursing home.

The first time he walked into his wife's room, he found himself looking at a face he barely recognised. She'd been biting her lips again, and the lower one was swollen. Her face was puffy, too, from a course of steroids, according to Colin. But these were only superficial and temporary changes, it was not as if her appearance really had altered much in those three weeks.

No, it was more that he'd been seeing Delia every day since the accident, and this lack of distance had blinded him to the way her features had transformed gradually over time. Now these weeks away had given some clarity, and he saw with a shock that her face had wasted, her body was shrunken, her limbs twisted despite the physiotherapy. She was, in short, the husk of her former self.

He sat down with the force of the blow, and gazed at her. He thought, She's buggered. Unseeing, unhearing, unfeeling, she's un-everything. For the first time, he contemplated the permanency of her position, and realised how deluded he'd been all these months. He took a deep breath. When he spoke, his voice was little more than a croak.

"Hello, love. I've been away for a few days. A bit poorly, but I'm right as rain now. You look well. How've you been? I hope they've been looking after you."

He reached down and put his hand on hers.

"Of course they've been looking after me," she said. "You think the whole world stops when you're not around?"

"No, no," he said. "To tell you the truth, it's the other way round. It's me that can't cope without you, love. I've missed you."

"Get away with you," she said, just like she used to, when he got too soppy. "Silly old fool."

"Here, I've brought you your magazines," he said, to lighten the mood. "It was nice of Gloria to pop by, wasn't it? Fancy a bit of music? How about *Sgt Pepper's*? I spoke to Eric yesterday. You'll never guess who called him up last week."

And he was off, the usual patter, like he'd never been away. He let his voice drone on and on, the same cheery tone, the same old guff, anything to drown out the voice in his head, the one that whispered that Delia would not get better.

But a single new seed of hope had been sown that day. It hadn't yet germinated, remained more a feeling than an idea. If he could have put it into words at that stage, he would have told Delia something like this: *Yes, I get comfort from this hellish limbo, but at what cost to you? I thought we were living this half-life for your sake, but now I'm not so sure. Carrying on like this, whose needs am I really putting first?*

At around this time, he first heard the term *permanent vegetative state* when he accidentally eavesdropped on a husband and wife discussing their son's situation in the visitors' break room. Up until then he'd heard the terms *persistent* and *prolonged* vegetative states, but not this new one. He thought, I'll google it when I get home. But when it came to it, he found himself unwilling to probe any deeper. He thought, Persistent? Prolonged? Permanent? They may each have their own distinct definition, but did understanding the nuances really make any difference to Delia's situation?

Once, in the early hours of the morning as he lay on his side of the double bed, hope of sleep abandoned, he began to wonder why the doctors brought Delia back at the time of the accident. He got up and Googled *Hippocratic oath*. He read: *I will use my power to help the sick to the best of my ability and judgement; I will abstain from harming or wronging any man by it.* He thought, Did they really help Delia by doing what they did? Who decides what harms or wrongs a person like Delia?

None of these doubts showed in his routine, which remained unaltered. Indeed his visiting was so deeply interwoven into the pattern of his existence, that if someone had prevented him making the daily trips to Headington, he'd have been at a loss to know how to fill his days. Hope had given way to resignation, but he was as yet unable to contemplate a change in the status quo.

Colin was more sensitive than most to the subtle change in Guthrie's mind-set. One day, seeing the weariness on Guthrie's face, he said,

"You look a little deflated, man."

Guthrie forced a smile.

"I'm alright."

"You don't have to visit every day, you know?"

"What do you mean?"

"She won't know if you aren't here."

Guthrie gazed at him for a long moment. Colin looked braced, as if for a furious response. But Guthrie felt less anger than a deep fatigue. He found himself sighing and nodding a reluctant acknowledgement.

"You understand, don't you? That's not the point. *I'll* know, won't I?"

Because Guthrie still hadn't revealed Delia's situation to Abi and Garai, home remained a place of escape. The only invasion of this sanctuary were the phone calls from Eric and other relatives, which he took in the privacy of his own bedroom.

There were occasional calls from two of Delia's old friends who now lived up North, as well as a niece in Scotland

and a cousin in Eastbourne. At first he appreciated their efforts to cheer him up. They'd ask, "How is she? Any better?" and Guthrie would say, "No, she's the same." Then they'd say, "Well that's good, isn't it? She's no worse, right?"

At the beginning, he'd feel the same. But as time went on, he understood that 'the same' was a curse, a purgatory that shifted day after day towards something closer to hell. After that, the more they tried to bring comfort to Guthrie, the more alone he felt.

At around this time, three people came to visit Delia.

The first few times the niece asked if she could come and see Delia, Guthrie put her off with one excuse or another. Apart from Eric, he didn't want anyone who knew the old Delia to see what she'd now become. Then the day came when he could no longer fob her off with excuses. They sat together in Delia's room, the niece on Guthrie's favourite armchair, the old man relegated to a straight-back seat in the corner.

"She's there. I can see it. Auntie Delia's in there," the niece said afterwards in the carpark. Was she trying to make Guthrie feel better? If so, it had the opposite effect. He thought, Christ, if she's really there, imagine the horror of what she's going through.

Soon afterwards, the cousin paid a visit. It was evident to Guthrie that he saw it as a difficult duty. On that occasion, Guthrie spent the visiting time in Luisa's office going over some paperwork. When the man came out of Delia's room, he was pale and trembling. He never visited again.

Eric flew home for another short visit. A few sweet days that passed only too quickly. With both spare rooms now occupied in Rose Hill, Eric slept with Guthrie on Delia's side of the double bed in Rose Hill, but most of the days were spent in the Headington nursing home. Listening to the news of his son's life in New Zealand, tales of grandchildren, the challenges of the infant business, was a sweet distraction for Guthrie. Father and son sat either side of Delia's bed. Eric held her hand and addressed his family stories to his mother. On the final day, he bent and kissed her cheek.

"Bye, mum."

On the way home, in the car, he began to cry.

"It's not right. It's not fair on her. Not fair on either of you."

"Stop that talk, son. I'm fine. Your mum's fine."

"That's not mum. That's just a ... ."

"I know. That's what makes it easier. Wherever she is, she's not here."

Back at home each evening after the visiting, Guthrie would pick up fish and chips from the Rose Hill chippy, or they'd cook a simple meal and talk long into the night over a shared bottle of whisky. They re-traced old stories of family life from Eric's childhood. Memorable holidays in Devon, trips to the football, scrapes Eric and his pals got into, older stories of Guthrie's own juvenile misdemeanours. And without fail the stories would somehow end up with things Delia had said or done, occasions they'd shared together as a family. Many times Eric dredged up memories that Guthrie had forgotten, and it struck Guthrie after a time that his own mind was erasing those memories and replacing them with newer ones of hospital and ill-health. It was an awful realisation, and he shared it with Eric.

"The old Delia, the one you can conjure up so easily, it's getting harder and harder for me to do the same. Ah, Christ, son. I don't want to lose her."

Eric nodded to show he'd understood but his only response was to top up their glasses from the whisky bottle.

For those few days with Eric, Guthrie slept like a well-fed cat, but as soon as his son departed, the old man felt lonelier than ever.

The hours Guthrie spent away from Delia, he busied himself with domestic chores, began to make tentative preparations for his garden beds, and tried unsuccessfully to sleep. Getting to know his new lodgers was a slow process, hindered by Garai's evening working hours and Guthrie's unwillingness to engage with Abi's cooking, despite her regular invitations to share her meals.

During all his years of marriage, Delia had cooked for him, and ever since the accident, he'd filled the freezer with ready meals-for-one. He preferred the classics of British cooking. Cottage pie, beef casserole and dumplings, bangers-and-mash, liver-and-bacon, fish pie. Occasionally he'd try something more exotic like lasagne or beef stroganoff, but he preferred to stick with what he knew, even though the meals were pale imitations of Delia's versions.

Abi, who'd waited until she moved in before announcing that she ate no meat, cooked pots of aromatic lentils and vegetables that seemed to last for weeks. In Guthrie's eyes, there was something suspicious about the overuse of exotic spices, just as there was with vegetarian cuisine. And veganism was beyond the pale. If Guthrie was in the kitchen at a time she was eating, she'd offer him a plate without fail, and he'd always decline.

"I like my meat-and-two-veg," he explained, the first couple of times, and this seemed to amuse Abi, because after that, whenever she offered him her food, she'd begin,

"I know you like your meat-and-two-veg, Mister G, but can I offer you something a little different today?"

Garai, when he did have an evening off, seemed to eat little more than macaroni or instant noodles. Occasionally he'd roast a chicken, then pick off the cold carcass little by little over the course of the week.

In the early days together, these eating habits seemed a little odd to Guthrie, but he was an African boy, after all. A black boy. And what did Guthrie know about how black people lived? And anyway, the lad seemed normal in other ways. He kept a toothbrush in the bathroom, he washed his clothes regularly, took showers, drank tea with milk and sugar. Guthrie still wasn't quite sure whether the boy was working or studying or both. After all he was away all hours of the night, yet had his nose in a book all day. Still, he paid his rent on time, caused no trouble and was willing enough to chat, so the old man put aside his doubts.

When he couldn't sleep, Guthrie delved into his history books. He was still curious about the Irish ancestor in Burma, so he re-read *Forgotten Voices of Burma: The Second World War's Forgotten Conflict* by Julian Thompson. That lit a fuse of interest, and he found a second-hand copy online of *Wingate and the Chindits: Redressing the Balance* by David Rooney.

One evening he came down from his bedroom to make himself a hot drink. His mind was awhirl with acts of military heroism in the worst of conditions. He found Garai in the kitchen, just returned from his job and working his way through a plate of pasta and tinned tuna. He began to tell the young man about his reading, and the conversation drifted to the wider topic of British Empire.

"They say the nineteenth century belonged to Britain, the twentieth to America, and the twenty-first will be Chinese," said Garai.

"You can't compare our colonialism with the Chinese," said Guthrie, and began listing the benefits of British civilization. Garai had heard it all before and listened without interrupting. When Guthrie finished, the young man offered to lend him his most recent library acquisition.

"That'd be great," Guthrie said. "But remember, you've got to take one of mine in exchange?"

Guthrie went to fetch Garai a copy of Niall Ferguson's *How Britain Made the Modern World*. In exchange, Garai fetched him a library copy of David Anderson's *Histories of the Hanged: Britain's Dirty War in Kenya and the End of Empire*.

"Thanks," said Guthrie, examining the cover. "That looks exciting. A different world then, eh? A man's world."

There were nights when Guthrie was too tired to read, and yet still he couldn't sleep. Once, in his twenties, when things were slow with the decorating, he worked on a building site for a few months. Now Guthrie lay awake and thought of that time, working as a brickie, using his memories as a kind of counting-sheep exercise to soothe his mind. A dollop of muck on the trowel, spread it and lay it. *Knock knock* it into place. Check that it's level. Brick after brick, course after course. No thoughts, no worries, you emptied your head, zoned out, your mind at ease.

One day Gloria phoned to arrange a visit to the nursing home.

"Have you thought about what I said? You know, about me taking your place?"

"I have."

"And?"

"If the offer still stands, I think I'd like to try it," Guthrie said, surprising himself. "Once a week. Just a trial. The garden's a mess and-."

"Excellent," she interrupted. "I'm off next week on Wednesday. I'll visit Delia in the morning. You plant some seeds or whatever."

"Thank you, Gloria."

And then, not long after that, he found out that his lodgers knew about Delia.

It was late on Sunday night and Guthrie, exhausted but awake, was downstairs making himself a whisky mac in an attempt to induce sleep. He had poured an inch of Teachers into a glass and was adding a top-up of Stone's Original when he heard the front door opening, then footsteps in the hallway. He was used to Garai arriving home late from work, and he'd thought that Abi was asleep in bed, but to his surprise, both lodgers came into the kitchen. Abi's face was flushed, and Garai's was etched deep with fatigue.

"Hey, Mister G," Abi said. "OG, the Original Gangster."

"Excuse me?" Guthrie said, puzzled.

"Don't mind her, Mr Guthrie" Garai said. "We've been to the pub."

"Have you now?" said Guthrie. "Well nothing wrong with that. I used to like a regular night at my local when I was your age. I've slowed down a bit since then."

"What are you drinking, Mister G?" Abi said, peering at his glass.

"Whisky mac. Fancy one?"

"I sure do. What is it?"

"Whisky and ginger wine," he explained. "The name's short for Whisky Macdonald. It's named after Colonel Hector "Fighting Mac" MacDonald. He came up with it while serving during the British Raj in India."

"Well if it's good enough for Fighting Mac, it's good enough for Battling Abi."

"Righteo. What about you, Garai?"

"Water for me," said the young man, filling a glass at the sink.

It started with a drink, but went on long into the night, and by the time they all climbed the stairs to their beds, the bottle was empty, the first fingers of light were playing across the mottled sky, and a lone robin was starting up his dawn chorus.

Afterwards, Guthrie could remember only fragments of the night's conversation. He recalled the moment Abi revealed that they knew about his wife.

"Your son called a few days ago, remember? I gave you the message? I told him you were at the hospital and he asked how his mother was doing. I didn't know what he meant, of course. Then he explained. He seemed surprised that you hadn't talked about it. I guess you wanted to keep it private, right? I mean, it's none of our business."

"Yes well, it doesn't matter."

They didn't probe, but the whisky was loosening his tongue, and in the morning he recalled that once the floodgates were open, he'd talked a lot about the situation. It hadn't been a strain to keep the secret, but still, it felt good to be listened to by someone other than Eric or Colin or Gloria. A sharing of the burden.

Heavy-headed and foul-mouthed the next day, he had a bad feeling the whisky may have drawn out a thread of maudlin self-pity. At one point, he recalled saying,

"Why did they revive her? Why did they keep her alive? Why did they induce the coma after she got pneumonia? My life is just a series of whys. And there are no answers. There'll never be any answers. No answers, just guilt and regret."

He recalled that they'd talked about regret, and the two youngsters had both made passing reference to their own remorse. Garai had talked about a friend of his that he'd let down, and Abi about her relationship with her mother. Later, Guthrie said,

"It's a funny thing, regret. When Delia was alive, she never regretted a thing. She wasn't that sort of person. She was content, she had a simple mind-set. Do the best for yourself and for others. Be the best person you can. If things go wrong, don't dwell, just work twice as hard to make things right. No regrets. It was a good philosophy, I tried to copy her. Then the accident happened, and everything's become so much more *complicated*."

"Complications," Garai said quietly.

"Complications," Abi said, and raised her glass. "Here's to bloody complications."

Abigail 3

Abi's working life dragged slowly, each day a misery of tedium. Over the weeks of spring, the boredom fossilised into something more sinister, an almost physical revulsion at the thought of the office environment. She knew she ought to move on, yet felt powerless to act. The depression that enveloped her was insidious, like the steady but relentless onset of hyperthermia.

She angsted over the first sickie she pulled, a Monday morning after a poor night's sleep. An hour of hesitation in the early hours, more guilt and shame, before she emailed her line manager from her bed and clicked 'send'. The immediate relief was intense. She put aside her laptop, lay back on her pillow and slept like a stone. It was only when she woke again at midday that the self-loathing returned. She thought, Your job's so basic, anyone with a pulse could do it. Yet you can't even hold that down.

Having signed herself off sick, she realised she lacked the courage to leave the house in case she was spotted. Instead, she stayed in her room and by mid-afternoon she was desperate to escape her own company. Down in the kitchen she ran into Garai, a rare occurrence given her usual nine-to-five existence.

"Hey," she said, as she filled her kettle. He was sitting at the table eating from a bowl of porridge and gazing down at an opened book. "What are you reading?"

He flicked over the cover to reveal the title: *The White Tribe of Africa*.

"Intriguing title. What's it about?'"

"It's a kind of history of the Afrikaaner people. It sort of explains how they ended up like they are."

"You're interested in history?"

"I'm interested in politics," he said. "Someone said, 'history is past politics, and politics is history of the present.' Besides, I like reading. It helps me relax."

"Are there many Afrikaaners in Zimbabwe? I thought they lived in South Africa."

"Yeah, there are not many back home. Most are Down South."

"And the book? Is it good?"

"It's interesting. It explains how come they've always been so ... *ruthless* in their politics. As a community, they came to Africa as refugees from Europe. They'd been persecuted there on religious grounds. Unlike the British settlers, their bridges were burned. They had nowhere else to go if things didn't work out in Africa, no place to call home. Backs to the wall, eh?"

"Right. Still, I don't believe they were any more ruthless than we Brits," said Abi, who shared her generation's contempt for Empire, though lacked much in the way of specific detail to back up her point of view. "Surely we were world-beaters when it came to bullying our way around the globe."

"Yes, that's the other interesting thing I've learned. The Afrikaaners really suffered at the hands of the Brits before they took power in 1948. You know, by the end of the Boer Wars, the British army had killed forty-eight thousand Afrikaaners and destroyed thirty thousand of their homes. Most of the casualties died in concentration camps."

"What? Like Nazi concentration camps?"

"Yes, but forty years earlier. And even after the British beat them into submission, they continued to discriminate against them. Afrikaaner children were punished at school for speaking their language, adults were treated as second-class citizens, only one step up from the blacks. You could even call it a system of apartheid amongst the whites."

A fortnight after her first episode of truancy, Abi called in sick again. Once more she lacked the courage to leave the house, but again found Garai at home, and spent a pleasant few hours in his company, a leisurely brunch as he spoke about his latest readings on colonialism in east Africa.

After a while, without quite knowing how, the conversation moved on from the political to the personal, and she found herself speaking a little more about her family. She painted a picture of her easy middle-class childhood, mentioned again her father's betrayal and the arrival on the scene of his unpleasant replacement. She spoke mostly of her relationship with her mother, their intimacy when she was a child, the drink problem, the guilt she now lived with ever since her flight from home. As she spoke, Garai nodded, occasionally made a comment.

"You're a good listener," she said when she'd finished. "You have a gift. You should become a therapist."

It was a joke, but he looked at her without smiling.

"Thank you. I'd like to be a journalist or an oral historian. I suppose listening's a good skill for either job."

Her first flare-up with Guthrie came soon after yet another sleepless night. She got into a pattern of three or four poor nights, then one decent enough to provide hope that perhaps she'd broken the cycle. That morning, she sat at the breakfast table, strung out and jittery, and wondered how she'd get through another day at her office. Just then, Guthrie came into the kitchen holding a newspaper.

"Top o' the morning to you," he said in a bogus Irish accent. He had a limited repertoire of expressions that he liked to use, accompanied by a foreign inflection, each dependent on the occasion. Apart from the morning greeting in the Irish brogue, there was a sing-song Indian 'Goodness gracious me!' that he used to express surprise, and a Chinese-style 'Ah so!' he'd offer to indicate understanding. Most unsettling and peculiar, he had an odd tendency to acknowledge a request made by one of the lodgers with a brusque Germanic, '*Jawohl, mein Kommandant!*'

And there were references Abi did not understand at all. Each month when she mentioned that she'd paid her rent into his account, he'd start singing, 'If I was a rich man' in a strange accent that she thought might be eastern European. Once, when admitting to Abi that he didn't know what *TikTok* was, he said, 'I know nothing. I'm from Barcelona,' in what Abi suspected was supposed to be a Spanish inflexion. The impressions made her uncomfortable, but still she did not challenge him.

It was a comment about a newspaper headline that morning that caused Abi to snap for the first time. She was sipping tea, and he was bent over his cereal, his copy of the *Daily Mail* laid out beside the bowl.

"Would you believe it," he began, pointing to the lead story. Abi peered over and saw that it was something about migrants in Calais, another spat between the British and French authorities about how to partition responsibility for the problem. "The Frogs want us to stump up even more cash to pay for the policing. Nobody's asking why they let 'em into France in the first place."

Usually Abi would have bitten her tongue, but today she was too tired to restrain herself.

"Jesus, Mr Guthrie, where do I start? I just don't get you. One moment you're a decent guy, the next you're just so bloody bigoted. You don't like the French. You don't like immigrants. Would you really be so happy in your little fortress?"

"Steady on, love," said Guthrie, visibly shaken by the vehemence of Abi's attack. "I didn't mean-"

Abi peered over at her landlord, saw the pain of his face and felt her anger puncturing.

"Ah, I'm sorry. It doesn't matter. You caught me at a bad moment."

"I'm sorry too," Guthrie continued. He still looked mortified. "I talk a lot of nonsense. Frogs, it's just a manner of speech, I don't mean anything by it. And I've got nothing against the pour souls who end up at our borders. It's not their fault."

"It's OK," said Abi. She got up. "I'm going to be late for work."

That evening, before Garai went out to his job, he knocked on Abi's bedroom. It'd been an achingly slow day for Abi, she'd come close to handing in her notice, and now, filled with a kind of reckless desperation, she was wondering whether to head into town to drown her sorrows at the Jolly Farmers.

"You had an argument with Mr Guthrie this morning?" he began.

"How do you know?"

"He's just been telling me about it. He said something about immigrants and you got angry? I think he's quite upset. He feels bad. He's just apologised to me, and I wasn't even there."

He looked at Abi and almost smiled, and she saw that he'd come to make the peace.

"It's OK. I told him it was OK. You know, I was just feeling tired. Another bad night," she explained.

He stood at the threshold of her room and waited.

"You know, sometimes he reminds me of my step-father," Abi said. "I told you about him, right?"

Garai nodded.

"It doesn't matter whether it's racist or sexist or homophobic or whatever kind of small-minded dick-headed intolerance, sometimes I just feel I've had enough."

Garai nodded again. Abi looked at him and swallowed hard.

"Roger, my step-father, he discovered something about me, and he used that to get rid of me. When I left, he hurt me. Not just with words, but physically."

"What did he discover?"

Abi took a deep breath.

"That I'm gay. A lesbian. You understand what I mean?"

"Of course," said Garai. "That's OK. I don't mind."

She gazed at Garai and felt a flush of irritation.

"You don't mind? Well, that's great. It's such a relief that a man doesn't mind how I live my life. Of course, I spend my days hoping and praying for his approval."

"Hey, chill out," said Garai, frowning. "I didn't mean-"

"Don't tell me to chill out. There's nothing more irritating than being told to chill out by a man, like my default position is hysteria." She felt her anger fizzing now. "There's nothing more fucked up in this world than the arrogance of the fucking patriarchy."

Garai, she saw, was still frowning.

"I think if you were black, if you were poor, you might think of one or two things that are more fucked up," he said slowly.

No one spoke for a long minute. Eventually Abi broke the silence.

"I'm sorry."

"I'm sorry too. And Guthrie really did want to apologise. He's also sorry."

"That makes three of us," said Abi.

They exchanged weak smiles.

"OK."

"OK."

*

It was around this time that the political debates between Garai and Guthrie began to heat up. They always took place in the kitchen, and were always ignited by Guthrie's blathering, some foot-in-mouth remark tossed into the discussion like a spark into tinder. Sometimes Abi found the arguments an entertaining distraction. At other times, she thought, Oh Christ, another power display between competitive men.

A typical exchange began as an innocuous prelude, ran on as a lively extended middle section, then petered out with a damp-squid finale, Garai exasperated and Guthrie, huffy, concluding that he didn't know why people couldn't just get on with life without harping on about things that were long over and done with. One such argument took place in the kitchen, as it always did, one Saturday mid-morning in April. Abi was making a flask of coffee in preparation for a bike ride. Guthrie was reading the *Oxford Mail* while half-listening to the radio. Garai had just emerged red-eyed and yawning from his bedroom.

"Another long shift?" said Guthrie.

Garai nodded.

"Good on you, son. A lot of kids these days, they don't know the meaning of hard work."

"Thanks."

"It's true. I left school at fourteen to start my apprenticeship. Did I ever tell you that?"

"I think you might have mentioned it, Mr Guthrie."

"Yes, well. I'm not saying I was special. We were all like that, my generation. You got a job, and you worked hard and when you met someone nice, you got married and started a family. Nowadays, no one's prepared to put in the graft. You work for a year and then decide you need to go off travelling, or you quit because you're not running the bloody firm yet, or you get signed off with stress. In my day we didn't even have mental health."

"It's harder to get a job these days, Mr Guthrie"

"And why's that then? I know I'm not supposed to say it, but we've too many folk coming here looking for work and not enough jobs."

Abi watched Garai sigh. She thought, Oh here we go.

"The UK has agreements about free movement with other EU members. Are you talking about them? Or are you still talking about immigrants from ex-Empire? Mr Guthrie, we both know Britain never had any problem breaching other countries' borders when it came to grabbing new colonies. There were never any problems when the British settled in those places. So why was it a crime when people from those colonies came here? They were citizens of the British Empire, remember? They had a right to come, yet still they were resented when they arrived. And their children and grandchildren and great-grandchildren are still resented today for daring to make a home for themselves here. You've read *Empireland*? I gave you the Sanghera book, right?"

"Yes, it's upstairs," Guthrie answered.

"And? How far have you got in?"

"Well, I've been busy. I've just been dipping in and out. Did you know that in the early 1920s, the British Empire covered thirteen point seven one million square miles? That's twenty-four percent of Earth's land area."

"What's your point?"

"And did you know that little parts of the British Empire still exist today?" Guthrie went on. "They call them the British Overseas Territories, like the Caymans and the Falklands and Gibraltar. I think that's amazing. It's heart-warming."

Garai looked at the old man and shook his head.

"*That's* what you've taken from the book so far? Well, let me give you the gist of Sanghera's arguments."

"I know what you're going to say. How terrible the Empire was."

"No. Many people all over the world benefited from the British Empire. The point was, those benefits were incidental. Britain always got much more than it gave."

"In what way?"

"Well, economically mostly. In simple terms, the British Empire was a means to make the British middle and upper classes richer."

"You sound like a Communist," said Guthrie.

Abi thought he looked a little uncomfortable and was trying for a lighter tone. But Garai was in no mood for retreat.

"A Marxist interpretation of imperialism often makes the most sense," he said solemnly. "But Sanghera's no Marxist. He just understands the power of money. He says the African World Reparations and Repatriation Truth Commission estimated reparations to cover compensation for lives lost and resources looted during the African slave trade as seven hundred and seventy-seven trillion dollars. He quotes other academics who've calculated that between 1835 and 1872 Britain received approximately seventy-seven billion pounds in today's money of goods from India annually. Annually."

"That's business," Guthrie interjected.

"Between 1765 to 1938, it's thought that Britain drained nearly forty-five trillion dollars from India. It's what paid for all those English country houses and estates. One third of National Trust houses and gardens are tainted by wealth from slavery or plunder. Companies too. Household names like Lloyds Bank, RBS, the law firm Freshfields, the Greene King brewery, Glasgow University and All Souls College, Oxford. You know when the slave trade was abolished, the slaves received no compensation, but the traders and owners were paid twenty million pounds at the time. That's two point two billion pounds in today's money. Those on the receiving end included seventy-five baronets, fifty MPs and a hundred and fifty Anglican clergymen."

"Money isn't everything," Guthrie said.

"No, but look what it paid for here," Garai cut in before Guthrie could elaborate. "Manchester wouldn't be what it is without the cotton industry, Glasgow without sugar. I've seen pictures of Liverpool and Bristol. All those beautiful buildings paid for by the slave trade."

"We gave as good as we got. All those roads, railways, bridges... ."

"They were investments, to make controlling the country easier and to boost the economy. Everything the British did in the colonies was an investment, carefully calculated to bring maximum profit to the British government, and to the shareholders of the companies involved. And it goes without saying that those shareholders included men of government. Gladstone's father made money from the slave trade. So did Peel's."

Abi glanced at Guthrie. He looked a little crushed.

"It wasn't all bad," was all he could manage. "Everyone benefited one way or another. We offered law and order, an end to criminality and violence, protection to the vulnerable."

Garai sighed.

"Who was protecting who? You'd have lost your wars without the people you colonised. Three million soldiers from the colonies fought on the British side in World War One. Roughly the same number in the Second World War, plus all the raw materials and food to supply the troops and the civilians in Britain."

"Really?" said Guthrie, clearly surprised at the scale of the support. "That's great. All good citizens of the world coming together to fight Nazi tyranny. We should all feel proud."

Abi hoped that the argument had run its course, but she watched as Garai shook his head sadly and saw that there was more to come.

"The First World War was fought for imperial reasons. Britain wanted to preserve its Empire. Germany wanted a bigger slice. It had nothing to do with the Nazis."

"I know. But still... ."

"I doubt if many colonial troops felt much pride in fighting for the British. It was a job. Their families were hungry. Some would have been conscripted or coerced. They were under no illusions about their 'mother country'. They'd have grown up with the stories of the atrocities carried out by British security forces and their local deputies."

"Ah come on. Next you'll be saying we were no better than the Nazis."

And just as Abi thought the men were running out of steam, they were off again. She sighed as Garai launched into a list of imperial massacres, outrageous incidents and campaigns of violence, making references to their shared reading of Gott and Sanghera and Newsinger all the while. Abi took in fragments of the diatribe. The Jallianwala Bagh Massacre of April 1919 in the Punjab, where a peaceful demonstration of men, women and children was fired on by British troops. The Myall Creek massacre of 1838 when fifty indigenous Australians, including women and children., were slaughtered by colonial cattle ranchers. The ritual dismembering of the Xhosa chief, Hintsa's body after the Sixth Frontier War, when troops removed his ears as souvenirs, as well as his manhood and some of his teeth. The habit of strapping intransigent rebels or mutinous sepoys in India to the barrels of cannons that were then fired so that the body parts were scattered and unusable for funeral rites.

"Sanghera calls all these tactics exercises in ritualized racial humiliation," said Garai, at one point, before launching into an account of the genocide of Palawa indigenous Australians in Tasmania at the start of the nineteenth century, a campaign that involved a shoot-on-sight policy.

"Women were systematically raped. Men were hunted on horseback or used for target practice. Those that survived were forcibly removed to the barren Flinders Island. The last Palawa died in 1869. Tell me that's not genocide."

"Cases like that weren't common," said Guthrie. "Otherwise we'd all have heard of them."

"During the campaign against Kandyan kingdom in Ceylon, the Brits killed ten thousand people in 1818. The campaign against the Mau Mau uprising in Kenya involved torturing prisoners to death."

You think the natives weren't capable of just as much violence? There were a hundred and one stories of uprisings. Civilians slaughtered, white women raped."

"Were they not provoked?"

"Not to mention the wars between tribes that had been going on for centuries."

"Of course, war is universal. But before the Europeans came, no one had the Maxim gun."

It was Guthrie's turn to sigh.

"I don't know. I'm not saying we were perfect. But it's all in the past. Isn't it time to move on."

"But that's my point," said Garai. The animation in his voice had increased. "What started in the past has repercussions today. You made all of these natives British citizens. You told them they were equal, that they could make this country their home. That they could become British. But when they came to live in the 'mother country', it wasn't long before they were kettled into the worst accommodation, denied all but the hardest jobs, resented for sending their children to the local schools or for visiting the local doctors' surgeries. And all the while there were National Front skinheads beating up immigrants for kicks."

"Yes, well, that's a disgrace."

"Read Sanghera. They've never been allowed to become equal here. Less than five percent of the most senior jobs in UK are held by ethnic minorities. There's no ethnic minority leadership in healthcare, education, criminal justice. The Met Police and the Home Office are institutionally racist. That's not me talking, that's the conclusion of independent enquiries. A third of companies on the FTSE 100 Index lack ethnic minority representation on their boards."

"People wouldn't want to come here if it wasn't a great country. It didn't become great by accident. It took centuries of strength and courage and determination. Of course, you can't cook an omelette without cracking a few eggs. But there's a lot to be proud of too."

At last the kitchen fell silent. Abi looked at the two men. Garai, tight-lipped, glared at Guthrie. The older man looked as if he'd disturbed a wasp's nest for fun, and now wished he hadn't. She thought, Oh God, I've had enough of this. She looked over at Guthrie.

"It's not your fault you're fascinated by Empire," she began. "You've been brought up brainwashed by stories of colonial adventure. And you're a man. You've got all this testosterone. It's telling you that it's good to fight. War is fine, so long as it's for a noble cause. You put the two together - the need to fight and the belief in the moral goodness of Empire - and it's no wonder thousands of young men went out and committed acts of terror. And it's no wonder men like you still dream of colonial times. But Christ, can you imagine what the world would be like if all that testosterone was focused on a different kind of war? On protecting the environment, or looking after the old and sick, or on parenting properly?"

There was a long pause. Guthrie and Garai looked at Abi, and then at each other. Guthrie spoke first.

"Steady on, love."

Even Garai looked a little abashed.

*

Sometime over the spring, Abi began to take more days off work. At first she justified it as a reasonable response to the physical exhaustion brought on by her insomnia. She wasn't yet ready to acknowledge the depression that was engulfing her, knew only that the very thought of sitting at her desk made her feel so anxious she thought she'd be sick.

Things came to a head when she took an entire week off. When she returned, no healthier than before but now tense from guilt, Emma called a meeting and asked how she was feeling. Abi mentioned the sleeplessness. To her surprise, Emma showed genuine empathy.

"I'm really sorry, that must be awful," she began. "Why not make an appointment with occupational health or your GP?"

"Thanks, I will," Abi replied. Her boss's concern only increased her feelings of guilt.

Then Emma grew a little uncomfortable.

"Look, I hate to ask, but I'm afraid if this continues, you'll need to get a doctor's certificate. It's just for our records, you know."

Reluctantly, Abi registered at the Donnington surgery and went along for her first appointment. The doctor was a locum, a young man not much older than Abi, with narrow shoulders, a stooped back and a jolly manner.

"Might be worth trying a short course of sleeping tablets, just a few days, to see if we can break the cycle."

Desperate for a way out of her downward spiral, Abi agreed. He wrote out the prescription, five zopiclone, passed it over and began to write notes in her file. He did not look up when she slipped out of the door.

The sleeping pill worked a treat the first night, not so well the second, and by the third Abi's tolerance had built so successfully that she barely noticed its effect. On the morning after the fifth and final tablet, Abi phoned in sick again.

A pattern emerged. Three or four poor nights, then when she thought she could take no more, the body would switch off, the brain would flip, and she'd sleep right through until seven o'clock. That day, fuelled by hope, she'd feel a different person. But evening would fall, and by midnight she'd realise she was back to square one.

On bad mornings, when she'd wake from an hour or two's rest, she'd lie in bed and think, If I can just get through this day, if I can survive it without injury to myself or others, that's all I must focus on. That's all I can hope for. She'd bathe and dress and eat breakfast like an alien creature trying its best to be as human as possible. At work she'd force out smile after smile, focus on being polite and helpful, on carrying out her duties as if she was normal. From the outside, no one could imagine the strain it put on her.

Occasionally when she slept, dreams of childhood would visit, safe and comfortable scenes. Car journeys, her parents in the front, Abi dozing in the back. Picnics in the park, warm lemonade and cold chicken drumsticks. Games in the back garden, swing-ball and a tea-party for the dolls.

And in the centre of all these memories, there was Abi, but an Abi she no longer remembered. A different person, before her father's betrayal and all that followed. She'd forgotten what a joker she'd been, always happy to play the fool herself. She'd forgotten the pleasure she got from making others laugh, the joy of an appreciative audience. And in those days, there was always an audience, for Abi shone with happiness and friends came easily. In her dreams, Abi was again that person, but when she woke, that old self felt like a stranger. She wondered, What has become of her?

Mostly, though, sleep brought nightmares. When Roger's attack was not replayed over and over, she dreamt of new assaults, each generating the same raw feelings of helpless humiliation. Teddy's vitriol came back too, all close-up snarl and coiled violence. But worst were the dreams of her eviction. Empty streets she trudged along, lonely and miserable from the knowledge that she had nowhere to go.

With little to distract her, Abi allowed her dark thoughts to stew, knowing this could only exacerbate her depression, yet unable to focus elsewhere. A mounting stress at work as she played her role of forced good cheer, all the poison bottled up until she'd snap at some innocuous remark, then wallow in guilt and shame. She longed to stand at her desk, open her mouth and scream until there was nothing left inside.

Tension showed itself in different ways, mostly as health conditions. Headaches, stomach pains, heart palpitations. For a month in June, she kept seeing Roger everywhere she looked. She'd sense something in the corner of her eye, turn and glance, and for a split-second she was certain the man had appeared. Outside the chippy in Rose Hill, at a zebra crossing in Headington, at the entrance to the hospital where she worked. Then she'd peer more closely and of course it was a stranger.

More absences, another meeting with Emma. No threats or warnings, no ultimatum, just an urging to get more expert help. Another GP appointment, this time a middle-aged woman shoehorned into a matching tartan jacket and skirt. When Abi set about describing her insomnia, she found, to her surprise, that she was crying.

The doctor was kind and patient and they spoke for twenty minutes. She asked Abi about her family and friends, how she spent her leisure time, but almost nothing about the sleeplessness.

"Do you ever think about harming yourself?" she asked at one point. Abi opened her mouth to answer without quite knowing what she'd say. Those feelings she'd been having, a desire to just disappear, to no longer exist, did they count? In the end, she shook her head.

The doctor began to talk about talking therapy, on-line support groups. At the end, she suggested that Abi try a course of medication.

"It's called sertraline. It's designed to help reduce anxiety. I think it might help."

Abi had come along that day determined to refuse all offers of medication, but she found herself agreeing to take the prescription. Before she left, the GP warned her that during the first few days, her symptoms might feel exaggerated.

"If you experience any urge to harm yourself, call the surgery, OK?"

"OK."

"I'll give you two months' supply. On the way out, book an appointment at reception. We'll review how things are going at that point. Is that OK?"

Abi stopped off at the pharmacy to pick up the prescription. Only then, reading the information pamphlet, did she understand that she'd been given antidepressants. She read, *...for the treatment of depression, panic attacks, obsessive compulsive disorder (OCD) and post-traumatic stress disorder (PTSD).* She thought, Is this what I've come to?

At the Rose Hill parade of shops, she dropped the pill packets into the bin outside the Co-op. She took half a dozen steps before she turned and retrieved them from amongst the empty crisp packets and cola cans. As soon as she got home, she swallowed the first tablet.

That evening, before bed, she felt a rise in her levels of anxiety. By the early hours of the morning, she had to fight the urge to get up and pace her bedroom. She slept little that night and the next morning she called in sick again. She spent the day alone in her bedroom wondering how long this downward spiral would last.

Dark thoughts. By day three she was wired. Waves of panic coursed through her body like pulses of electric pain. Her thoughts were jumbled and acute. Fear and melancholy fought a battle as she rocked back and forth on her bed like a demented zombie.

Helpmehelpmehelpme.

When she could stand it no longer, she called the doctor's surgery and spoke to the receptionist. It was afternoon on day four and she was alone in the house. She explained about her medication, repeated what the GP had warned her about the early side effects.

"I'm getting like a big panic attack. It's just going on and on. It feels like it's never going to stop," she said.

"A GP will call you back," the receptionist promised.

She repeated the same thing when the doctor phoned back an hour later.

"Are you having any thoughts of harming yourself?" he asked, when she'd run through the same details.

"No, I don't think so," she answered, with less certainty than she let on.

"What you're going through is quite normal," he told her. He sounded tired.

"I'm afraid it's a question of riding it out for the moment. If there's no change after a week, call the surgery and we'll arrange an appointment. It may be we need to try a different medication. For the moment, though, just try and hang in there."

"OK."

"Of course, if you do start to feel, you know, like you might want to hurt yourself, then call us back at once, right?"

"OK."

"But really, once you get through these first few days, it should get better."

And he was right. She peaked on day five, and the night of day six she slept nine hours straight. She woke up and thought, Can this really be working? The relief that she'd slept so well, that the panic had quietened, was so great that she began to cry. Different tears now, of relief not despair. Oh God, she thought, let this be over.

Garai 3

One night Garai fell asleep in the small hours and dreamed that he and Teddy and Tafadzwa were travelling into the provinces to interview young lesbian women about their experiences of intimidation by the Zimbabwe police. The women told harrowing stories of violence and sexual assault. Teddy took pictures and Tafadzwa conducted the interviews, and afterwards, when the bus came to take them home, Garai and Teddy climbed on board but Tafadzwa remained standing at the bus stop. Garai, looking out from the door of the bus, and saw that there were tears in his friend's eyes.

"Come on," Garai called. "What are you waiting for?"

"I can't," Tafadzwa replied. He was sobbing now. "The bus is full."

"Are you crazy?" said Garai. He glanced at the rows of empty seats. Now the driver was revving the engine. "Quick! It's about to leave."

He looked back at Tafadzwa and saw now that his friend was undergoing a peculiar transformation, both shrinking and reversing the aging process. Soon he stood barely a metre high, his physique that of an eight-year old with a face to match. Garai leaned out of the door and held out a hand to pull his friend on board, but the boy shook his head and continued to weep.

"Don't leave me," he kept repeating. "I'm afraid."

The scathing guilt and piercing melancholy that hit Garai when he woke remained with him throughout that day, then lingered on in traces in the week that followed.

At least there was Abi for friendship, and Guthrie for distraction. Anything to take his mind off the thoughts of arrest, detention and deportation.

Abi's disclosure to him about her sexual orientation played on his mind. Of course there were such people back home, but the voices that prevailed as he'd grown up in Zimbabwe were those of the pastors and politicians denouncing these practices as un-African. A Western disease. He knew that was wrong, yet when Abi had revealed this about herself, his knee-jerk reaction had been to reject. Was he so shallow that he'd allow the poison of others to taint his own judgement?

Though Abi had never told him the details of her break with her parents, and her flight to Oxford, he could see how this had hurt her deeply, and suspected it was all related to her sexual identity. He ought to offer himself to her as a shoulder to cry on. And yet he hesitated, torn in his own mind between sympathy and aversion.

And this guilt at his lack of empathy was only compounded by her own kindness towards him. Damaged though he knew she was, she was only too happy to lend him her laptop, offer him the food she cooked, listen to him ramble on about his nights at work, his daily reading, his future study plans. He'd still not confided everything to her about his life before Rose Hill. Tafadzwa and the reasons for his flight were still too raw. And his illegal status in UK, the dangers that would face him if discovered, were too terrifying to articulate.

His study plans were the fuel that kept his spirit burning, even though they felt temporarily stymied. He supposed he'd have to pass his A levels, and would need the backing of a school or further education college to overcome that hurdle. Yet in order to enrol him, any educational facility would need evidence, at the very least, that he'd applied for leave to remain, that his case was pending. And that alone left university entrance a pipe dream, without even factoring in the need for loans to pay the student fees and maintenance costs while he studied.

An agony of frustrations. At times he felt like handing himself into the authorities, if only to end the ever-present fear of capture. But then he'd read the latest news from Zimbabwe, and realise that such an act would not fall short of suicide.

Economic strangulation and political repression, that's how Garai would have described the Zimbabwe he read about. Hikes in electricity tariffs put the cost of using electric stoves outside the means of ordinary urban Zimbabweans, who were forced to cook on wood fires in their back yards. Lighting, televisions and refrigerators were switched off and sat idle.

Hyperinflation combined with foreign currency shortages, local currency devaluations, frozen salaries and soaring prices to create a climate of spiralling misery and despair. The Zimbabwe Congress of Trade Unions announced that unemployment stood at ninety percent as a growing population looked to casual and informal jobs to survive. Garai thought of his parents and wondered how they were doing. With a teacher's or nurse's salary no more than fifty US dollars, and with monthly pensions set at around ten dollars, he saw a bleak future ahead of them.

And then there was the politics. Each month, the attacks on opposition figures, rights activists, and lawyers seemed to grow in number, part of a government campaign to strike fear into a restive population. Garai read the report of a human rights monitoring group that had documented almost eight thousand cases of abuse, including the abductions of around a hundred activists and opposition figures by suspected state agents.

The first Christmas in Britain, Garai read about the misery of daily life back home. Hospitals and clinics understaffed and emptied of medicines. Shops stocked with goods only available for the richest few. Parents unable to pay their children's school fees. Petrol shortages and power cuts. He read the stories and remembered the festive seasons from his childhood. His mother's feasts of fried chicken and rice and bottles of cream soda. Parties next door at the house of his friend, Chipo. Presents of new clothes and shoes and books and toys. The thought of how his parents must have scrimped and saved made him flush with shame.

And so he'd come full circle, back to his need to make amends, to turn his misfortune to his advantage. To make something of himself here so that if and when he made contact once more with his mother and father, he'd be in a position to help them, to prove himself not a burden but the powerhouse of the family.

The weekly trips to the Central Library continued, a stream of books so steady that he began to lose count. Which Saturday did he borrow *Inglorious Empire: What the British Did to India* by Shashi Tharoor? How long ago since he read Sanghera's *Empireland: How Imperialism Has Shaped Modern Britain*? Was that before or after Richard Gott's *Britain's Empire: Resistance, Repression and Revolt*?

The scribbled notebooks continued too. As they filled up, he made a decision that when he finished his studies, he'd write a book, a defining account of colonialism. He realised he'd need to widen his reading to take in French, Spanish, Portuguese, and Dutch imperialism. Turkish and German, too. And what about modern Imperialism? America and China and Russia? Iran and Saudi Arabia in the Middle East? The challenge ahead left him dizzy.

He began to focus in his readings on how the British Empire ended, noting how the government at home became ever more brutal in its frantic efforts to keep its territories in order. He wrote in his notebook:

It reminds me of the way a spoilt boy at the end of a party throws a vicious fit when his mother comes to pick him up and it's time to put his coat on and leave. It's an act of desperate ferocity by someone used to getting their own way.

He read about the Black and Tans in Ireland, the shooting of sporting spectators in Croke Park in 1921. The brutal suppression of rising nationalism in Egypt with tanks on the streets and the indiscriminate shooting of protesters. The use in Iraq of gas shells to subdue the rebels, and of aerial bombing by the RAF resulting in the destruction of whole villages, every living soul blown to hell.

He read about the government's suppression of the Palestinian revolt because it believed wrongly that the Jewish settlers could be manipulated as puppets. How the British bombed Palestinian villages accused of aiding rebels, and turned a blind eye to settler atrocities against native Palestinians, thus paving the way for the mass expulsion of Palestinians in 1948.

And he read about the famine in India in 1943-4, three-and-a-half million civilians dying from starvation while Britain continued to export food grown in India.

This last fact he told Guthrie when next they began one of their regular discussions. Guthrie began it one late afternoon after he got back from his hospital visiting.

"Just been reading about Churchill. Now there was a great man."

"*I've* just been reading about him too," Garai said. "I was re-reading a section of that Newsinger book I lent you."

"Course, he had help from the Yanks and the Russkies, but he showed what a small island of plucky folk can do when faced by the Nazi menace. The whole world owes him a debt of gratitude."

"I'm not sure that every nation looked at him with such appreciation. He once said, 'I hate Indians. They are a beastly people with a beastly religion.' You know, in his victory speech in 1945 he thanked Australia, Canada and New Zealand for their war effort but made no mention of India, though it provided more material and men than the other three put together."

"That doesn't sound right."

"I can look up the references."

"Oh well, the point is, we fought alongside the Yanks, and that gave birth to our Special Relationship. Two equal nations fighting for a free world."

This time, Garai could not hide his snort of derision.

"You really believe that? As the Empire crumbled, the Americans undermined Britain's efforts to prop things up. They wanted the benefits of imperialism. They wanted to take over. Their lack of support led to your Suez humiliation, and to the loss of Iranian oil after the CIA engineered the Shah's rise to power. The US took over from the British as the number one colonial player. Newsinger calls the CIA the most powerful terrorist organisation in the world. Just look what it's been responsible for in South America, the Caribbean, Indochina, Afghanistan, the Middle East. Things haven't changed, the bully still wants the oil and other natural resources, and the strategic positioning for his military bases. There may be a new boss in charge but it's business as usual."

"You've really got it in for democracy, haven't you? Would you really prefer to be living in Russia or China? What about your own country? There's nothing stopping you from going back there if we're so dreadful here."

"Mr Guthrie, That's not what I'm saying. I just think it's important to know what went on back then, and to trace the links that connect those past events with the present."

"That's why I like my history books."

"Yes, but we have to be careful. Your books offer one version of the truth, but it may not be as accurate as you think. There's a distorted narrative that gets peddled about the British Empire, about how it started, and grew, and about how it ended too."

"What do you mean?"

"I'm talking about the myths that exist around the British Empire. Like how independence was given to the natives like a generous gift. But the truth is, it was *won* not given."

"Hm."

"Like the British applied consistent principles to its governance."

"What are you getting at?"

"Well, for example, I was reading Newsinger and he was talking about how there was always one law for Black rebels and another for the Whites."

"Whites? There were never any White rebels."

"Compare what happened in Kenya to my country. By the end of the Mau Mau rebellion, fifty thousand Africans were dead versus twelve white soldiers, fifty-one white police, and thirty-two white settlers. The torture and killing at internment camps was hidden for a long time, it's only been acknowledged by the British government in recent years. There were wholesale massacres at Hola and Manyani camps, Mr Guthrie."

"That's news to me."

"In Rhodesia, the same brutality was shown to resisting Blacks, starting with the machine gun-against-spear massacres of Ndebeles at Shangani and Imbembesi in 1893. But when the Whites rebelled, it was different. You've read about the Unilateral Declaration of Independence in 1965, right? The Smith regime snatched power from the Empire, but this illegal act was not only permitted, it was secretly supported by the British government. There were clandestine sanctions-busting deals for oil, arms and technology right the way through to Zimbabwe's real independence in 1980."

Guthrie shook his head sadly.

"Those books of yours, Gary. They always paint us as the villains. Maybe Britain just decided it was time to give the locals their independence. Maybe it just waited until it thought they were ready for it."

Garai stared at the old man and counted slowly to ten. Then he glanced at his watch and saw that he needed to get ready for work. He thought, Just as well. If I spend another minute arguing with this man, I'll end up strangling him.

Sometimes he felt like strangling the people who ordered the food he delivered, too. Most folk were appreciative. They'd smile as he handed over the bags of food, thank him properly, even press a pound or two into his hand as a tip. But there were always the odd bad apples who'd get shirty and shout abuse.

"Fucksake, where've you been? They said half eight on the phone and it's nearly nine. It better not be cold."

He wondered about his customers, their lives lived inside those rows of identical red-brick houses. The same wheelie bins parked in the patch of each front garden, the same curtains in each front window, the same cars parked at the curb. Probably they were no different from folk back home in Mabelreign and Greendale and Ardbennie, their dreams and fears and expectations quite similar. Only here the electricity ran all day, the water was clean, people had jobs, and hope for their children.

He stood on the *stoeps* and rang the doorbells and smiled as he passed over the pungent cartons of food. The customers had paid with debit cards or online, so there was no fiddling with money and he didn't linger. Sometimes he caught a glimpse of the home within the house. A framed picture of a fishing boat in the hall. The bark of a pet dog. A whiff of stale fat, or tobacco, or fresh coffee. The clatter of dance music or the cries of a wailing child.

Only once did he get invited inside. It was early evening, one of his first deliveries, and it was pouring with rain. An old black woman with a Caribbean accent opened the door and asked him if he was hungry.

"You look like a drowning rat. Come and have a plate, boy. We ordered too much."

His phone pinged with the latest order.

"Thanks but I've got to get on."

That whole evening he rode around in wet clothes, and soon after that he fell ill with a cold that went to his chest. He tried to work through it but two days later he took to his bed. He lay there worrying about going to a GP, and about the loss of earnings, of his job even. Abi looked after him. She fed him paracetamol and orange juice and warming soups. Even Guthrie poked his head round the bedroom door once a day.

"Touch of flu is it, son?"

Garai tried to speak but his voice was gone and he could only produce a weak cough, gungy and crackling with phlegm.

"That doesn't sound too good. I'll get you some Vicks."

"Vicks?" Garai muttered.

"You rub it on your chest. It's kosher, works a treat, Delia always swore by it. I can't promise a dolly bird to administer it, you'll have to do that yourself."

"I know what Vicks is," Garai croaked. "We have it back home."

"Well, then. You know it works a treat then, son, don't you?"

The day he was well enough to leave his bed, he wandered down to the kitchen where he found Abi shelling chestnuts.

"I collected these this afternoon," she said. "There's a posh school at Radley, a couple of miles outside Oxford. You should see it, it's amazing, it's got its own golf course."

"Wow."

"Anyway, if you walk through the grounds, at the far end there's a row of sweet chestnut trees. Loads of them. I'm going to do a chestnut and parsnip soup for starters, then chuck some in a mushroom risotto, followed by a chestnut chocolate tart. I hope you're hungry."

Garai took a seat at the table and began to help her shell the nuts.

"Oh, I nearly forgot. I bought you a present."

She went to her food cupboard and took out a five-kilo paper sack. He peered at the label and smiled.

"Maize meal," he said.

"You said it was your favourite food. I found it in one of those corner shops on the Cowley Road. You make some kind of porridge with it, right? I've forgotten the name."

"*Sadza*."

"*Sadza*, right. Well how about you teach me to cook it? I'd love to learn."

"It's a deal. But don't get your hopes up, I'm a poor cook. My mother makes the best *sadza*, but I usually make a mess of it. I burn it or it goes lumpy or there are uncooked parts to it, what we call *mbodza* in ChiShona. Anyway, I'll do my best. I'll buy some chicken drumsticks and we'll have *sadza ne huku*."

"I'm vegetarian, Garai."

"Of course, sorry. I'll buy some nice greens and do *sadza ne muriwo* instead. I wish I knew my mother's recipe for *dovi*."

"What's that?"

"It's the homemade peanut butter we use to make a relish. We cook the greens in the sauce."

"I bet we can use shop-bought peanut butter and get a recipe off the internet."

"OK," said Garai. "We'll try."

After a week in bed, it felt good to be alive, to talk to someone, to make plans.

The following Sunday, Garai cooked his Zimbabwean meal for Abi and Garai. The sadza wasn't up to his mother's standards, but neither was it *mbodza*. Abi helped with the greens. Altogether, it was a success. Even Guthrie, who poked at his plate of food with great suspicion at the start, ended up tucking away almost half of the dish.

"It's not bad at all," he said. "I thought it'd be spicy. I can't say I've heard of putting peanut butter on your vegetables, but it's really quite tasty."

The conversation moved, as it so often did, to Empire, and they began to list the food and drink that Britain had acquired from its colonies.

"Potatoes."
"Sweet corn."
"Tea."
"Coffee."
"Hot chocolate."
"Tonic water."
"Curry."
"Chop suey."
"Chutney."
"Biltong."
"Chai latte."

Most of the items came from Abi. Guthrie listened but didn't contribute much.

"I haven't heard of most of those, but it goes to show the British Empire wasn't all one-way. We gave railways and British law and we got back gin and tonic, and a nice cup of tea."

"Well, it's good to hear that it wasn't all one-way," said Garai. "Though heaven knows what we'd have done without Britain to provide its wise counsel and protection. We'd be like motherless children, right?"

"Well, I don't know about that," Guthrie began. He was frowning, studying Garai's face for traces of irony.

From there, the argument grew more heated.

"Look, I know not everyone who went out to the colonies was a decent chap. There were a few bad apples, you'd expect that, wouldn't you? But most of them went out there with good intentions. You've read some of those memoirs I lent you. Remarkable men leading remarkable lives."

Garai bridled at this, and as happened occasionally, his self-control slipped.

"First of all, most of them who went out there were conditioned from birth to see themselves as superior to anyone with darker skin. At best, some of them might have viewed the locals with a paternal sympathy. You know, 'You can't blame the ignorant savages. They don't know any better.' They may have genuinely wanted to help. But for every one of them who cared, there were a dozen who viewed a native's life as worthless."

"Oh, come on, you can't-."

"And second of all, it's not about the individuals who were sent out from here. It's about the Government's *intentions*. They were based on self-interest, a hundred percent. I mean, come on, Mr Guthrie. You really think there was any sense of altruism?"

"Of course there was. We wanted to spread Christianity. To end polygamy and cannibalism."

Garai sighed.

"After the industrial revolution, Britain needed raw materials for its factories. It wasn't going to pay market price for them, was it? Not when it had gunships and repeating rifles. And besides, it felt it had to grab what colonies it could, otherwise the land would be seized by France or Holland, Portugal or Belgium."

"You do have a jaundiced view of the world, Gary."

"It's Garai. *Garai*. How many times do I have to tell you?"

Garai had never raised his voice like that.

"Well, what about slavery? We took it upon ourselves to end it."

"Only after you'd profited hugely. Sanghera says that for one hundred and fifty years, the British carried as many slaves across the Atlantic as all the other slave-trading countries combined. And anyway, did you not read the Gott book I gave you? The first nation to end slavery was Haiti. Self-liberated slaves rose up and overthrew the French plantation owners. The Haiti Revolution began in 1791 and ended in 1804. The Slave Trade Act of 1807 abolished the slave trade in the British Empire, and the Slavery Abolition Act of 1833 began the abolition of slavery itself, but really the Government's hands were forced by slave uprisings and pressure groups in Britain. And even after 1833, slaves weren't given any support to make new lives for themselves. Does that strike you as fair, Mr Guthrie?"

"Well, I don't know. I mean... ."

"There's a book you should read. Douglas Hall's *Thomas Thistlewood in Jamaica 1750-86*. It's an abridged version of Thistlewood's diaries. He kept them for years and years. He owned a slave plantation in Jamaica. He was a serial rapist and a sadist. He branded his slaves when he first bought them. As punishment he'd whip them and then flush their open wounds with lime, hot pepper and salt. If one slave misbehaved, he'd get another one to defecate into his mouth. He even gave this punishment a name, *Derby's dose*, after one of the slaves who provided the faeces. He lists in his diary a total of three thousand eight hundred and fifty-two sexual encounters with his slave women, none of which would be considered consensual in the modern definition of the word. His average annual tally of rape attacks worked out at a hundred and eight sexual assaults on fourteen different women over a period of thirty-seven years."

Silence.

"You know, Sanghera argues that the British Empire was also a way of getting rid of all its own native rejects. Not just the convicts to Australia, but also the misfits and failures given a second chance to botch their lives in the colonies. And Christ, the rejects included some psychopaths. Read Gott on some of the outrages, like the treatment of indigenous Australians by the settlers."

"Gott? I knew a fellow with that name."

Garai was used to this tactic by now. When confronted by something unpalatable, the old man simply shifted focus. But the fight had left Garai, and he sighed and almost managed a smile. He thought, Little by little, I'll get through to him. It's like throwing mud at a wall. Chuck enough of the stuff, and something will stick.

"Don't tell me, you painted his house for him?"

"Well, it was his kitchen. How did you know?"

"Just a hunch, Mr Guthrie."

"I'm boring you, Garai. Delia used to give me stick sometimes, when I rattled on with my stories. 'Give over, you silly old fool,' she'd say."

"You're not boring me."

"Well, you're kind to humour an old man."

Silence.

Guthrie got to his feet and began to tidy away the crockery left to dry on the draining board.

"Go on, Mr Guthrie. I'm waiting."

"Eh? What for?"

"This man Gott. The paint job. Tell me about it."

"Blue lagoon, the colour. Bit too dark, I remember thinking. But it's what he asked for, and the customer's always right."

Frustrating though these encounters could be, Garai relished them. It was social interaction, which he knew he needed, like a slaking of thirst. But it was also an important intellectual exercise. He was honing his debating skills, preparing himself for his academic future.

And it was also a diversion from the instability of his life. Outside the four walls of his home, away from the circle of his adopted family, he lived in fear. As he cycled to and from work, whenever he passed a police patrol car, he felt a wrenching in his stomach, an escalating panic. At least once a day, he'd feel the terror of his predicament and think, How long can this go on?

Abigail 4

Abi never thought she'd say it, but that medication had kept her sane. Nine hours' sleep each night, and like a miracle, it continued. True there were some odd side effects. Abi developed restless feet at night, a kind of mild spasming in her calves that lasted anything up to an hour before she could drop off. She felt a little bloated, and needed the toilet more often. Did she get more headaches than usual? But the anxiety was gone, and though she was still as lonely as ever, still hated her job and felt that her life was stalled, she could view it all with an equanimity she'd never before possessed.

Summer eased into Oxford like dripping honey. One day she arrived at work hot and sweaty from the cycle ride and thought, Why am I still wearing this thick winter coat and gloves? She was still tired at work, but now it was spring warmth and boredom that made her sleepy, not acute insomnia. A change in routine for her lunch breaks. Now she'd find a grassy spot on the hospital grounds and lie face up, enjoying the burn of the sun's rays on her pale cheeks. She'd stare up at the empty sky, or squeeze her eyes shut and let the pulsating orange circles explode behind her eyelids.

It was July, and every day now she'd go back out as soon as she got back from work. She'd watch the dragonflies hover over the pond at Rivermead, catch the discordant chatter of sedge warblers from the reeds near Sandford, note the pissy reek of fox as she made her way past the horse field at Meadow Lane. Once or twice a week she'd grab her swimsuit and towel and bike, head for the towpath, then stop wherever the mood took her for an early-evening dip.

At weekends, she cast her net wider. She had three favourite cycle rides. The first took her over to Brill, the second past Horspath to Wheatley, the third to the RSPB reserve at Otmoor, where she'd be serenaded by chiffchaff and blackcap and grasshopper warbler.

Usually though she preferred to walk, as it meant she could stop when she liked to forage. She picked elder flowers and made cordial and fritters, both praised by Garai and Guthrie. They were less enthusiastic about her chickweed salad, and wouldn't touch the chanterelles she fried in olive oil.

"No offence, love," Guthrie said apologetically. "But I've never seen the point of mushrooms."

She fared better with the ground elder she cooked in butter and served on toast.

"It's good," said Garai. "A bit like *covo* from home."

Guthrie's reaction was less complimentary.

"Weeds? You trying to kill me? If you're after my inheritance, I think you're in for a disappointment."

Abi's favourite walk remained along the towpath to Abingdon. It was a rugged, muddy slog in winter, but now that the ground had dried and the flora had exploded into life, she found it delightful, new discoveries to be found on each successive trip. The newt she spotted in the shade of a woodpile. The buzzard soaring overhead. The first ripe blackberries bloodying her fingers. A pair of Egyptian geese afloat on the water, their bodies marked as if by war paint.

When she fancied a change, she'd veer off the towpath at Kennington, walk through Bagley wood and out to Boars Hill, then return to the city through Chilswell Valley and South Hinksey. She'd stop to forage or just to savour the peace, to eke out the trip and make it last all day.

And somehow, over these months, her head began to clear and she found the strength to turn thought into action. She made the decision to apply to Brookes for the Conservation course, was surprised when they offered her an interview and then an unconditional offer. Her student loan came through. For the first time in years she felt - what was the word? - *purposeful*. She'd work right through to September as she'd need every penny she could earn. The thought of quitting her job was as sweet as the prospect of returning to study.

Was she happy? There was certainly no one-eighty turnaround. True, the sleeping was much improved, but what she'd left in Pangbourne was still an unhealed wound that brought up guilt and shame and anger in equal measures. And yet, where she was now, in time and space, no longer felt so alien. Not quite home, but not a foreign country.

Part of why she felt better was the house, and those she lived with. She'd come to understand that Guthrie, despite his clangers, was not only harmless, but a kindly soul at heart. Sure, he could be annoying, but only in the way that she'd found her own father irritating at times. Above all, she'd come to trust him.

And as for Garai, she valued the time they shared together, the weekday windows between her return from work and his departure, the weekend afternoons when she wasn't out on an adventure. Was he a friend? Well, he was the closest thing to one, given that there were no other eligible candidates.

And then something quite unexpected happened.

It was a Friday, the last day at work for one of the lunch-break quartet of women. Tammy, the one with the cats and camping anecdotes, was moving on. There'd been a card and a gift presentation earlier, and now Abi had been press-ganged into drinks at the White Rabbit in town. She cycled home and changed into jeans and tee shirt. She hesitated at the front door, tempted by the prospect of a solitary walk. The thought of boozy bonhomie felt oppressive. Only guilt dragged her back on her bike and into the city centre.

Her colleagues had taken taxis straight from work into town, and there were a dozen or so sat around two tables in the garden. Abi guessed they were on their second round of drinks. She bought herself a pint of lager and joined the mob. One or two of the more dominant personalities held sway at the start, a steady stream of office jokes and teasing.

An hour passed and Abi went to the bar for another pint. As she queued for the barman's attention, she turned and saw that Tammy was waiting at her side. They exchanged awkward grins.

"You having fun?" Abi asked. Since she'd ditched the lunchtime socialising, she'd spent little time with any of the women, and often wondered whether they resented her snub.

"I'll be better once this is over," said Tammy. "I hate being the centre of attention."

Abi looked at her more carefully. She supposed they were the same sort of age. She reminded Abi of a girl she'd had a crush on at school, what was her name? Angie? Yes, Angie. She had the same clear pale skin, the explosion of chestnut frizz, a sharp nose and thin lips. Her expression just now was warm and knowing, like one of two friends sharing a joke.

"How come you're leaving?"

"I had a kind of epiphany at the start of the summer. Part of it was that I realised that I hate offices. There were lots of other things I wanted to change in my life, the job was just one part of it."

"Wow, that's great. So what's the great plan?"

Tammy smiled.

"My plan is to have no plan. Me and my boyfriend, we got together in sixth form. Our whole life together we'd been planning every step. Everything from holidays to saving up for a mortgage, it was all calculated, right down to the spreadsheet we updated every fortnight listing what we'd eat for dinner each day."

"Wow, that *is* planning."

"I'll probably sign on with a temping firm so I don't eat into my savings. After that, the world's my oyster. I might travel, or study or just go and live on top of a mountain."

"That's so cool. You're really brave," said Abi. "I'm leaving soon too. I haven't told anyone yet." She went on to explain about the course at Brookes.

Just then Emma joined them at the bar.

"Hey, no running away, Tammy. I'm buying shots and we're expecting a speech."

Tammy threw Abi a look of horror and the conversation ended.

Abi drank her pint quickly, then bought another. She knew she ought to eat something, but that the moment was passing. At nine o'clock she finished her third pint and went to the toilet. As she washed her hands, she realised that she wasn't going to re-join the party. She slipped out of the pub and walked the streets for a while, stopping at a kebab place near Gloucester Green for a falafel wrap. That was when she got the idea to grab a last drink at the Jolly Farmers.

The place was crowded when she entered, and she didn't see Tammy at the bar until she herself was queuing. She saw the back of her head, the curls she'd so recently been admiring, and at that exact moment, Tammy turned and met her eyes. For a split second, Abi read a curious expression on the woman's face. There was confusion and surprise. Was that alarm, too? Then her features relaxed and she smiled a smile that was warm and sweet and, dare she say it, welcoming.

"Hey," said Abi.

"Hey. You escaped too?"

They laughed.

"Drink?" Tammy asked.

"Thanks. I'll have a vodka and cranberry."

The drinks came and they stood side by side and there was an awkward moment before Abi spoke.

"Is this your local?" she asked. She was aware that there was another question wrapped inside this one.

"No. This is new to me. You know, I told you about my epiphany, right? That I didn't like offices. Well I realised I didn't like other things too. Cats and civil war enactments." She paused and took a sip of her drink. "And sleeping with men."

Abi said nothing for a moment while she digested this.

"That must have been hard on your boyfriend."

"Yes, I feel guilty. He's a good guy. We went through a sticky patch but things are OK now. Still on speaking terms," she grinned.

They drank another drink after that, and then they went together to collect Abi's bike and pushed it back to Tammy's new flat, a bedsit above an estate agent's on Cowley Road. The sex that night was good, and the next morning it was better. Afterwards Tammy went out and bought rolls and orange juice, and they cooked scrambled eggs washed down with OJ and coffee.

"Have you tried sprinkling wild garlic on the eggs?" Abi asked.

"No."

"It's really good," she said, and told her new friend about her interest in plants.

"I'd love to go foraging with you," said Tammy.

"How about tomorrow? We'll go to Bagley Wood, and I'll cook you a meal with whatever we find."

"Is that a date?"

Abi looked at Tammy, felt something in her heart she didn't yet have a name for.

"I guess it must be."

*

July stretched into August. At the review appointment with her GP, she told her that she was feeling much better.

"You know, I never thought I'd be the type to need medication to function properly. I grew up with the idea that happy pills were for the weak. For nineteen fifties housewives and neurotic New York TV characters. Now I'm like Little Miss One-a-Day, and it feels OK."

She said this, and it did feel alright, though the doubts and the guilt remained tucked away in the far corner of her mind.

Abi was in love. She stayed over at Tammy's three or four times a week, but didn't invite her back to the Rose Hill house, explaining that her landlord was old-fashioned and might object.

Guthrie, for his part, presumed that Abi had a boyfriend and teased her relentlessly.

"When are we going to meet him?" he kept asking. "I want to make sure I approve."

She told Garai about Tammy, and about the pills, and he nodded in his sober way and said he was glad for her. She was seeing less of him these days, and when she did, she found him a little withdrawn. She kept meaning to invite him out for a drink, to find out if he was OK, but what with the job and Tammy and her outdoor adventures, she never quite found the right time.

The main source of entertainment in the house remained the political arguments between Guthrie and Garai. They could get heated, but neither of the men seemed to bear a grudge after one of their battles. Often Abi would tune out, and the words would pour over her like dissonant music. But sometimes she listened carefully. And as the disputes continued, she found she was gaining an education, and even joined in from time to time.

One Saturday morning, Guthrie provoked a reaction from Garai when he mentioned, again, his admiration for Winston Churchill. There'd been an attempt to damage his statue in Parliament Square during a demonstration, and Guthrie was fresh from reading a condemnatory editorial in the *Daily Mail*.

"The whole world owes him a debt of gratitude," he said. "Without him we'd be living under Nazi jackboots."

Abi remembered Garai's previous comments, and prepared herself for a forthright reaction.

"The man openly admitted that he detested Indians, Arabs and Africans. He was a duplicitous, racist thug," he concluded. Abi, keen to curtail the coming rant, interrupted her friend.

"Hey, Garai," she began. "Surely the times that Labour were in power, their policies were anti-colonial."

Garai shook his head sadly.

"You'd think so, wouldn't you? But more often than not, that wasn't the case. The Newsinger book addresses this point. Of course, there'd be Labour supporters who were against imperial expansion. Some Labour politicians, too. But on the whole, when Labour was in power, it tended to support the colonial agenda. They resisted Indian independence as forcefully as the Tories. Same for their policy in the Middle East when the liberation movements grew strong in Iran and Iraq and Palestine. After the Second World War, the army brutally attacked leftist and trade union groups in Malaya, Indonesia and Indochina. It actually used captured Japanese troops to help carry out its violence and killings. It was a Labour government that gave the orders."

"No way!" said Abi.

"I'm telling you. In 1965 under Labour the SAS fought a covert war to put the Indonesian army in power under the dictator General Suharto. On the pretext of stamping out communism, the army killed half a million men, women and children."

"Jesus."

"In 1950 Attlee sent troops into Korea to bolster the alliance with America, just as Blair did into Iraq fifty years later. It was a sign of just how enthusiastically Labour clung onto the myth of the Special Relationship. Since the beginnings of Empire, Labour has paid lip service to liberal ideals but its actions have always supported imperialism, even if you could call it a slightly more ethical version."

A moment of stunned silence.

"How did I manage to get through all those years at school knowing so little about the British Empire?" Abi asked. "All we ever learned about was the bloody Tudors."

"If I wanted to give you a diplomatic answer, I'd say it's because it's easier to learn dates of kings and queens than about imperialism. The British Empire is *complex*, man. Historians can't even agree when it started and ended, let alone all the more controversial aspects."

"And if you weren't being diplomatic?"

"You don't learn the truth at school, because it would be ugly and unpalatable. The white British psyche is built on a belief that it is a magnanimous but superior people. Learning about the contributions of non-whites to civilization is bad enough, but having to study the long history of European brutality and treachery and greed, that's a step too far. Maybe it will change one day, but it seems that today, this country's not yet ready. It's just too sensitive. No one likes to be reminded of their failings."

Guthrie had said little so far, but now he spoke up.

"You like to blame white Europeans, as if we're the devils. What we did, for better or worse, isn't it just human nature? Isn't it human nature, right back to cavemen, to fight for your family, your community, against the next one along."

Garai looked at him and waited.

"The industrial revolution came to Europe first, right?" said Guthrie. He spoke slowly, as if keeping his ideas unjumbled took an effort. "We developed machinery and factories and needed raw materials to process. We didn't have them at home, so we went looking for them. Don't you think if that development had happened in India or Africa or South America, they'd have been just as quick to hunt out what they needed? How do you know they wouldn't have behaved just the same?"

"It's true, we'll never know," Garai said quietly. "I suppose-"

Abi, following a train of thought, interrupted.

"Surely it doesn't matter what might have been. The only useful thing we can do is accept what happened in the past, think about how it's affected the present, and work to deal with the consequences."

"You mean things like paying reparations and changing the school curriculum?" Garai said.

"Not just that. I mean you've talked about how the British behaved in the colonies. Tying people to the mouths of cannons and blowing them up. Mowing unarmed locals with machine guns. Ethnic cleansing and genocide. Starving people into submission. Where does that come from? What's the urge that makes such behaviour possible?"

"Not every white man in the colonies behaved like that," Guthrie said. "Maybe some people are just born evil."

"White *man*, you said. Not white woman. You know all that stuff you were talking about last week, Garai? About what the white policemen did to the women suspected of helping the Mau Mau fighters? The gun barrels and knives and glass bottles in the vaginas, the use of rape as a weapon?"

Abi glanced over at Guthrie, and saw how uncomfortable he looked.

"Sorry, Mister G."

"That's quite alright," he answered.

"It's never women who do these bad things, is it?" she continued. "But it's women who get them done to them."

Neither of the men responded, so Abi continued.

"And there's something else. Of course we can't imagine the trauma inflicted on the victims, on the survivors and their families and the generations that came after. But it's just as hard to imagine too the effect of that violence on the colonialists themselves. No wonder the Empire was so psychotic."

"So are you saying we should feel sympathy for the oppressors?" Garai asked.

"No, just that it explains how we ended up poisoning our own society."

"'When the white man turns tyrant, it is his own freedom that he destroys.'" Garai quoted. "That's George Orwell."

"Yeah, that's what I'm saying. We can see the link between what happened over there back in the day, and the culture that emerged back here even after it was all over. No wonder it came back and infected us here. That whole wogs-out Paki-bashing culture on the streets, the ghettoization of property, the institutional racism in the police, in the Home Office and business and commerce. And it's still the men doing most of the oppressing."

"Oh, come on. It's always the same with you feminists," Gut6hrie scoffed. "When in doubt, blame the men."

"But it's true. No offence, Guthrie, but your generation, you don't even know how deeply it's embedded inside you. It's not your fault. It's just the society you grew up in. The education system, the media, the Government, the people with power. All men, of course."

"Ouch," said Guthrie

"Truth hurts, Mr Guthrie," said Garai.

"No pain, no gain," Abi added.

A pause.

"So what's the solution?" Garai asked.

"Castrate all men," Abi answered.

That comment earned a look of horror from Guthrie.

"Only joking, Mister G," said Abi, smiling. Then she looked at Garai and winked. "Or am I?"

"I don't know what's what any more," said Guthrie. "Why can't people just get on? Anyway, who's for a nice cup of tea. I've just got time before I head off out."

"Hospital visiting again, Mister G?" Abi asked.

"Yes," said Guthrie. "The usual."

*

A few weeks after that, the landline phone rang one afternoon after Abi got home from work. Guthrie was out so she picked it up.

"Dad?" said the voice. "Hello?"

"No, it's me, Abi," she explained. They'd spoken on the phone once before, when Guthrie had been at home, and she'd passed over the phone straight away. "I'm sorry, he's at the hospital."

"Oh, right. I should have known. Dad said mum had a poor chest. How's she doing?"

"Sorry? Who?" said Abi.

And that was how she found out.

"I can't believe he never said anything to you," Eric said, after he'd filled her in.

"I'm so sorry," Abi said. "I won't say anything."

"Don't worry. It shouldn't be a secret."

That evening, Abi told Tammy about the conversation as they cooked pasta in the Cowley Road flat.

"I guess you've just got to respect his privacy. Maybe he doesn't want the pity."

It was an undreamt-of luxury to have Tammy in her life. Someone to talk to, to love and be loved by. Tammy was filled with a zest for life that was contagious. One day she was learning chess from a book, the next signing up for badminton classes, or a course in Urdu, or drumming lessons. She was working part-time for a temping agency, just enough hours to pay the rent and food bills. Every day she had a new life plan.

"I'm thinking about getting a job teaching English in Costa Rica," she'd say. Or, "I've been reading about volunteering in a refugee camp in Lebanon." Every idea seemed to be pencilled in for the following year. "But until then, I'm all yours!" she'd say each time she described the plans.

Abi had told Tammy early on about her mental health issues, and the medication. At first she treated it lightly.

"It's no big deal, if you don't count the weight gain," she laughed. It was a side effect she'd noticed, and she was trying hard to pretend that it didn't matter.

"I like you any which way," said Tammy. "But insomnia's a bummer, and the anxiety sounds tough. Tell me what it's like."

Abi had to think hard. She picked her words carefully.

"It's like a sort of permanent thing that stays mostly in the background. There was a time when I was younger when I

187

lived without it. But it started maybe around the last year of uni. It's a bit like the humming of a striplight, it's there even when you're not aware of it. And then this last year or so, before I took the pills, it just got worse."

She'd told Tammy about Roger, and Teddy, but had couched it in terms of bad stuff she'd put up with and moved on from, in a tone of anger, not pain. This time, she was able to put into the words the damage inflicted, the nature of the wounds, the lack of healing.

"I went to the doctor because I couldn't sleep, but that was a symptom of something deeper." Abi explained about the manic first five days of medication. "All the bad feelings were magnified a thousand times," she said.

"Wow, that must have been terrifying.

"Yeah it was tough at the time. But after that, it was like that anxiety had been excised. Like the removal of a cyst."

"And now? You don't feel all kind of drugged-up?"

"Not at all. It's not like that cliché. You know, the chemical cosh. It's more like some chemical was missing in my brain, some magic ingredient. Like it's the lubricating oil that helps the machine run smoothly."

"It's brave of you to admit you have a problem And I'm glad you could talk to me.. I admire you."

By now, Abi was spending as much time at the Cowley Road bedsit as in Rose Hill. And every time she returned home, she faced the same Guthrie teasing.

"Gosh, he must be a fine young fellow, all the time you're with him. When are we going to meet him?" he'd say. Then he'd add, "Mind you, I wonder whether he knows how lucky he is. Want me to tell him?"

And each time, she'd bite her lip, smile but say nothing.

Until, that is, she found the right moment to reveal her truth. It was a deliberate act, a mark of her confidence that the time had come for honesty. And it was, too, an opportunity to challenge Guthrie's ignorance, and end the shame she felt at her own cowardice.

It was Tuesday breakfast. Abi had slept poorly and she'd been up for hours. She made tea and toast while Guthrie browsed the *Mail* and worked his way through his cereal.

"That Sandi Toksig's on the warpath again," he said, breaking the silence. "It's not enough forming the Women's Equality Party." He pronounced the name like it was a joke. "Now they say she's thinking of standing as an MP."

"What's wrong with that?" said Abi, trying not to rise to the bait.

"Don't get me wrong, I like the woman. She's very amusing on the telly. But she should stick to that. You know she's married to a woman? I can't get my head round that. Maybe it's normal back in Holland."

Abi stared at him .

"Where do I start? What's marrying a woman got to do with standing as a politician? And she's *Norwegian*, not Dutch. And you can be funny *and* want to make the world a better place. Even a woman. "

She took a deep breath.

"And by the way, I'm a lesbian too."

"Pardon?"

"You heard. I'm a lesbian."

A long moment to process, but to his credit, Guthrie was quick to respond.

"Well, that's fine. It takes all sorts, I suppose. Good for you. I hope you'll be happy," he said, blustering so much that Abi burst out laughing.

"I won't bite."

"It's not that," he said. He seemed to be struggling to find the right words. "I don't care. Really I don't. It's none of my business, is it? It's just I don't know the right things to say. We just didn't have these complications in my day. Not so's you'd notice, anyway."

"They're not *complications*. And you *did* have those things, it's just that the people who felt different didn't feel they could talk about it. They kept everything bottled up. You didn't notice, but it was hurting them. It was *harming* them."

For a moment Guthrie didn't speak. Then he nodded.

"Yes, I imagine it was. Look, I suppose what's important is that people love each other. So long as they're adult and they know their own minds and there's no hanky-panky going on, no bullying or whatnot, I don't suppose it matters if it's a man or a woman or two of each. I'm not explaining myself very well, but I'm just saying if there's love involved then it's fine by me, because this love makes a difference to everyone. You know, the more the merrier. It spreads and makes the world a healthier place for everyone. I suppose it's a bit like compost in the garden, if you know what I mean."

Abi said nothing for a long moment. Then she reached out and laid a hand on Guthrie's arm. It was the first time she'd touched him.

A few days later, Abi finally got round to inviting Garai out. He'd grown steadily quieter over the past few weeks, she was convinced that something was bothering him, and she wanted to find out what it was. He took some persuading but eventually agreed to go out for a drink. At the last minute, as they left the house, she got a call from Tammy. Garai hovered beside her while she spoke to her girlfriend.

"Everything OK?"

"I thought we might go out this evening. I just realised it's our anniversary. Two months! I booked a table at *Pierre Victoire*. You ever been?"

"Wow, amazing," she said. She still marvelled at how happy Tammy could make her feel. Then, catching sight of Garai's face, she bit her lip.

"Ah, look, I'd love to do it, but I've got something on. Can we postpone it? How about tomorrow?"

"Sure," said Tammy. "I'll call the restaurant."

That was another thing Abi loved about this woman, the way she understood without needing to know.

"Thanks, Tam. And happy anniversary."

They chose a quiet pub within walking distance, the Jolly Postboys in Florence Park. Abi, for reasons she didn't quite understand, found herself drinking more than usual, first pints and then double vodkas. She'd never seen Garai drink more than a single pint, but that evening he managed three.

It was an evening of shared confidences. Lubricated with alcohol, Abi spoke first about her feelings for Tammy, and this led to a fuller account of Roger and Teddy than she'd ever offered. Garai in turn opened up about his past, about Teddy and Tafadzwa, that awful day in Harare, his escape to Britain. Then he told her that he was living as an unregistered migrant, that his status was illegal, and that he could be arrested and deported at any moment.

"Jesus," she said, when he finished. "You've been through the wringer. I had no idea. Can't you go to a solicitor? Surely if they can prove that your life in Zimbabwe would be in danger, then they'd never send you back."

"I wish it was that simple," was all he'd say.

They drank more and talked more, and she found herself telling him what she'd learned about Guthrie's wife. By the time they set off home, Abi was declaring that they should make an appointment with a solicitor first thing in the morning, and that she'd go along to give him support.

"We need to find a good one, someone who specialises in immigration law. I'll lend you the money."

"I have a name and number of a good firm. A guy I work with recommended them. I've just never had the courage to call," said Garai.

"Well, maybe it's time."

"I'll think about it. And thank you."

Abi looked at her friend, read the fear in his eyes, but something else too, a glint of determination.

When they got back to the house, they found Guthrie sitting at the kitchen table, nursing a strong drink.

"Hey, Mister G," Abi said. She knew she was a little tipsy, and it felt good. "OG, the Original Gangster."

"Excuse me?" said Guthrie.

"Don't mind her, Mr Guthrie" Garai said. "We've been to the pub."

Guthrie's invitation to sample his whisky tipple soon loosened tongues. Afterwards, Abi could remember only fragments of the night's conversation. She recalled the moment she told Guthrie that she and Garai both knew about his wife.

"I'm sorry I found out. I guess it was none of my business. You wanted to keep it private, right?"

"Yes. But it doesn't matter."

Summer at its zenith, autumn around the corner. A time for stock-taking, to prepare for change. With the start of her course at Brookes on the horizon, Abi made the decision to stop taking her medication. Her life was back on track, she'd exorcised her demons, and she felt strong enough to deal with whatever she'd meet in the next chapter of her life. Still, remembering the horrors of those first five days on the medication, she couldn't help but feel a little frightened at the prospect of withdrawal.

She spoke to the GP and to Tammy, took her last pill and waited for some kind of mental firework display. But as the days passed, she was shocked at how easy it was to end the treatment.

"It's because you're happy," said Tammy. "You needed it at the time, and it worked for you. I guess the need's just gone now."

"I suppose you're right," said Abi. "You know you're a big part of that happiness, don't you?"

"Aw shucks, thanks."

"Well, it's true."

We should celebrate," Tammy said, producing a bottle of prosecco from the fridge. And so they ate and drank well that night, and when they went to bed much later, Abi fell asleep in the crook of Tammy's arm.

Garai 4

Six months went by for Garai without much change in status or fortune. He dreamt less of Tafadzwa, found it hard to remember exactly what he looked like, and the fading memories brought their own remorse. He wondered where Teddy was. Garai knew he'd be taken care of, but he couldn't help wondering whether his one-time friend carried his own burden of guilt.

His nights remained barren deserts, though when he did sleep, there were fewer flashbacks. No, it was worries about the present that tormented him more than memories of his past. He read articles about the savage journeys that migrants made to get to Europe, trekking across the Sahara, held to ransom in Libya, rotting in the jungles of the northern French coast,. There were items in the news about flimsy boats pulled out of the Channel. He'd followed the story of the young men and women asphyxiated in the back of a lorry, watched TV footage of Home Office raids on buildings housing the undocumented. He felt he was walking a razor-wire tightrope above a pit of black mambas. He thought, Life is so *precarious*. Deportation was ever on his mind. He woke up each morning and wondered whether it'd be his last day of freedom, and when sleep finally came at night, he dropped off with the thought that tomorrow would bring no change.

One day he arrived at work to find his boss engaged in an animated conversation with a young fellow countryman. After a while, the old man retired to the kitchen and the younger one turned to Garai.

"Hello, my name's Jing. Call me Jimmy. The old man's my father."

"Oh, hello."

"I've just finished an MBA in London. Now I'm going to help my father run his business."

Garai nodded.

"It won't be easy dragging him into the twenty-first century," the young man said. "He's always run the place as if he was still in Hong Kong."

Garai returned Jing's smile and thought, Should I be worried?

Back home, the discussions with Guthrie continued, though Garai couldn't help but feel that the old man's attitudes were changing. He still loved to boast about the benefits of imperialism on British society, but spoke less about the backward savagery of the natives. What jarred most for Garai now was that his landlord never stopped harping on about the importance of Britain's global position in contemporary politics.

"The Empire may be over, but we're still a major player in world affairs," was a typical statement from Guthrie.

"Explain yourself, Mr Guthrie" Garai said. "Give me an example."

"Look what happened after the Twin Towers thingie. We teamed up with the Americans. Together we punished Saddam Hussein and brought democracy to Iraq."

"Are you serious, Mr Guthrie? Saddam Hussein had nothing to do with 9/11. There were no weapons of mass destruction. It's all documented. George W Bush wanted to play the gun-toting cowboy, and the American government wanted Iraqi oil. Bush needed an ally to give some kind of legitimacy to the invasion, so he played on Blair's ego. But it was all a scam."

"Now wait a minute, son. Saddam was an evil man. I read about what he did to the Kurds. Chemical warfare."

"That may be true, but it's not the point. Bush broke international law by fabricating a pretext for the war. When Blair backed him up, he became equally culpable."

"I'm not so sure. You should give the man the benefit of the doubt."

"That's the way Britain has always behaved towards the USA. It was never *forced* to hitch its horse to the American wagon, it *chose* to. You read the Newsinger book, right? After America engineered the Suez humiliation, France and Britain took different paths. France rejected America. It ordered American military bases on French soil to close, it created its own nuclear arms and sought closer ties within Europe. Britain went the other way. It embraced the USA, all that Special Relationship rubbish. You've never been equal partners. You got your nuclear weapons from America, you allowed US bases on UK soil, and when Bush said 'Jump,' Blair said, 'How high?'"

Guthrie shook his head.

"I don't know what to think, Garai. "You say one thing, the papers say another. It's downright confusing."

Around this time, the dull routine of Garai's life was disrupted by a number of blows, like the first waves before the tsunami's arrival. The first one struck a week or so later, one early afternoon when Garai arrived at work to pick up his first delivery order. His boss, the old man, called him over.

"Look David, I need to take a copy of your passport. And bank details for your wages, and your national insurance card for paying contributions. No more cash in hand."

The man must have seen the look on Garai's face. He shrugged apologetically.

"My son is meddling," he continued. "I've opened the door and let in a tornado. My advice, never work with family."

Garai was too busy absorbing the news to speak.

"I must have the documents by Friday. Is that OK?"

"Oh sure, yes," Garai answered. He thought, So this is it. No papers means no job. No money means I can't pay the rent. This is the beginning of the end.

The second blow came the next day, a casual conversation with Guthrie in the kitchen as Garai ate a late breakfast.

"How's your morning?" Garai asked.

"Not bad. Just been up to the shops," said the old man, indicating the loaf of bread and pint of milk on the table. "I was posting the forms for the electoral register."

"What's that?" Garai asked.

"You know, for voting in elections. There's a form that gets sent to each household. You fill in all the people staying in the house. That way they can make sure everyone gets a polling card next time there's an election. We've got local ones coming up in May," Guthrie explained. And then, seeing that he could score a point, he added, "It's called Great British democracy."

It took all of Garai's self control to keep the horror from his face. A register of householders? He could picture the process unfolding. His name on the form. The envelope opened in some town hall office. Names typed into a database. And then his own flagged up, alarm bells ringing, the security forces informed. If he was already sleeping poorly before that conversation, things plummeted afterwards.

No respite for Garai when he trawled the internet for news from home. National strikes called by government opponents in response to the growing economic misery, civilians taking to the streets to demonstrate, protestors fired on with live ammunition. A crackdown on human rights activists and opposition politicians followed, and this sparked more demonstrations and, in turn, more military reprisals. Garai felt his time in Britain drawing to an end, with no safe alternative destination available.

All he had to distract himself were his visits to the public library. Lost in a book, he felt temporarily weightless. The filled notepads in his bedroom multiplied, though he felt his dreams of study fading.

Garai's growing desperation insinuated its way into his arguments with Guthrie. Two particularly fiery ones stayed with him afterwards.

The first one was sparked by a comment Guthrie made about Jamaican gangs running a nationwide drugs ring from London. He'd read an article in the *Daily Mail* about the county lines phenomenon.

"It's not right, all these coloured boys spreading poison round the country. I don't know why they don't just round 'em up and send them back to the West Indies."

Garai, stung by the mention of deportation, reminded Guthrie of Britain's part in the opium trade in China, but the old man cut him short.

"Yes, yes, I know all about that. But it's like I always say, you've got to weigh the negatives with the benefits. I've done my homework like a good schoolboy, I finished your Sanghera book. Even he can't deny all the great things about the Empire. Science and technology. All sorts of innovations. The Empire gave us so much and we shared it with the world. It's called civilization, and that's a fact.

"A fact?"

"You can't argue with facts," said Guthrie. "And that's what history is. History is facts."

"No, it's not. History is interpretation. History is *politics*. Plumelle-Uribe said it best. Let's see if I can remember. She said that in history, the definition and characterisation of facts, along with their historical substance, are a question of *power*. I've just finished her book. I'll lend it to you, Mr Guthrie."

"I'll stick with Sanghera and British innovations, if you don't mind. Let's see if I can remember. There were advances in shipping and insurance, medical breakthroughs, scientific leaps in botany and zoology, great dietary changes including all sorts of techniques for food preservation that we still use today. Oh, and Indian Pale Ale. Things we can be proud of."

"Did you read the part in Sanghera where he talks about all the contemporary political and military crises left as a legacy by Empire? Iraq, Nigeria, Sudan, Hong Kong, Kashmir, Myanmar. Places where the British decimated the old ruling class, destroyed the system of government, then left a vacuum to be filled with chaos and conflict."

"Oh here we go."

"And it's not just the British. Look at the Portuguese in Angola and Mozambique, the Italians in Abyssinia, the Spanish in Equatorial Guinea. Look at the French in Central African Republic and Mali, the Belgians in Rwanda and Congo. Look at the new imperialists, the Russians in Afghanistan and Chechnya, China in Tibet and Xinjiang. And of course the US, from Korea and Vietnam to the present."

"It's easy to lay blame when things go wrong."

"And even after Empire ended, those white settler colonies didn't stop subjugating the indigenous peoples. Canada and Australia, the USA and New Zealand, none of them have seriously addressed past injustices, nor fought to create more equitable societies today."

"Now wait a minute. The white man gave law and order, democracy, education. Compare India to Afghanistan. One's on the up, the other's a mess. It's a pity we never colonised Afghanistan. It'd be in a lot better shape now if we had."

This was one oversimplification too far.

"Mr Guthrie, really, sometimes I have to bite my tongue. First of all you're ignoring all the suffering that followed Partition in India after independence. Hundreds of thousands died. Millions were forced from their homes. The seeds were sown by the British. Secondly, every nation's journey is different, you can't generalise. Zimbabwe was colonised with all your so-called benefits of Empire, but it's in a terrible state today. You know why?"

Guthrie shook his head.

"Because the British botched the land issue when it handed back the country in 1979," Garai began. He remembered Tafadzwa's lecture in the dorm all those months ago, the clarity of his rhetoric, the facts and figures to support his argument. "At the time, ninety-seven percent of the population held a quarter of the land. The rest was mainly white-owned farms on the best land. The freedom fighters fought to win back their land. At Lancaster House the black leadership agreed to hold off seizing the white farms for ten years in exchange for a pledge that the British government would use its influence to raise the money from the international community to buy back the land from the farmers. It never happened. That's what caused all the mess afterwards. Mugabe's bitterness, the political violence, poverty and corruption, the rise of the Army and Mnangagwa. My own history, the disaster that led me here, it can be traced directly back to colonialism."

As soon as he'd finished, he realised that he'd let his mouth run away with him.

"Disaster? I thought you chose to come here. You told me you wanted to see a bit of the world, get a better education, earn some money. I thought this was an adventure, not a disaster."

"Yes, of course. It is an adventure. I just meant I had some problems back home. Just forget it."

Guthrie looked at him carefully.

"You know, Garai, if you're in some kind of trouble, you can talk to me about it. We're sort of family now, aren't we?"

"Yes. No. I mean. There's no trouble. And thank you."

The last time the two of them swapped books, it was towards the end of summer. Garai gave Guthrie Rosa Amelia Plumelle-Uribe's *White Ferocity: The Genocides of Non-Whites and Non-Aryans from 1492 to Date* and received Ian D Colvin's *Cecil Rhodes* in return. A week or so later, he found Guthrie and Abi at the kitchen table, the Plumelle-Uribe book between him.

"How did you get on with it?" Garai asked, gesturing towards the book.

There was an awkward pause.

"It's an interesting premise, right?" he continued

"What's that?" asked Abi, who was pulling the leaves off a bundle of parsley.

"Plumelle-Uribe argues that the aim of white oppressors throughout history was the eviction or banishment of Blacks from the human family. In other words, modern history is underwritten by racism. She uses the slave trade as an example, along with the annihilation and subjugation of native Americans in north and south America. She gives the example of Mexico, which had a population of twenty-five million. That fell to a million after the Spanish conquest. I've got that right, haven't I, Mr Guthrie?"

He paused and looked at Guthrie, hoping for encouragement, though expecting a rebuttal. When Guthrie didn't speak, Garai continued.

"And she goes on to suggest that this idea that certain peoples were unworthy of consideration as humans was the template used by Nazi ideology. She then argues that because the violence against Jews was white-on-white and within Europe, it took on a far greater significance in the writing of World History than the anti-black violence. That's why the term 'genocide' was first coined in 1948. And why they came up with a special term, the 'Holocaust', in order to give this white-on-white violence more significance than the centuries of self-same genocide towards Blacks."

"Interesting," said Abi. She'd momentarily stopped picking the parsley leaves.

"She argues that what an African American faced in nineteenth century America was no different from what a Jewish person faced in Dachau. America was like a giant concentration camp for blacks. A white in America held a black person's life in his hands the same way that the camp guard held the Jewish person's in his. That's more or less what she's saying, I think. Right, Mr Guthrie?"

Another long silence, and then Guthrie spoke.

"I'm sorry, Garai. I just looked at the title and I couldn't bring myself to turn the first page. I mean, don't get me wrong, I'm not saying it's poppycock. I can imagine what it says, and I'm sure there'll be a lot of truth in it. If I've learned one thing from our little chats, son, it's that when it comes to understanding the nitty-gritty of things, I haven't always seen the full picture. There's a lot more to history than meets the eye. Or maybe I'm just a silly old fool."

Garai shook his head.

"I didn't say that."

"Oh, I know that, son. That's the conclusion *I've* come to. And that's fine with me. You know what? I think I've just about reached saturation point, if you know what I mean. I think I need a break from history books. I dug out my old PG Wodehouse omnibus this morning. I just feel I need a bit of light relief."

Garai nodded.

"So no more book swaps?" asked the younger man.

"A temporary suspension, that's all. Is that alright?"

"Sure. Of course," said Garai. Then, grinning, he added, "So, I've finally ground you down."

They looked at each other and now both men smiled.

"You could say that, son. And don't think I'm not grateful. It's been a real education. It's good to see both sides, isn't it?"

Garai nodded.

"I've learnt an awful lot from you, son."

Garai knew what he ought to say.

"And me from you, Mr Guthrie."

Guthrie looked pleased. He got to his feet.

"How about a nice cup of tea?"

"A cup of tea sounds good to me, Mr Guthrie."

"Smashing."

Despite what felt like a small victory, the important aspects of Garai's life were spiralling out of control. Every day now, Garai's boss was pressing him for his documents, and though Garai put the man off for a fortnight, the day came when Jing gave him an ultimatum.

"Tomorrow if you don't bring your documents, I won't let you work here," he said. "My father could get into trouble."

Mounting tensions back in Zimbabwe added to the pressure that Garai was already feeling. Trawling local independent media sites, Garai learned that a member of the main opposition party had disappeared, last seen getting into a police van. Inflation had risen again, and two civilians demonstrating against rising prices were killed by stray police bullets.

Closer to home, Garai's paranoia over Home Office arrest and deportation had grown so raw that he'd begun taking elaborate routes home from work, doubling back several times when he grew close to the house so that he could check that no suspicious vehicles were loitering in his street.

The night he finished his last shift at work, he hit rock bottom. How would he find another job? How could he pay the rent? It was two in the morning when he found himself home in the kitchen, filling a glass of water to take up to his room. He saw the night ahead, the ticking clock, the hours of fretful wakefulness. He thought, Oh God, I've reached the end of the line.

Before he knew what was happening, he began to cry.

He didn't hear Abi come in. Lost in his tears, he felt the hand on his shoulder. He started as if he'd been shot.

"Sorry," said the young woman. "I didn't mean to freak you out. What's wrong? Are you worried about the Home Office?"

That night, filled with despair, Garai tried to put into words the everyday dread he lived with. He spoke about his parents, how much he missed them, and the guilt that plagued him. Then he told her about the loss of his job, his looming eighteenth birthday, the terrifying fear of arrest and deportation. Once in a while, she asked a question, but mostly she just listened.

By the time he finished, he'd stopped crying. He'd had his head bent when he spoke, to hide his tears, but now that he looked up at her, he saw in her eyes both sympathy and fire.

"Listen," she said. "I've heard about these cases. We could get married, me and you. Then they can't send you home."

Garai felt himself welling up again.

"You'd do that for me?"

"Sure, why not? It's not as if it means anything."

Garai shook his head.

"It's not as simple as that. They'll do everything they can to show it's not a real marriage."

"How can they prove it? We're already living together. Our toothbrushes are in the same mug in the bathroom. We share the same toothpaste."

"I ran away from the care home. I've been living here illegally. That will count against me."

"Look, marrying me may not solve the problem, but it'll complicate things for the Home Office. You'll buy some time, right?"

"I don't know. I don't think it will help. And you could get into trouble. But thank you, anyway. That's an amazing offer."

"Well, look. Whatever happens, tomorrow we'll get an appointment with a solicitor. We'll get the ball rolling so at least you're not living in limbo. I can't imagine how hard that must be."

And that's exactly what they did. The step that Garai had lacked courage to take felt manageable with Abi at his side. Garai still had the solicitor's name that his colleague had given him, so the next day Abi called the number, and made an appointment for Monday morning.

"I'll call in sick and come with you," Abi offered.

"You don't have to. You've done enough."

"I'm on to you, Garai. I know you're planning to do a runner and leave me alone with mad Mister G," she said.

It took him a moment to see that she was joking.

"You have read me like a book," he said. And then, "Thank you, Abi."

The solicitors' office was in a side-street at the town end of Cowley Road. Abi and Garai chatted on the walk there, but nerves silenced them in the waiting room. Abi scrolled through her phone while Garai sat taut with fear. He thought, I'm about to put my life in a stranger's hands.

"Mister Hove," announced the receptionist. She pointed towards a closed door. "Ms Oluwa will see you now."

Garai and Abi sat side by side facing a middle-aged woman with shoulder-length braids, frown lines on her forehead, and the darkest skin Garai had seen since his arrival in Britain. The woman got straight down to business.

"OK, my name is Simisola Oluwa. Call me Simi. You're Garai, right? And this is a friend?"

Garai nodded.

"I think it might be best if Garai and I spoke alone," she continued, this time addressing Abi. "Please take a seat in the waiting room."

Once she was alone with Garai, Simisola asked him to explain his situation.

"Tell me everything, as much detail as possible. There are things that could help you that you may not think are important."

It was hard at first, opening himself up to this outsider, but she listened well, her head cocked, a nod here and there for encouragement. Occasionally she interrupted Garai to ask a question. He spared nothing, from the tragedy at home to the terror that ate away at him as he approached his eighteenth birthday. When he'd run out of things to say, and she had no more questions, she sat for a while in silence making notes on a pad. He watched her fill three whole sides before she put down her pen and looked at him. What he saw in her expression was compassion and determination, and a calm self-assurance he knew he lacked.

"Look, I'm going to be straight with you," she began. "You're right about the importance of the birthday. The Home Office often uses that transition to deport unaccompanied minors. They often arrive years before they reach adulthood, they grow up in Britain, feel this is their home, may not even have any contacts back where they came from originally. The way they're treated, it's a crying shame."

Garai waited.

"What you've done, coming here today, you've taken a big gamble. Once you're back on the radar, you can't predict how the Home Office may react. But what we do know for sure, is that if you carry on as you are, living *under* the radar, then you're consigning yourself to a life in limbo. You may never get caught, but you'll never live free of fear, and never have access to the things you need to make a good life here. Things like legal employment, access to health and welfare services, and so on. It's a brave thing you're doing."

Garai swallowed hard.

"The bottom line, if we can find evidence to support your account of what happened at the demonstration, that your friend was murdered, that you were there, that your life is therefore at risk, then I think we have a good case."

"What about running away from the children's home?"

"Well, legally-speaking you were … are … still a child. It sounds like it was a frightening incident that prompted your flight. I don't think we need worry too much about that. The important thing is to get your case moving again. The Home Office must have you on file. It's still six weeks to your birthday. By then we'll have the case back up and running. What we need to do in the meantime is look for evidence to support your claims."

Now she handed Garai a sheet of paper and a pen.

"Can you write down the full names and addresses of your two friends in Zimbabwe, the one who got killed and the other one? Also can you read through my notes and see if all the facts are accurate? Names of places and people, dates, times, it's important that they're all correct."

When Garai finished, the solicitor explained that the Home Office would no doubt want to interview him again, that social services would be in touch, that a social worker would be appointed.

"You're not legally permitted to seek employment, but you'll be entitled to an allowance. Housing's a bit trickier. You'll have the rent paid, but you've got no choice where they send you. If you insist on staying where you are now, the government's under no obligation to pay."

Before Garai left, Simisola asked him about his ambitions for the future. He spoke about his study plans, the dream of a university education. He told her about his visits to the public library and she asked him what books he'd been reading. To his surprise, he discovered that she'd read most of the same ones. She recommended a book about French neo-colonialism in Gabon, another about Chinese foreign policy in Africa, a third about American interference in South America and the Caribbean. She wrote down the details.

"You know once the Home Office have spoken to you, you should go down to the further education college in Oxpens. You're entitled to enrol for ESOL classes. There's an Access course they run there specifically for people in your situation. They'll assess you, but you should be eligible and it's fully funded."

"Thank you, Madam." Garai said. "I'll do that."

"It's Simi, remember. Look, I can't make any promises, but I'll do everything in my power to help you. In the meantime, you keep on with your reading and get on a course. We need all the future leaders we can get."

Before he left, he asked her,

"Where are you from?"

A half-smile on her face as she answered.

"Birmingham."

"I meant, you know, your roots."

"Nigeria. My parents came over in the fifties. He drove a bus, she worked in a care home. We didn't have a lot but they understood where education could get you. I hated my childhood, all those hours of extra homework, the weekend tutors. But now I realise what they sacrificed for me."

A last word before Garai left.

"I've got your number," she said. "I'll give you a ring in a week to let you know how we're doing."

Abi was waiting outside. On the way home, he told her what had happened.

"How do you feel about it?" she asked.

"I don't know. Good, I think. And scared to death."

That evening, with no job to go to, Garai stayed in the house. Abi was cooking soup, carrot and coriander, and when it was ready, she called up to his bedroom to come and eat. It was early, sixish, but they'd been too nervous to eat during the day.

He came into the kitchen smiling.

"You look like the cat that got the cream. What's up?" she asked.

"I'm happy."

"You won the lottery?"

"No, I just messaged my parents and they messaged back. I haven't done that since just after I came to Britain."

"What! Why not?"

"It's complicated. I don't want them to get into trouble. I guess I'm a political criminal in Zimbabwe. Also I just wanted to, you know, feel I had something positive to tell them. And today, after the solicitor, I feel I do."

"Christ, all that time dealing with this on your own. That must have been hard, Garai," said Abi.

She looked up and saw tears in his eyes. She made no comment, just waited.

"Well, I feel I've got past that now. You know, it's not like I have anything to celebrate yet. But at least I'm taking steps to sort things out. I made a new email account so it can't be traced back to me, and I messaged my father. He answered straight away, like he'd been waiting."

"That's great."

"Everyone is well back home. It's such a relief."

"Are you going to call them?"

"I don't know. I'm still worried about getting them into trouble."

"Give them my number. You can use my phone."

"Really?"

"Of course. Let's eat and you can do it after."

Garai smiled, an explosion of joy, and Abi saw now that all the times he'd done so before were poor imitations of the real thing.

"I'll message them your number," he said. "Thank you."

They ate the soup with a crusty loaf that they'd bought from the Co-op on the way home.

"You know, you'll have to tell the OG, now that it's out in the open," Abi said.

"I know. I'll do it when he comes home. I should have done it a long time ago. I've felt guilty all this time. You know, I was afraid if I got caught, he'd get into trouble."

At half six Guthrie returned home.

Garai sat him down in the kitchen while Abi made him a cup of tea and a bowl of soup.

"I have something I need to tell you," Garai began.

"Ooh, this sounds serious," said Guthrie. He looked more tired than usual, a greyish tinge to his pallor, his mouth set tight, but he tried to smile as he spoke. Then his face clouded over.

"You're not thinking of leaving us, are you, son?"

"No, no. At least, I hope not."

Garai ran through the full story again, the third time in a short while after almost a year of secrecy.

"Look, Mr Guthrie," he said at the end. "I know I should have been honest with you. I understand if you want me to go. All I ask is that you give me a bit of notice, a week or two to find somewhere else."

"Notice? Somewhere else? What are you talking about, son? Have you gone doolally?"

"No. I mean-."

"You're not going anywhere, son. This is your home. You did the right thing today, going to the solicitor. It's all above board now. And anyone who heard what you've been through would say you should be allowed to stay here. I mean, this is Britain. No, I've got faith in the Home Office. You're stopping here while they straighten things out, and that's my final word."

"I lost my job too, Mr Guthrie. Because I don't have the right papers. I've got enough saved up for next month's rent but after that, I don't know."

"Well, we'll suspend the rent for the time being, shall we? I'll keep a record, don't you worry. In the meantime, if you want to pay your way, you can help me out in the garden. I'm thinking of making a new bed this year. For potatoes."

"How about planting some maize?"

"Like home, eh?"

"Yes."

"Well, alright. I suppose this is your home now."

Guthrie 5

A year had passed since the accident. The pattern of Guthrie's life remained unchanged. The visits to Delia provided the foundation to his routine. The conversations continued. The same light banter they'd always enjoyed, a kind of mutual preening with words.

"Hello, love. You're looking lovely today," he might begin." Gosh you don't look a day over forty."

"Get away with you. Silly old fool," she'd scoff, and he could see the look in her eye, the hint of a smile, as clear as day. "So what nonsense have you brought with you today?"

"You'll never guess what I saw in the paper today," he'd continue, and then he was off. News that a favourite shop of hers was closing, or an Oxford landmark knocked down to build flats, or whatever other titbits he'd gleaned since the last visit. Then there was last evening's Whatsapp call to Eric, or a phone call from the niece, or a passing chat with a neighbour.

In between the visits to Delia, there was the garden, his research, his breakfast chats with Abi, the political wrangles with Garai. A recent exchange was quite typical of their debating tone.

"Don't get me wrong, I'm not a racist," Guthrie began. "But I do believe there are too many immigrants in this country. I'm not talking about folk like you who've come here to escape danger. I mean the ones that sign on for housing as soon as they get here, pocket the dole, then sit back for a cushy ride. They've got their own language and their own ways of doing things, and they won't make the effort to adapt. We don't need that sort. They're changing the character of this country. We used to know who we were. Now we're neither one thing nor the other. I just want some limits. That's fair, isn't it?"

"You have to see all that British Empire stuff in the past, and the current issues of immigration and multiculturalism, they're all part of the same thread," Garai countered. "It's a thread that's been going back for centuries, from the time the first Romans arrived up to the present."

"What do you mean?"

"It's never been one-way traffic, Mr Guthrie. This thing that happened to Britain, its people coming and going for whatever reasons, it made connections with other parts of the world that led to what we have today. I'm talking about the hundreds of thousands of native Brits who made their lives in all corners of the world, those who died, and those who lived and multiplied and put their stamp on their new homes. You know between the mid-nineteenth century and 1920, nine point seven million Brits migrated to the colonies? Sanghera says that a quarter of the white miners in South Africa at the end of the nineteenth century were Cornish. They sent the equivalent of eight to twelve million pounds home to Britain in remittances with every single mail."

"Well, I never!"

"So what's the difference between them and the ones that left their homes to come to Britain? The native Africans and Europeans and Asians, the Muslims and Hindus and Sikhs, the Protestants and Catholics, who came here to make new lives and earn a living?"

"I'm only saying... ."

"The only difference is that the British arrived pointing rifles. There was no 'Can we come in, please?' No discussion at all. As soon as they arrived, they started taking over the land, charging taxes, forcing the locals to work for them. The migrants arriving here come in peace. Most just want an opportunity to make their lives better, the lives of their families."

Guthrie listened but did not reply.

"That book I lent you, the one by Sanghera. You read it, right?" Garai continued.

Guthrie nodded, though in truth he'd fallen behind in his reading.

"He says it better. We have to accept colonial history for what it was, warts and all. And we have to accept that British society today is a direct consequence of that history. You either accept the whole package, or reject it all. You can't pick and choose."

"Yes, I see."

"Look, I know we're not swapping books any more, but the Sanghera book's over there on the counter. It doesn't have to go back to the library until Tuesday, so feel free to give it another browse."

Guthrie thought about the conversation later that night. Before he went to bed, he retrieved the book from the kitchen. He looked at the cover. *Empireland*, he read. Yes, he'd flicked through it first time round, but hadn't read it in any depth. Now he opened it at the first page and began to read.

*

A few days later, Guthrie arrived at Delia's bedside to find her masked-up on oxygen. He'd taken a rare day off from visiting, so that he could spend some time in the garden, and he'd worked his way through a list of chores. He'd bagged up the contents of the compost bins, raked up fallen leaves, cleaned out the birdboxes. Now he drew close and listened to Delia's laboured breathing. A moment of raw panic, followed by an equal measure of guilt. He'd abandoned Delia and look what had happened. Just then Colin appeared.

"It's OK. She was a bit chesty overnight. We've given her IV antibiotics. The mask's just to help her feel a bit more comfortable."

"Does she need to be in hospital?" Guthrie asked. The thought of returning to the chaos of the wards filled him with dread.

"Not for now. We're monitoring her. Try not to worry. I think she'll be fine. She's a tough cookie, right?"

A little later, Colin brought Guthrie a coffee, and they sat together by Delia's bedside.

"How long will she need the mask?" Guthrie asked. He knew how much she'd hate wearing it.

"I don't know," Colin answered. "As long as it takes. We don't want to lose her, do we?"

Guthrie looked down at his wife. He took in her gaunt cheekbones, the dry mop of hair, the pale skin. He reached out and held her hand, stroked her gnarled and twisted fingers. He thought, I lost you a long time ago.

A week or so later, after the antibiotics had done their work and Delia had rallied, Guthrie found himself unable to sleep at midnight. Rather than read a book or research his beloved Empire history, he googled *traumatic brain injury* and began trawling through the websites. One site particularly caught his attention. It featured a series of interviews, mostly family members talking about their experiences of dealing with a loved one who'd suffered these sorts of injuries.

One of the interviewees, the mother of a hit-and-run victim, talked about a curious phenomenon she called the 'miracle mind-set'. She said that from the very first day, she believed that every single moment, every event, was a stage on the way to a miracle recovery. Likewise, for her every setback was just a delay, nothing more. During the course of the next year, as her son remained in a vegetative state, her attitude gradually changed. Fourteen months after the accident, she agreed to withdraw treatment. She said that the erosion of hope was cruel, but that she had to go through it to rid herself of the miracle mind-set.

The next visit, at the end of the day, Guthrie had one of his periodic conversations with Delia. He'd brought a new CD, an Ella Fitzgerald compilation, as well as a couple of the latest magazines and a box of Quality Street to offer to the care workers when they popped in. Now, towards the fag-end of the afternoon, he got to his feet.

"I'd better be going, love. Eric said he'd call at six."

"Thanks for coming to see me."

"Don't thank me, love. You know it's what I want to do."

"Yes, but still."

"Still what?"

A long pause. Guthrie picked up the empty shopping bag.

"Let me go."

He thought he'd misheard her.

"What?"

"I said, *let me go*."

He stood, frozen, and gazed down at the shell of his wife. He opened his mouth, closed it, gulped. Just then, Colin poked his head around the door.

"You off, Mr Guthrie?"

"Yes," he said, his voice a whisper. When he got home, Eric called. Guthrie told him about the conversation.

"I think your mother's had enough. I think she wants to … to… ."

He didn't know how to end the sentence.

The line stayed silent for a moment, and Guthrie feared he'd said something awful. Then Eric said,

"I think so too, dad. I didn't want to say anything."

For a week it was enough just to carry this new thought around in his head. When he next spoke to Eric, his son brought up the conversation.

"I've been thinking about what you said. About mum having enough. I've been looking into it. About withdrawing treatment. Reading up on it, talking to people about it, that's really helped me get it clear in my mind. I think you should do the same."

Eric paused. When Guthrie didn't answer, he went on.

"I'll send you the links, dad. They'll help you understand what we'd be getting into. Whatever decision you take, it won't be easy. It won't be clear-cut. But you need to feel it's the best decision of the alternatives. Is there someone you could speak to at the nursing home?"

A few days later, the opportunity came up with Colin, as they were getting Delia ready for bed.

"I don't know how long I can put my wife through this," Guthrie said. He didn't know how to edge into something as brutal as this, so dived straight in. Colin looked at him carefully, and then nodded.

"It's hard, man."

"It's hard on me, sure. But I don't mean that. I mean it's *inhumane* what we're all doing. We think we're being kind and caring, but it's wrong to subject her to this … this *non*-life."

Colin stopped what he was doing and waited in silence.

"If we withdraw treatment, how will she, you know… ."

"Unless something unexpected happens, she'll die of organ failure. A body needs fluid and the withdrawal of ANH will do it. But it won't hurt her. If the medical profession have got one modern advance sorted, it's pain relief. Morphine pumps are little minor miracles. They'll be no pain."

Another long pause.

"How do these things happen?" Guthrie asked at length.

"You mean the process? It's regulated by National Clinical Guidelines. They were brought out by the Royal College of Physicians in 2013. Now, let me get this right. The most important principle is that after a year in a permanent vegetative state, it should be considered not only appropriate but *necessary* to consider withdrawal of treatment and end of care. If the family comes round to thinking it's the best way forward, there's a legal process. The case goes to a Court of Protection to decide whether it's the right course of action."

"So this whole situation, this awful bloody situation, it comes up all the time?"

"Of course. There are cases like Delia's all over the country. For the families, it's the hardest thing they'll ever go through. The whole thing's a minefield. It's a sensitive issue for the medical practitioners to know when it might be right to bring it up, so often they just carry on keeping the patient alive just because it's the easy option. Of course, people refuse to consider it for different reasons, cultural or religious or whatever. Or people think, Miracles *do* happen, right? You can imagine, even those folk who decide it's the right decision, they all get there in their own time, and sometimes that's a long process."

They talked more. Guthrie's hesitant probing, Colin's gentle explanations. At the end, when Guthrie got up to leave, he offered the nurse his hand and thanked him for all his help.

"No problem, man."

Then Guthrie took a deep breath and asked,

'Hey, I meant to ask. How's Tracy?"

"Eh?"

"Tracy. Is he well?"

"Sure."

"Well, that's good. Give him my regards."

That evening, when Eric called, Guthrie described the conversation he'd had with Colin. When Eric responded, Guthrie couldn't help wondering whether this was something his son had been waiting for.

"I think we both know mum's not coming back. All I want is to help her find peace. I know how hard this is for you, dad. It's one thing to want an end to the suffering, it's another to take on the responsibility for driving the thing forward. That's more than you should have to deal with. But if you're absolutely certain, then leave it with me. I'll speak to a solicitor and get some advice on how to proceed."

"Thank you, son."

Once the decision had been made, it was a relief that nothing dramatic happened too soon afterwards. He was not yet ready for the unspeakable consequence of his resolution. Life continued as normal for Guthrie, and although he was aware from Eric's comments that the legal process was underway, he tried not to think too much about it.

Then one day a document came in the post. He tried to read it but got bogged down in the legal jargon. When Eric called that evening, he explained that it was an affidavit for Guthrie to sign.

"You're not having second thoughts, are you, dad?" Eric asked. "It's OK if you are. No one's saying this is easy. If you need more time, I get that. Just know that I support you."

More time? For what? For this hell to continue? Guthrie tried to speak, but had to clear his throat before any words would come.

"I appreciate that, son. So what is this affi-wotsit?"

"It's what we discussed, dad. It basically says you believe it's best for mum to stop suffering. But like I said, you don't have to sign it. We don't have to go through with this. It's up to you."

They talked of other things for a while, and then, before they hung up, Guthrie said,

"The document thing. I'll sleep on it. I'll let you know in the morning."

Guthrie expected a sleepless night. He was determined to read through the affidavit carefully, but to his surprise, he fell asleep almost at once and enjoyed the best night's rest in a long while. In the morning, still without reading the document, he signed it, put it in the stamped envelope that it came with, and walked down to the post box.

A few weeks later, the Court of Protection sent a nervous woman called Jenny Jarvis to check on Delia. She was small and scrawny with pale skin and thin mousy hair cut into the shape of a helmet. She spoke with Delia's doctors, with staff at the home, spent a while observing Delia, and then asked Guthrie if she could talk to him. She began by explaining that his application to the Court was for deputyship.

"That means that you get the legal right to manage Delia's affairs and make decisions about her wellbeing."

"I see."

Jarvis asked him a number of questions about his finances, and Delia's too. Who owned what, the various savings accounts, the annuities and insurance policies they'd taken out. And though none of them amounted to a great deal, the questions still felt intrusive. He understood, of course, what she was digging for, to calculate whether he stood to gain financially from her death. After all, he wasn't stupid.

They sat together in the visitors' room, and Jarvis ran through a list of questions on a form she produced from her briefcase. Some of them, he felt, were too personal, and he would have got cross if she hadn't looked so apologetic. Instead, he took deep breaths and answered as best he could. She took copious notes. At the end, she said,

"I'm sorry about this line of questioning. I find it awkward, but it's the process we have to go through. Do you understand?"

The look in her eyes, genuine discomfort, was enough to chase away his growing indignation.

"I understand," he said.

Jarvis glanced at the form again.

"I'd like to ask you a few questions about your wife's medical condition now, if I may?"

"Go ahead."

"Mr Guthrie, do you know what's actually wrong with your wife?"

"It's a brain injury. Is that what you mean?"

"Can you be more specific?"

Guthrie said something about vegetative states.

"What's her prognosis?" Jarvis asked.

Guthrie shook his head.

"You tell me. I must have asked the doctors that question a hundred times. I don't think they like to commit themselves, in case they're wrong."

"What do you mean?"

"Well, at the start, those first few weeks, they were happy enough to say she was in a coma. But after that, when she first opened her eyes and started responding a little to things, that's when I could never get a straight answer."

Guthrie paused to draw breath. The woman scribbled away for several minutes. Then she looked up.

"Go ahead, Mr Guthrie. I'm listening."

"I've heard people say she's in a persistent vegetative state, and a prolonged one, and a permanent one. I've heard people call it unresponsive wakefulness syndrome, and apallic syndrome, and someone said she was in a minimally conscious state. I've given up caring about the labels. All I know is my Delia's gone. Sometimes I think there's nothing beyond the body on the bed. Sometimes I wonder whether maybe there is something, a spark of her left inside. But then I think, Jesus, what a nightmare for her. To be trapped like that with no hope."

"No hope?"

He shook his head.

"No," he said. "She's not coming back."

At the end, the final question before she left.

"This whole process you've been through, what have you learned from your experience?"

"I've learned that there are worse things than death."

Afterwards, to Eric, he said,

"I suppose they're checking I'm not trying to murder her. Well, in a way I suppose I am. But you know, for the right reasons. To give her peace."

"You're not a murderer, Dad."

"Well, I feel like one."

A fortnight passed and then Eric called Guthrie one evening. The Court had ruled that Delia's treatment could be withdrawn. From now on, she'd receive only palliative care. After the call, Guthrie sat at the kitchen table and poured himself a stiff whisky. *Palliative*. The word was a shock. He felt wracked with doubts, and the whisky did little to soothe them.

When Abi returned later that night, she asked, as she always did these days,

"How was your wife today, Mister G?"

Usually Guthrie would fob her off with something meaningless. He didn't resent the question, indeed he appreciated her concern, it was just that he never knew how to answer it. After all, what do you say about a body that's as lifeless as a living thing could be without being dead?

Today, though, was different. At first he didn't answer, just beckoned for her to take a seat at the table while he fetched a glass and poured her a drink. They sat together in silence for a while before he began to speak. He told her quietly about the process that he'd started, the decision that had been made today. When he finished, she laid a hand on his arm and squeezed.

"I'm sorry," she said. "Can I do anything?"

Ah, Christ, he thought. I'm not going to cry.

Instead, he poured another drink for them both.

"Yes, you can," he said. "If you don't mind, I'd be very grateful if you could just sit here with me for a while. You don't have to say anything, not if you don't want to. And you don't have to stay too long. Just for a while. Is that alright with you, love?"

"Of course it is, Mister G," she answered, and raised the glass to her lips.

*

They began end-of-life care on the Friday of that week. Guthrie was there when they withdrew the feeding tubes. Colin sat with Guthrie and explained that from now on, there'd be no oxygen masks or IV antibiotics if Delia picked up an ailment.

"She's on pain relief," Colin said. "That'll continue. We'll monitor dosage, and increase it if we think she's showing signs of distress."

"How long?" Guthrie asked.

"Usually around a week. A fortnight tops. Like I said, she'll be sedated so there'll be no discomfort. At the beginning you won't notice any difference."

The next few days took on a surreal and disjointed air, a little like the days after the accident. Most of the time Guthrie remained convinced that he was doing the right thing, but there were still moments of crisis. One evening, at the kitchen table, he confessed that he was having doubts. Abi, who was eating some kind of suspicious-smelling curry, laid down her fork and put a hand on his shoulder.

"There are more important ways to show her you love her than to keep her alive."

Eric had booked a flight home, leaving the day after, but he called to say his pregnant wife had gone into labour three weeks early and had needed an emergency C-section.

"Jesus, dad, I don't know what to do," he said. His voice sounded thick with emotion.

"It's an easy decision, son," said Guthrie. "You can't be in two places at once. Lizzie's conscious and anxious and needs you by her side. Your mother wouldn't want to drag you away from that."

"I hate to think of you on your own there, dad. I'll be over as soon as things are OK here."

"I'm not on my own. I've got Abi and Garai and Gloria, and all my friends at the nursing home. I'll be alright. You come when you can, son."

Each day he arrived at the home first thing in the morning. He opened Delia's door bracing himself to see some grotesque degeneration in his wife's appearance since the night before. In fact, change was almost imperceptible. She appeared to maintain her weight, her expression remained the same, she just slept more than usual.

Though ashamed to admit it to anyone, that period was far easier to navigate than he expected. Delia looked more at peace than before, and he felt a lifting of pressure. In fact, he wished that this stage could have lasted for a lot longer than it did. Even his conversations with Delia seemed less strained than they had been for a long time.

"Nearly over," she'd say cheerfully.

"And then what?"

"Then I can relax."

"Really?"

"You think I'm lying?"

"No. I mean, I don't know."

"Trust me, love. You've done the right thing. You tried your best. You showed patience and kindness, I'd have expected nothing less."

"You don't feel ... disappointed?"

"Disappointed? Ah, be quiet now, man. This has gone on too long. It's not disappointment I feel, but *relief*."

Guthrie's nights were not so easy. Several times he woke from grisly nightmares. Delia, skeletal, was holding out her hands and pleading,

"I'm hungry, feed me!"

On the fifth day, he noticed that her breathing was shallow. She seemed stiller than she'd ever been.

"You're leaving, love," he told her. "I can feel it."

"It's all right, Oswald. Think of it as me going for a nice long walk. Remember how I always liked a nice walk? "

"I do."

"Remember how we'd sometimes take the towpath all the way to Abingdon when we were younger? In the summer I'd pack a picnic and we'd stop halfway. We'd swim at that boathouse. What was it called?"

"Radley?"

"Yes, Radley. We'd swim and I'd lay out the picnic and the day seemed to last forever. In autumn we'd wrap up warm and buy fish and chips in Abingdon. Then we'd catch the bus back."

Eric called every day. His wife was healing well but they were keeping the new baby, a son called Ralph, in the newborn intensive care unit.

"It's something to do with his breathing," Eric explained. "They say it should sort itself out but you know how Lizzie panics."

"She needs you there, son."

Gloria sat with him on the Sunday she wasn't working. Abi and Garai offered to come but he said no. He wasn't sure why. He preferred to talk to them at home about Delia. He knew they were busy, that they had better things to do than listen to the prattle of an old man, and he was grateful for their patience. He liked to describe what his wife was like before the accident. Her personality, her strengths and foibles, the silly bickering as well as the love they shared.

"I was always proud of her," he told them. "Not just of her kindness and loyalty, the good she brought those around her. But her strength, too. Christ, she was a strong woman. Stronger than me. I tell you, that woman had spirit. A fighter to the end."

Delia died on the tenth day, a Wednesday. The final two nights they'd given him a bed at the nursing home so he wouldn't have to keep coming and going. He was at Delia's side for hours at a time, getting up only for the toilet. It was hard, on his own. Delia had grown quiet and the conversations had ceased, and he felt very alone. The staff would take it in turns to sit with him, once they'd seen that he welcomed the company.

It was after midnight and he was dozing in the armchair when Colin shook him gently awake.

"She's gone," he announced quietly.

Guthrie leaned forward and took Delia's hand. It was still warm.

*

Eric flew home for the funeral. Delia's friends were there, the relatives, several neighbours, and Barry came down from Yorkshire with his wife. Gloria took a day's leave to attend. Abi wore a long rainbow dress, and Garai a suit that looked three sizes too big. They sang *All Thing's Bright and Beautiful* because it was Delia's favourite hymn, and they left the crematorium to the sound of the Beatles' *Here Comes The Sun*. They went home to the house in Rose Hill for sandwiches and scotch eggs and pork pies, tea and beer and whisky.

Before the funeral, Guthrie had been too tied up with arrangements to dwell much on his loss. He'd thought it would hit him during the service, but he remained calm throughout while all around him tears were shed. He'd thought he'd be grief-stricken, but instead he felt a hollow relief.

Afterwards, when the last guest had left, Eric and Abi and Garai helped clear away the leftovers and wash up the crockery. It was only when Guthrie tried to pitch in that he realised how exhausted he was.

"You look fit to drop, dad," said Eric, eyeing his father's greyish pallor. "Why don't you go up to bed? We can finish up in here."

"I thought we might crack open a bottle of Teachers, the four of us," said Guthrie. "Put the world to rights."

"We can do that tomorrow evening, dad," Eric said. "I'm not leaving until the day after."

"Well, if you're sure," said Guthrie, relieved. He wondered if he even had the strength to drag himself upstairs.

"I'll be up in a while," said Eric, who was sleeping with his father during his visit home.

Guthrie got undressed and crawled into bed. He couldn't stand on his feet much longer, but he was certain he wouldn't sleep either. He was expecting to lie awake for hours as the reality of what had happened hit home. He thought, Oh well, and now it starts.

He closed his eyes and fell into a long deep sleep.

Epilogue

They scatter Delia's ashes in late January. It isn't a special anniversary, but the time feels right. They set off after breakfast, Guthrie and Garai and Abi. A cold morning, a clear blue sky, the grass grey with frost. Guthrie's got the ashes in an old biscuit tin that he tucks beneath one arm. Later, they'll take it in turns to carry them.

They follow a route of memories, a pilgrimage to love. From the house they walk down to Rivermead, traipse through the small nature park, clamber up the path onto the ring road, across the bridge and down the footway to join the Thames towpath just below Iffley Lock. Thin eerie whistles of a red kite riding the sky, grunts from Canada geese and greylags on the water.

"We walked this route a thousand times, me and Delia," Guthrie explains to his lodgers. "We liked the way the weather made it a different journey every time."

Kennington meadow is awash with winter rain, and they have to navigate their way cautiously around the ankle-deep pockets of marsh. They pass the lock at Sandford. Guthrie points to the Kings Arms pub on the far side of the water.

"I took Delia there for her birthday once." He's talking as much to himself as to the others, but they listen politely. "Delia had a gammon steak, and sticky toffee pudding for afters. I had a mixed grill and apple crumble. They did a nice custard, if I remember. Tasty."

They talk as they walk, the water on their left, the fields of Kennington and Radley on their right. Abi points out the spots where she swam during the summer. Garai's never been this far down river. He admits he's never learned to swim and Abi promises to teach him.

"The first warm day in June, we'll all have a dip," says Abi. "There's a woman I've been watching at Rivermead, she swims all year round. In winter she wears a woolly hat and does the breast stroke. If she can do it, so can you, Garai. The first day in June, we'll begin your lessons. What about you, Mister G? Are you in?"

"Sure, why not. It'll probably kill me, but what the hell."

"Somebody said what doesn't kill you, makes you stronger," says Garai. "I can't remember who."

They all chew on that in silence for a while.

"Are you OK?" Abi asks the old man, after a few minutes have passed.

"Yes, I am," he says, surprising himself. "I really am. You know, it feels like I did a lot of grieving before she died."

Abi is leading the way, and when she stops and points to the water ahead, she says,

"Do you see them?"

"What?"

"Egyptian geese."

"Ah yes," says Garai. "Right over by the reeds. Got them, Mr Guthrie?"

Guthrie scans the water until he spots the birds the other side of the river. There are two on the water, each a striking patchwork of colours. Guthrie can make out dull yellows, shades of brown, chestnut and cinnamon, as well as sections that are black and metallic green. The eyes are patched brown, as if they're wearing masks. Their bills are pink.

"They were introduced into this country from Africa a few hundred years ago," says Abi. "Now they're naturalized. Handsome, aren't they?"

"Very."

They stop at the Radley boathouse, the picnic spot for Delia and Guthrie all those times before. Here, Guthrie opens the biscuit tin and tips the pale ash into the water.

"Goodbye, my love," he says. No one else speaks. It's too cold to linger long, so they set off home almost straight away.

Back in the kitchen, Guthrie makes tea while the others sit at the table.

"One thing I want you both to do. You'll think I'm being morbid, but I'm serious," Guthrie begins.

"Go on," says Abi.

"End of life wishes. You both need to make them," he continues. "Now, don't laugh. I'm being serious. And no, I'm not planning murder. And yes, I'm sure you're both feeling fit as a fiddle, neither of you's planning to kick the bucket any time soon. But that's the whole point. There are things you can't plan for. So what I've learned, if I've learned anything, is that it's worth setting things down in stone. For yourself. But also for those you leave behind, the ones who love you."

"Like what?" asks Garai.

"Like decisions about how you want to be treated at the end if you're not able to express them at the time. Delia's social worker spoke to me about it once, and it got me thinking. I don't remember all the right lingo, but she talked about a living will or an advanced statement or decision or something. I looked into it myself. Google 'end of life care' and you'll see. The NHS has webpages."

"What did the social worker say?"

"She said it better than I can. She said how none of us are new-born babies, we're adults with wishes and desires and opinions about everything. About favourite foods and politics and religion. And about how we want to end our lives. Like *where* do you want to die? A hospital? A hospice? At home? Like what to do if you can't breathe or feed yourself, if you're in a vegetative state. Like if you want to be pain-free, for instance. What treatments you don't want. If you stop breathing, do you want to be resuscitated? She had lots of lingo I forget. DNR and DNAR and DNACPR and whatnot. Do you really want to live for years fed through a PEG tube and breathing through a mask? They gave Delia antibiotics to fight infections long after anyone believed she'd come back. I wish I'd said no to that. Promise me you'll write something down."

"Is it legal? Do I need to get a lawyer?"

"I don't think so. Just write down what you want, then print your name and sign it at the bottom."

And that's exactly what they then do. They sit at the kitchen table, mugs of steaming tea at hand. Guthrie fetches paper and pens and envelopes and they write and stop, and think and write, the silence punctuated by questions about the right spelling of this and that. When they've finished, they each fold their sheet into an envelope, scribble their name on the front, and leave them under the biggest of Delia's Beatrix Potter figurines on the mantelpiece.

It's lunchtime now.

"Listen, it's a special day. I'd like to mark it properly. How about I treat you two to fish and chips from the chippy. Fancy that?"

Abi offers to fetch the food and she writes down the orders. Fried chicken for Garai, Veggie burger for herself, battered haddock for Guthrie, and chips for all.

"How d'you want your chips?" Abi asks. "Salt and vinegar? Ketchup? Curry sauce?"

"Curry sauce? Oh no thanks, that spicy stuff doesn't agree with me," says Guthrie. "Drop of malt vinegar for me. I'll do my own salt."

Later, as they eat their takeaway, Guthrie asks,

"What are you doing this afternoon?"

"I've got an appointment with my solicitor," says Garai. "She's got evidence to prove what I said about my friend's killing at the demonstration in Harare. Someone filmed the beating on a phone and it was posted on Twitter. You can see me clearly in the footage. That'll really help my case."

"That's wonderful news."

"Simisola thinks he has a good case to be granted Leave to Remain. She needs to interview him again," Abi goes on. "Just to check a few details, right, Garai?"

The young man nods. He says,

"Abi's coming for support."

"Oh well, good luck. Maybe if you're both out all afternoon, I might make a start on the spare bedrooms. I thought I'd give them a lick of paint. It's good to freshen things up every now and then. Especially since it looks like you're going to be around for a while."

Abi looks at Garai and winks.

"What colour were you thinking about, Mister G?" she asks.

"Well, I thought I might do the walls in an off-white, maybe Hint of Magnolia? And for the woodwork something earthy. Maybe Mulberry. What do you think?"

"I think that sounds perfect, Mr Guthrie," says Garai.

Abi nods in agreement.

"Perfect."

© MZ Pevsner 2021

Printed in Great Britain
by Amazon